for David,
my brother from
another Mother!
Enjoy :)
xo —
Birgit

Turtle Key

A Novel about Love, Family
…and Rescuing Sea Turtles

Birgitt Van Wormer

This is a work of fiction. Names, characters, businesses, locations, events, locales and incidents are either products of the author's imagination or used in a fictitious manner. Any resemblance to actual persons and/or businesses, living, dead or defunct, or actual events are purely coincidental.

Acknowledgements

This novel has been a work of friendship. I am truly humbled by all of my Florida friends who have stepped up to help with and improve this story:

Cherie Blickenstaff who generously gave me permission to use her beautiful oil painting "Turtle Key" as the book cover (Tropical Impressions on FB and www.tropical-impressions.com),

Charlott Fisch Cadiz who shared some great stories and insight about growing up in the Florida Keys and some fun tales such as Cleatus the Crocodile and Fred the Tree,

Jane Harm Barr and Stephanie Rivers Luberger who have both proofread and edited several of my novels,

Barbara Whitesell and Valerie Preziosi who provided valuable information on Key deer (www.saveourkeydeer.org),

Roger Silvi who generously permitted me to print the lyrics of his song "Fred the Tree" (Rogersilvimusic.com),

my beloved mother-in-law Lucille Van Wormer who is always the force keeping me on task and demanding to read a new chapter nearly every day and, of course, my husband Paul who had the great idea of the prologue!

Thank you everyone!

© Birgitt Van Wormer, August 2021
First Edition

Prologue

The Kenworth T680 18-wheeler semi-truck, pulling a 53-feet long trailer full of perishable groceries hurtled down US1, the highway that traverses the entire length of the Florida Keys. The turquoise colored ocean glistened on both sides of the road and 42 bridges dividing the Atlantic Ocean from the Gulf of Mexico.

The driver, on his way from Pensacola to Key West, rubbed his eyes and took another sip of his coffee in a thermos as he drove slightly over the speed limit through picturesque Islamorada. He didn't pay any attention to the beautiful sites on both sides of US1. The drive was routine for him and this was not a vacation. He could barely stay awake and knew he was breaking the law and acting recklessly but he kept going, mile by mile. Not only had he not followed his seven day work period/34 hour rule which stipulated he had to take a 34 hour break after working for seven days straight. Traffic on 75 South and the Turnpike had been extremely heavy, delaying his usual 12-hour drive for more than two hours and he hadn't taken his mandatory 30-minute break after eight hours either. He was on a tight deadline to deliver his perishable trailer-load by 6 pm in Key West tonight and had previously gotten in trouble for not making the deadline. He yawned a loud and drawn out yawn as he briefly looked at his GPS to see how far it still was to his final destination. He usually took a break and gassed up the truck in Homestead but wasn't paying attention and had missed that exit. It didn't help that he had a splitting headache and had taken a few Tylenol. He knew there was a larger gas station near the airport in Turtle Key and he just wanted to make it there and take a cat nap before he continued to Key West. Just after crossing Toms Harbors Cut Bridge and entering Grassy Key in front of the Dolphin

Research Center, he nodded off again. As the driver's chin rested on his chest, his massive truck drifted ever so slowly into the oncoming lane. He snapped awake and slammed his foot on his air brakes, but it was too late to avoid the collision with the sedan. The couple in the front seats were killed instantly as their vehicle was reduced to a mangled hunk of metal, glass, plastic and rubber in the blink of an eye.

The big truck pushed the wreckage 50 yards down the highway, barely avoiding other cars that were somehow able to swerve out of the way.

The truck finally came to a halt. The driver sat, wide-eyed and seemingly frozen, with both hands clutching the big steering wheel so tight, his knuckles were white. An acrid stench filled the air as onlookers ran to the wreckage...

*****

Turtle Key

Chapter 1

On a beautiful winter morning in mid February, Sienna Brantley, 36, sat down on one of the stools at the counter of her cozy, sunny, meticulously clean kitchen in downtown Boston with a freshly brewed cup of coffee and opened her laptop. The sun was shining on her beautiful red-brown hair, the reason her parents had given her the name Sienna. She stared at the headlines in bold capital letters, frowned and took a sip of the strong coffee.

Fatal car crash involving local couple on Grassy Key in front of Dolphin Research Center. Only street leading in and out of Keys shut down for hours.

Born and raised in the Florida Keys, the unique archipelago of islands extending from the southwestern tip of Florida, bordered on the west by the Gulf of Mexico and on the east by the Atlantic Ocean, Sienna still had the settings in her laptop set to the "Turtle Key Daily News" even though she had been estranged from her family in the Keys for nearly 17 years. She also followed several Keys pages on social media and checked if there was any more news.

"Wow, I hope nobody I know is involved," she mumbled to herself and drank another sip of coffee.

*****

Sienna's thoughts drifted off as she thought about her childhood in the Keys, riding bikes with her friends to the Seven Mile Bridge or one of the countless docks and boat ramps to go fishing on endless sunny summer days, smashing sea urchins on the concrete for bait or making a "cocktail", a combination of several pieces of bait on one fishing hook and just chilling, staring out onto the water for hours, waiting for a fish to bite. Every sunny summer afternoon ended in a monsoon-like rain, the palm trees would start blowing in the wind like giant paint brushes being shaken back and forth, the rain would start slowly splattering big drops, ramping up and evolving into a wall of water, soaking everyone from head to toe. Nobody cared though. It was so humid and warm. It was like walking through a sauna, but most had bathing suits on anyhow. Mist would rise from the heated asphalt that had stored so much energy that the liquid rain was converted into steam.

Sienna remembered meeting her first love Ricky, her soul mate, the cool guy who had moved to Turtle Key from Coral Gables in eighth grade and was the crush of many girls in Turtle Key Middle High School. Sienna remembered sneaking over to the high school building and watching his every move during lunch until he finally noticed her. Then, finally, their first tender kiss on the dock behind Sienna's family's cottage, concerts in Miami and Key West. Until he left for veterinary school in Miami and she left for law school in Boston and he betrayed her with her own sister...

She discovered their affair when, coming home from her first semester of college in Boston, Ricky was not at the airport, as promised, to pick her up. When she finally arrived home, she overheard her older sister Camilla and her mother talking about Camilla being pregnant. By Ricky. During the first weeks of this winter vacation her entire family and Ricky seemed to have turned against her. There were tears and terrible arguments.

Her father was on Camilla's side and made no secret of the fact that he thought Camilla and Ricky were a much better match and the perfect couple to take over the family business one day. Sienna's mother tried to remain neutral but both she and Sienna knew she'd never be strong enough to defy her husband's wishes. Ricky never spoke with Sienna or tried to apologize, even when she confronted him. He was too busy working at the Sea Turtle Sanctuary and went out of his way to not run into her. Finally, Sienna left early and never returned to Turtle Key until her parents' sudden death two years ago. In all these years she only spoke to her mother a handful of times, who tried calling her for Sienna's birthdays and for Christmas. Sienna never wanted to see the Turtle Sanctuary and her family again but had to face her sister and Ricky one more time when their parents both died within days of each other.

*****

Sienna snapped out of her daydream and started reading the article about a local couple that had been hit by a tractor-trailer swerving in and out of its lane as the driver had lost control of his vehicle right after the bridge leading onto Grassy Key, in front of the Dolphin Research

Center. Sienna and her sister Camilla had been there many times, running errands for their parents or swimming with the dolphins with their friend Jill whose parents ran the center.
Sienna clicked over to the social media page of the Dolphin Research Center and several traffic and news pages but nothing had been posted yet.

Her eyes wandered to the clock in the upper right hand corner of her laptop's screen. She realized that she was losing track of time, slammed the laptop shut, pushed it into a pretty leather briefcase with a padded laptop compartment and jumped up. Even though she was late for a meeting, she poured the rest of the coffee into the sink, rinsed the cup, placed it into the dishwasher, wiped off the counter where she had been sitting and neatened up a few other things. Everything had to be in its place. Her entire small, yet comfortable apartment showed that she was a neat freak, bordering on OCD, and everything had its designated spot. She looked at her beautiful collection of her favorite orchids, white Phaleonopsis, with countless flowers on various long stems, cascading like waterfalls, on a coffee table and the window sills. She walked over, checked if they needed to be watered, picked off a couple of dried up blooms and threw them into the garbage can in the kitchen. Then she grabbed her designer purse and her briefcase, stopping briefly at a mirror by the front door, checking her image. Sienna brushed a strand of her perfectly coiffed shoulder length red hair behind her ear and refreshed her pale pink lipstick. She turned in front of the mirror and frowned. Something wasn't right. She closed the upper button of her white blouse and the blazer of her classic dark blue pantsuit. That was better. She was now ready to go, but she didn't step out of the door before she had straightened a few pencils next to a notepad on a little table by the front door. Then she grabbed a dark blue cashmere winter coat that matched her outfit perfectly.

*****

Sienna locked the apartment door, stashed the key in her purse and quickly walked down the flight of stairs in front of her beautiful Victorian apartment building across the street from Boston Common. She made her way toward the Park Street subway station. She had a very athletic body that she kept in shape with regular yoga and a very consistent diet. Her whole life seemed very organized. She was a bit antisocial, not very spontaneous and got upset when something in her schedule suddenly changed.

She only had a few steps to the "T" but she still had a moment to enjoy the beautiful scenery in the park, which was sparkling in the morning sun, with birds chirping happily, jumping and flying from tree to tree. The snow that had been lying here for months had finally melted and, even though it was only February, it was a mild day and felt a little like spring. But she knew this was just one of New England nature's tricks. Winter was going to last for at least two more months and there were still some dark gloomy days ahead of the residents in the northeast. But Sienna tried to be positive and take one day at a time. She knew Mark Twain's quote: "If you don't like the weather in New England now, just wait a few minutes." That went both ways. Today was a good day, not only weather-wise but also in the law firm she worked for: Sienna was preparing herself mentally for the meeting she was about to have with her boss and some other managing partners of the law firm she worked with as an associate attorney. After successfully closing a big case and having been a very reliable hardworking member of the renowned law firm in Cambridge for almost ten years, she was sure her boss, Charles Chester-field Jr., was finally going to offer her a position as a partner today. Her job in this law firm was all she lived for. Sitting in her seat in the crowded subway, she imagined herself in court, finishing a long, brilliant summation with everyone in court hanging on her every word and then breaking out in applause after the judge declared the defendant innocent in this complicated and imaginary murder trial.

*****

Sienna's daydream abruptly came to a screeching halt, just like the subway, as an extremely dashing gentleman in his early to mid forties almost fell into her lap, spilling some of his coffee on the sleeve of her blazer. Unfortunately, she had taken her coat off because it was so warm in the subway. Sienna looked at her sleeve in horror and then at the man, as a voice delivered information in a thick Boston accent through the intercom system:

"There's a minor power outage on Beacon Street. We hope to be on our way shortly."

Sienna searched for a tissue and a Tide pen in her purse and tried to pat her coffee-stained sleeve dry prior to applying the Tide pen to remove the stain.

She was really annoyed. This was a major nightmare for Sienna who always had to have control over every situation in her life and felt like one of the possibly most important events in her career was now ruined.

The gentleman apologized profusely.

"Oh, no. What a bloody mess. I'm so sorry for ruining your jacket," said the man with a distinguished sounding British accent as he did a double take realizing how attractive Sienna was. As the subway started back up again, he handed her a business card. "Of course I'll take care of the dry cleaning. Please message me the amount and I'll reimburse you."

"It's okay," replied Sienna despite the fact that she was very upset and also took a closer look at him as she accepted the business card and stuck it into a little side pocket in her purse without looking at it. He was tall and clean shaven, with curly brown hair and reminded Sienna a bit of Hugh Grant, dressed in posh business attire with expensive Gucci shoes. He had a boyish face and the brightest blue eyes she had ever seen. She blinked as he turned around and exited at the next station that the subway was now rolling into, Harvard Avenue.

This was Sienna's station as well. She quickly jumped up and followed the man out of the subway. To her surprise, she bumped into him again a few minutes later at the entrance of her law firm's building, "Chesterfield & Partner." They both nodded as she quickly walked to the elevators and he stepped up to the reception desk to get a visitor's pass and ask for directions. Sienna was late for her meeting and she knew she'd be heading straight to the conference room where everyone was already waiting. She quickly pulled out her lip-gloss and reapplied it, using the metal panel of the elevator buttons as a mirror. Then she went through her hair with her fingers, pushed it behind her ears, straightened her jacket and took a deep breath.

*****

The door opened on the firm's floor and Sienna walked straight to the conference room where everyone was already waiting. Of course, she felt as if everyone was staring at her stained sleeve and wanted the floor to open up and swallow her.

"Good morning, Sienna, we've been waiting for you, but you're not the only one who's late..." said senior partner, Charles Chesterfield Jr., an older heavy-set gentleman with wavy white hair that was combed over a bald spot and was definitely too long for his age. Sienna always thought his hair looked like a British barrister's wig.

"There was a problem with the subway," Sienna replied, "It stopped in the middle of the tunnel due to some power outage..."

Suddenly, the door to the conference room was opened again abruptly and the British man who had stained Sienna's sleeve entered, walked up to Mr. Chesterfield and shook his hand.

"Hello, Mr. Chesterfield, I'm really sorry for the delay. Good morning, ladies and gentlemen," he said, his British accent coming through clearly as he nodded to the group, stopping his gaze briefly on Sienna. "There was a problem in the subway."

Mr. Chesterfield Jr. nodded and replied: "Yes, Ms. Brantley here was just explaining. Hello, Mr. Wilson. Well, let's get started with our meeting then since we're all here now. Ladies and gentlemen, I'd like to introduce you to Mr. Craig Wilson from London. He comes very highly recommended from our headquarters in England, has worked in Hong Kong, Paris and New York, and as of today he is going to be joining our local office as one of our partners. This is the position that I've been meaning to fill ever since Mr. Darden left us in November."

Everyone knocked on the table in an acknowledging manner except Sienna who was beside herself and so disappointed that she couldn't even think straight. She felt as if all of the blood in her head had rushed into her stomach and she might throw up, while Craig Wilson nodded to the group with a confident smile.

Mr. Chesterfield continued, making a hand movement toward Sienna: "Mr. Wilson, Ms. Brantley will show you to your new office and introduce you to the office staff after the meeting."

Sienna was barely able to nod but managed to remain professional and pulled herself together. Not only was she disappointed about not getting the job she had hoped for, but now she also felt like she was being degraded to a secretary. Usually, the office manager took care of these duties.

Mr. Chesterfield looked at Sienna as he explained: "Our office manager Ms. Smith is out sick today. Do you think you could step in and take Mr. Wilson under your wing, Sienna? I know this isn't your job but since you just closed your latest case yesterday, I thought you might be free for an hour or two this morning?"

Sienna replied short: "Sure." *I'm only going to be helping out a new colleague,* she thought, trying to calm herself down.

Craig Wilson smiled and stared frankly and curiously at her with his bright blue eyes. She blushed a little and looked down at her coffee-stained sleeve she had forgotten about. Now you have not only ruined my blazer but also stolen my job, Craig Wilson, she thought angrily as she looked back up and unknowingly glared at the handsome man with his complacent, almost arrogant smile.

Chapter 2

Craig Wilson was the type of man who was used to getting everything he wanted – including women. He had grown up the single child of wealthy parents in the upscale London neighborhood Highgate. His father was a lawyer and the job always came first. His mother had been a stay at home mom and then worked part-time in an art gallery when Craig started primary school. Craig never lacked attention or the means to get what he wanted. He was a mama's boy and was smothered with love by his proud and doting "mum". He brought some beautiful girls home in his teenage years but none were good enough for his mum, so from then on he kept his love affairs outside of their home. He had whizzed through secondary school and university, was one of the best players on his school's rugby team, played piano like a young Chopin (at least his mum thought so) and became one of the youngest lawyers in the history of Chesterfield & Partner, one of the UK's most prestigious international law firms with offices in Paris, New York, Boston, L.A. and Hong Kong. After interning for six months in New York and Boston right after college as a Junior Lawyer and working in both Hong Kong and Paris for a few years, it was time for Craig to get some more US experience under his belt and since the position as a partner was available and offered to him, he returned to Boston. He and his girlfriend Chloe just had a bad break up in Paris and one of them had to leave.

Unfortunately, it was Craig, since Chloe's father was the Managing Partner of the Paris office. He swore he was never going to date a coworker again - until he met Sienna.

*****

Craig certainly enjoyed being led through the firm by this very attractive, classy American woman, who was wearing a perfectly tailored navy blue business suit - although he could vividly imagine her in something a bit skimpier. He flirted non-stop and told her how great he was at basically everything he did and she was becoming annoyed. Could this guy not stop talking about himself or was he just an outright narcissist? And it seemed all fun and games for him, while Sienna had worked hard after leaving her home in the Keys and was now dealing with horrendous student loans.

She secretly wished Craig an incredibly hard case and couldn't wait to see how he would manage once challenged. Had he gotten the position as partner because he was a really good attorney? Or because his daddy had the connections? She would soon find out.

Sienna would also soon find out whether he was a big flirt or if he was really interested in her. He had proposed he take her to dinner, as repayment for showing him around the office and for dumping his coffee on her.

About a week later, after he had proven that he was a knowledgeable lawyer and returned from a business trip to Los Angeles, she finally caved and agreed to go out for happy hour right after work the next day. She hated to admit it to herself but she had actually missed him and the flirting a little. His charisma and impeccable manners that drew her to him like a bee to honey – and with dashing good looks made him very easy on the eyes.

*****

Sienna arrived in the office the next day and she had to admit that she was a bit excited to see Craig again and finally go out with him. Instead of the boring button up blouses that she usually wore, she was wearing a stylish low cut top underneath her blazer that showed off a hint of her cleavage in a subtle manner. She had thought of him so much during the past week that she blushed a little as they almost bumped into each other in the kitchen, both getting their morning coffee, which made her look even more beautiful.

"Oh, Sienna! Good morning. It's so good to finally see you again!" he said, sounding sincere. He talked in such a formal manner that she had to grin but she actually liked it. He tried to keep his eyes on her eyes, but couldn't keep them from wandering down a bit, first stopping at her lips with her bold red lipstick and then her nice outfit. "You look absolutely lovely today," he said, his British accent endearing as always, lifting his eyebrows a bit. He stepped up closer to her and looked around if anyone else could hear what he said and whispered into her ear. "May I give you a bit of advice? That lipstick looks really nice on you but I'd personally prefer something more subtle..."
Sienna just looked at him with a raised eyebrow. He was the first man who had ever given her advice on her lipstick color and red actually matched her hair color really well.

"Ummm, thanks, Craig. How was L.A.?" she asked to distract from herself.

He rolled his eyes. "I'll tell you later. I have a conference call with the London office this morning and have to get ready. They can't go into the last hearing of this very important case without getting my advice. See you later?"

"Sure," Sienna replied.

"I can't wait. Cheers!" He smiled at her, turned around and walked down the hallway toward his office.

Craig and Sienna had agreed on not leaving the firm together but meeting at the restaurant after work instead to keep office gossip to a minimum. Since Sienna was the one who knew her way around Boston, she chose Antonio's Seafood, situated in the Seaport District in Downtown Boston and one of the best restaurants in the city. She didn't really know where else to go since she never went out but decided against one of the stuffy old-fashioned steakhouses with dark wood interiors where the lawyers usually met.

Sienna stepped out of the office building, took the Red Line back into Boston, got off at South Station and walked across the Summer Street Bridge with a view of the Boston Tea Party Ship, a famous tourist attraction. She made her way along Summer Street and took a left onto D Street to the water's edge at Boston Harbor where she ran into Craig.

They greeted each other with a "long time no see" as they came up to the glamorous high-tech looking skyline in the area that used to be working fish piers 20 years ago.

"This all used to be fish piers. Developers turned it into a modern area with cafes, restaurants and bars," Sienna explained as they walked up to a flight of open metal stairs and he made a charming gesture for her to go ahead. Again, she was impressed by Craig's impeccable manners. The stairs led up to the waterfront restaurant "Antonio's Seafood" with big sliding glass doors across the entire length of the dining-room that opened up in the summer to an outdoor cocktail bar, high ceilings, a contemporary interior with halogen lights, metal tables with bar stools and a big mural depicting a nautical scene with breaching whales and frolicking dolphins on the inside wall. A young hostess led them to their table and Sienna was glad she had made a reservation. The place was abuzz with young urban professionals meeting here for happy hour or more. Sienna frowned and looked out of the window as Craig flirted with the hostess. *He obviously can't help it,* she thought annoyed. What she didn't know is that Craig pretended to be flirting but absolutely took notice of how men were stopping in their tracks and staring at his date, which made him feel very important.

*****

After a brief wait, the waiter came up and introduced himself.

"Good evening, folks. My name is Tom and I'll be your server tonight. Do you already have a drink preference or may I get you the drink menu?"

Craig ordered two vodka Martinis, some oysters and asked the waiter to recommend the main course, making sure everything was okay with Sienna. She just nodded, watching him and enjoying listening to his British accent. It made him appear so classy and she knew she was falling for him. He was funny and sexy and the conversation that never stopped went from office talk to Craig's work in the different offices around the world, his time in Hong Kong and Paris and then briefly to Sienna's childhood in the Keys.

"What made you want to leave the Keys? I have never been there, but I would kill to live in such a tropical place right on the water. As a matter of fact, my parents and I used to vacation a lot in the Cayman Islands," Craig said.

"Well, it would be like you coming from a boring small town in England and wanting to leave that town to see the big wide world. And can you imagine any colleges in the Keys? There's only a community college. Everyone that wanted to get a bachelor's or master's degree had to leave. Most kids were expected to take over their family's business," she explained. "Of course I loved growing up in such a beautiful place, but it wasn't anything special for us. I actually hated it because my parents worked non-stop and never had time for us. My parents were both veterinarians and they owned and ran a turtle sanctuary, which they lived for. We never went to the beach as a family or out in a boat – unless it was to rescue a turtle, of course," she added with a grin.

He nodded. "My father was a workaholic too but my mom was always there for me." He looked at her in a flirtatious manner. "And were there no high school sweethearts that you left? Handsome young tanned beach boys?"

She laughed briefly and her mind drifted off to Ricky as she looked out of the window. *Yes, there was.* For a second, some memories surfaced...

Flashback

20 years ago, 1998, Turtle Key, Florida Keys

Sienna, 16, long red hair with bangs, wearing a denim mini skirt and a tank top with spaghetti straps, had snuck down to the dock in back of her family's property to meet Ricky, 17, wearing a pair of loose fitting high-rise acid washed jeans and a short-sleeved cotton plaid. She had brought a blanket and some chips and Ricky had brought his discman, a little speaker that he had plugged into the device and two beers. He was playing "Everybody," by the Backstreet Boys, Sienna's current favorite song and currently at the top of the charts. She spread out the blanket and they both sat down on it. He handed her the second beer.

"I snuck these from my dad."

"Hope you don't get in trouble," she replied grinning.

They clinked bottles and both took a swig. Sienna didn't like the taste at all but didn't admit it.

"Oh, that's my favorite song. Can you play it from the beginning?" she asked.

"Sure." He pressed a button and the song started again from the beginning.

They just sat there, listening to the music, looking out at the Gulf.

"I really wish I could go to the concert next month," she said into the silence.

"Won't your parents let you go?"

"You know my parents, I think they're paranoid, just because of the big crowds and so..."

"Well," he said grinning and pulled two concert tickets out of his pocket, "I already got these, just in case. Otherwise it'll sell out."

Sienna looked at him with big eyes and her mouth hanging open.

"Wow, that's so awesome!" she said and hugged him as they looked in to each other's eyes and started kissing each other. They had already been dating for a while now but their kiss was still tender and shy. After a while, they stopped kissing and looked out at the Gulf where the sun was slowly setting. Sienna said: "Maybe I should just tell my parents I'm sleeping over at Hannah's..."

He nodded. "That might be a good idea. But aren't Camilla and Daniel going too? Your parents would probably let you go with them."

She nodded and took another small swig of her beer. She could feel the alcohol rising to her head.

The next song "All I Have To Give" began playing. It was incredibly romantic and they looked into each other's eyes as they started kissing each other again, this time more passionately, as the setting sun disappeared into the Gulf.

*****

Back to Present Time

Sienna shook off her memories. She certainly didn't want to discuss them with Craig and quickly changed the subject. He could tell that there was something but didn't inquire any further. He preferred talking about himself anyhow. They clinked glasses before they took another sip of their wine. Craig's voice became a bit raspy as he asked: "And how about now? Is there anyone in particular that you think of before you fall asleep?"

Yes, you, she thought, but she just shook her head. "No, work has been exhausting the past few months. Besides going to yoga regularly, there's barely any time left for a social life."

"I agree," he replied. "Between traveling and the long hours, I barely even find the time to work out. I hope in spring when the days are longer things will get better. I used to jog and even ran a half Marathon once. My dream would be to run the Boston Marathon one day..."

I can tell that you're athletic, she thought and just nodded.

Sienna truly enjoyed the conversation with Craig even though he did seem to talk a lot about himself and made sure she knew that he had been the best of his class, the best on his rugby team, the best in his college graduation year and how much his parents adored him. She wondered again if these were warning signs of a narcissist, but then she also realized how much he was into culture, how well read he was and that there were many favorite books and movies they both had in common and she threw all caution to the wind. After all, he was an only child and they were probably different and more self-centered than people with siblings. Sienna was truly impressed by the way Craig ate with a fork AND a knife, unlike most American men she had gone out with who ate like barbarians and held their fork like a spear, but she was embarrassed when Craig complained to the waiter about the wine and sent it back. She hadn't even noticed that they were already on their second bottle.

Finally, the waiter brought the check and, even though Sienna insisted on splitting the bill, Craig took care of it and said:

"You can buy dinner next time."

She nodded happily. Obviously he had enjoyed himself and there was going to be a next time. Craig extremely overtipped the waiter but then lectured him on taking too long to bring the check back after running the card through the credit card machine.

"We're in a hurry, man, if someone tips you that well you might want to give him more preferential treatment."

The embarrassed waiter thanked Craig quietly and slinked away.

Sienna frowned briefly. This was the second time that Craig had been rude and condescending to the waiter. She knew the saying about the way people treated waiters was an indication of their character, but she was too tipsy to really be bothered by that right now, even when Craig said: "What a wanker", loud enough for others to hear, as they walked out of the restaurant.

They both lived in the same part of Boston so they shared a taxi home and it went without saying that Craig got out with Sienna.

*****

They stood in front of her apartment building, light snowflakes dancing around them, gazing into each other's eyes as they finally shared the kiss they had both been dreaming about, at first gently and then more and more passionately. All doubts that Sienna may ever have had vanished as they walked up to her apartment and slowly undressed each other, moving toward the bedroom…

Chapter 3

Early the next morning, Craig jerked awake out of a deep sleep. He looked over to the side and saw Sienna's red hair next to him sticking out from underneath the comforter. Shocked, he realized where he was, quickly jumped out of bed and gathered his clothes that were scattered all over the floor leading from the bedroom to the hallway. He didn't know what to do about his feelings that were slipping away. He had to stay in control of the situation and feelings couldn't be involved. Last night was just meant to be a flirt and nothing else. Craig thought about some of the things they had talked about last night and how they had laughed about the same jokes and how smart and funny Sienna was under that prim and proper façade. He was starting to fall for her and that was exactly what couldn't happen. His last serious relationship with a beautiful French colleague in Paris had ended in a nightmare with his heart broken and him not being able to work at the firm in France anymore, one of the reasons he had come to Boston. He had sworn he never wanted a relationship with a coworker again...

He got up quietly, quickly dressed and looked around one more time, gazed upon Sienna's beautiful profile for a few more seconds and snuck out of the apartment. This had to stay a flirt and he couldn't get involved with her. He stepped out into the street and tightened his coat around him. The sun was coming up behind the trees in the park and it was going to be a beautiful day, but it was still chilly and there was a fresh dusting of snow on the ground. Quickly, he marched the few blocks along the park to his apartment that was just a five- minute walk from Sienna's.

*****

A bit later, Sienna woke up smiling. Her arm was stretched out to the other side of the bed. She carefully patted the spot where she expected Craig. She looked up but he was gone. Then she realized she had a splitting headache, put her hand on her forehead, closed her eyes and moaned. She slowly got up, walked over to the kitchen, poured a glass of water and got an Alka-Seltzer from the cupboard. Frowning, she watched the tablet slowly sizzle until it had entirely dissolved. She checked her cell phone. No messages.

It was a very awkward encounter that same morning when Sienna and Craig both walked into the kitchen to get their coffee at the same time as usual. Anita, a young intern, was making copies at the copy machine that was located right at the entrance of the kitchen and Craig acted as if nothing had happened and greeted Sienna with his usual stiff British demeanor which made her never know whether he was serious or joking: "How are you today, Madam?"

"Great, how about you?" she replied and tried to read something in his eyes, but he backed off and left the kitchen, since Anita was obviously eavesdropping.

Sienna understood and agreed that nobody in the office should know about last night so she played along with the game.

*****

Craig and Sienna continued to go out and since Craig was so charismatic and extremely charming, Sienna really had a great time, but she was so smitten that she never realized the extent of how much Craig talked about himself and had started belittling some things she did or said, obviously trying to make her feel bad about herself. Just some little things like her tripping on the curb as they were walking through the park, "Wow, we're a bit clumsy, aren't we?" or pointing out that she had a slightly crooked nose, which actually she didn't mind. She had always thought it made her face interesting. "Wow, did you ever break your nose? I just realized it has a little hump here." But then he corrected himself quickly and said: "But it makes you look even cuter."

The worst thing was that he was a partner in the firm and she wasn't which he liked to mention and it went like a dagger through her heart. This had been extremely important to her. It seemed so typical that men were preferred in large law firms when it came to promotions. Craig liked to say that women didn't belong in leading positions. Sienna wasn't sure if he was joking or not but just ended up ignoring these comments.

He was also notoriously late for everything and sometimes Sienna would just sit there, wondering why she was letting him do this to her. It was disrespectful of her time. But then he'd show up and be so charming that she forgot and laughed about his funny jokes and stories. Her heart was already too far into the relationship and it was too late for her to leave it without getting hurt...

*****

Chapter 4

A few days later, Sienna was sitting in her office. She was supposed to be working on a rather complicated case but couldn't concentrate because she was thinking about Craig. He was getting under her skin. They had had such a wonderful evening – and night - again but then he had disappeared again in the morning before she woke up and didn't text her or even acknowledge their previous night when they saw each other in the office. She hated not being in control of the situation. She wasn't sure whether she wanted more than he did and it drove her nuts. He constantly switched from being extremely charming to seemingly not interested in her at all and withdrew especially when their relationship seemed to be getting steadier. Maybe she needed to withdraw. She didn't need drama in her life. She needed to know where she belonged.

Suddenly the phone rang, startling her. She pulled herself together and answered.

"This is Sienna Brantley," she said in a very businesslike manner.

There was a slight pause but then the person on the line finally talked.

"Hola! This is Bianca Torrez. Is Anderson your maiden name by any chance? I'm looking for Sienna Anderson from Turtle Key. Do you remember me? Your old neighbor in Turtle Key, your mom's friend!"

For a second, Sienna was speechless but then she replied in an upbeat manner. Of course she remembered Bianca. She had loved her and there were times when she had hung out at Bianca's house and with Bianca's daughters more often than at her own home.

"Bianca! Of course I remember you! Yes, I got married about ten years ago and my last name is Brantley now. I should change it back, the marriage didn't last very long. You sound just like 17 years ago! What's going on?"

"Well, I don't have good news, unfortunately. Since we used to be close, I was chosen to contact you. It wasn't easy to find you because of your new last name. Even on social media, I just kept looking for a Sienna Anderson. Then I finally started looking for lawyers in Boston with your first name and I could only find the work number, so I apologize for calling you at work even though this is a private matter."

Sienna asked carefully: "Uh oh, what happened?" It could only be something regarding her sister's family, her only relatives, or maybe the Sea Turtle Sanctuary.

"Did you hear about a bad car accident in the Keys about two weeks ago?

"As a matter of fact, I did briefly read about it but then got distracted and forgot."

"Well, it was Camilla and Ricky."

Sienna froze and let Bianca continue.

"An exhausted tractor-trailer driver fell asleep at the wheel on Grassy Key by the Dolphin Research Center and hit them head on. Both of them were dead immediately. We would have called you earlier but nobody knew how to get in touch with you and there was so much going on. I'm so sorry..."

For a slight moment, Sienna felt like someone had punched her in the stomach and she was going to pass out.

Suddenly, several text messages came in on her phone but she ignored them.

"The Celebration of Life is in a few days," continued Bianca. "I've been taking care of the kids and can keep doing that as long as you need me to. Do you think you can come down?"

Sienna was too shocked to reply. A thousand things raced through her mind.

*****

Flashback

19 years ago, 1999, Turtle Key, Florida Keys

Ricky, one year older, and Camilla, two years older than Sienna, were off to college at University of Miami where they were both going to college for veterinary medicine. Everyone was standing at Ricky's car in the parking lot of the Sea Turtle Sanctuary: Sienna, Camilla, their parents and Ricky. They were all excited for Ricky and Camilla, Sienna didn't think much of her sister hanging out or going to the same college with her boyfriend. She was so sure of his love. They were soul mates, had already been dating for almost three years and nothing could come between them. Camilla and her friends often hung out with Sienna and Ricky. Camilla and Ricky were friends but nothing more.

Sienna and Ricky gave each other one last kiss, he got into the driver's seat of the old pick-up and he and Camilla were off. Sienna and her parents stood there, waving as the car took a left onto US1 and then headed north.

Sienna heard her father mumbling: "They make a much better couple anyway," but didn't really give it a second thought. Until a year later...

*****

2nd Flashback

A year later, 2000, Turtle Key, Florida Keys

Sienna had just come home from her first semester of law school in Boston. She was tired from the flight and two-hour drive from Miami airport to Turtle Key and was wondering why her girlfriend Maureen had picked her up instead of Ricky. After bringing her luggage up to her room and changing into something more comfortable, she walked down the stairs and overheard her mother and sister Camilla in the kitchen.

"You're going to have to tell her," said their mother, "she's going to find out sooner or later."

"She's going to kill me," replied Camilla.

"Get it over with and tell her. She'll be upset but she'll have to understand if you're pregnant..."

Sienna, who had already reached the kitchen, stopped in her tracks, shocked about what she had just heard.

"What did you just say, Mom?"

"Um, nothing. I think you and Camilla need to talk," she said, quickly gave Sienna a hug and left the kitchen.

"Why am I going to kill you, Camilla?"

Camilla burst out in tears. She stood in front of the kitchen counter, sobbing.

"You're going to hate me so much. You're going to hate me..."

"What's going on Camilla? Just tell me."

"I'm pregnant... by Ricky."

Sienna felt as if she'd been punched in the stomach and might have to throw up. She just stared at her sister, then she turned around, ran out of the house and down the path leading to the Gulf. Automatically, Sienna ran to her and Ricky's spot where they had hung out and listened to music or made out so many times. She dropped down onto the dock and just sat there sobbing, inconsolably.

Back to Present Time

Sienna had hated Camilla and Ricky for what they had done but over the years she had found peace with her life in Boston and her work at the law firm that she truly enjoyed. She wished she had been able to see them and talk to them one more time.

This whole time, Bianca was patiently waiting for an answer. Finally, Sienna remembered Bianca was on the line and said:

"I'm sorry Bianca, can you give me your phone number? I need to get out of the office to be able to talk better. I'll call you back when I'm home."

"Of course, honey, take your time. I'm here whenever you want to talk."

*****

As if in a trance, Sienna packed up her laptop, grabbed her briefcase, her purse and her coat and walked out of the office with long, quick steps.

Craig and Mr. Chesterfield were standing in the hallway, chatting as Sienna walked past them, still holding back the tears but as pale as a ghost.

Craig took one look at her and asked shocked:

"Are you okay, Sienna?"

"I just got some really bad news, I'll call you later, Mr. C. I might have to take a couple of weeks off," she said breathlessly and was gone.
Craig and Mr. C, as he was called by all of the coworkers, just looked at each other, quizzically.

As she rode downstairs in the elevator, Sienna briefly checked her phone. All text messages were from Craig, asking if everything was OK. When she didn't answer because she was too much in shock, he proceeded to bombard her with text messages.

She finally texted back: "Sorry, got some really bad news about my sister and her husband in the Keys. They had a fatal accident. Need some time to myself tonight."

"OMG. I'm so sorry," he replied. "Call me if you need anything."

*****

Two hours later, Craig, more than a bit tipsy, rang Sienna's doorbell with Thai takeout, since he knew it was her favorite, and a six-pack of beer. She had been sitting on her couch, staring at an old photo of her and her older sister Camilla.

"I really need to be by myself tonight," she said as she had buzzed him in and he came up the stairs skipping every other step.

"Can I just come in for a little?" he asked sounding like a little defiant boy. "I brought you something to eat."

"That's really nice of you but I'm really not hungry right now," she replied but opened the door further for him to come in. He gave her a quick peck on the lips as he walked in and walked toward her little kitchen where he set down the bag with the take out, got out a few dishes and cartons and started preparing a portion of Pad Thai by adding hot sauce, peanut sauce and some chopped peanuts.

Sienna had walked back to the couch and sat there, forlorn. Her eyes were puffy and red from crying but she didn't care. She seriously wasn't up to having company and just wanted to go to bed but also still had to call Bianca and make travel arrangements to go down to the Keys.

Craig carried two bottles of Singha beer and his bowl of Pad Thai over to the couch, sat down next to Sienna, offering her a forkful of Pad Thai, which she rejected, shaking her head. He drank a big swig of beer and didn't seem to get that she wasn't in the mood and not feeling well.

"Come on, have a bite," he tried to coax her, almost shoving the food into her mouth.

She shook her head again and he handed her the bottle from which she took a small sip to keep the peace.

"Well, there you go," he said smiling, shoveled more Pad Thai in his mouth, finished his beer and got up to get another one. As he walked back over to Sienna, he drank half of the second beer, sat down next to her, put his arm around her shoulders and tried to kiss her in quite an obtrusive manner she found disgusting since he was already drunk. She couldn't stand his advances and the way he didn't seem to have a thought or care about her feelings, freed herself from his arms, jumped up and said:

"I really appreciate you bringing the food but I think it's time for you to go now."

He just glared at her in disbelief. People didn't send him away. His blood pressure started rising for a minute. He grabbed her wrists and tried to kiss her again, this time a bit forcefully. She freed her arms from his grip, stepped back and yelled: "GET OUT!"

Once again, he just stood there, staring at her, his nostrils flaring, but then he pulled himself together, grabbed the rest of the six-pack and left without a word. Sienna just stood there for a while. She was shaking. She didn't know if he might have become more violent, but she was sure that he had a temper and this incident had truly scared her. Not really what she wanted in a relationship. She needed to end this as soon as possible. Before she flew down to the Keys.

*****

The next morning before work Sienna called Craig to tell him they shouldn't see each other anymore.

"Hi, Craig, I hope I'm not calling you too early?

"No, I'm getting ready for work. What's up?"

He seemed like a different person than last night with his usual charming British accent.

"I'm sorry that I'm telling you over the phone, but I wanted to talk to you before we see each other in the firm. I don't think we should see each other anymore."

"Oh, come on, Sienna, you're in shock from the news of your sister and brother-in-law being dead. You need me now more than ever. I'm sorry, I was a little drunk last night."

"No, I'm ending this. I'm sorry. Your behavior last night was unacceptable."

"You can't live without me, just admit it."

"Craig it's over. Please understand. I've got to go, bye."

She ended the call. He just stood there, staring at his phone for a while, then his face became angry and distorted and he smashed the phone onto the ground.

Chapter 5

Two days later Sienna stepped out of the automatic door of the main terminal of Miami International Airport and was hit by the extreme heat and a thick wall of humidity, immediately making her sweaty and uncomfortable, even though it was only the second week of March and theoretically still winter. She set her suitcases down for a second to gather her wits and check where the car rental counters were located. *Oh, yeah, something I didn't miss*, she thought to herself, *the terrible humidity...*

Even though it was overcast and looked like it was about to start raining, she felt blinded by the bright light in the subtropics and fished a case with a pair of designer sunglasses out of her purse. She took her sweater off that had served its purpose on the plane and wouldn't be needed again until her return flight, folded it neatly and stashed it carefully into her carry-on. Then she found the signs for "Car Rentals", grabbed the handles of her suitcase and carry-on and walked along the side of the building.

The airport was buzzing with activity and the lines at the car rental counters were long. Craig and she hadn't seen each other since the terrible evening two days ago but he hadn't accepted the fact that she had broken up with him and had started texting her as if nothing had happened.

Sienna read a few messages but didn't respond to them like others she had been ignoring for days. At some point she was just going to have to block him. He was acting like a stubborn little boy who wasn't getting his way and she could not forget about how badly he had behaved on that last evening.

*****

Finally it was Sienna's turn. She stepped up to the car rental counter, waited as the employee pulled her reservation up on his computer, then she initialed her car rental agreement in at least ten different spots. She got the key fob for her car and walked over to the rows and rows of rental cars. Her heart leaped when she saw the sleek red Mustang Convertible that she had been upgraded to and which would be a blast to drive around in the Keys. It was a bit hard to fit both suitcases into the small trunk but she managed. With a quick look into the black sky, she made the wise decision to leave the top closed for now. Then she was ready to depart, pressed the ignition button, slowly drove out of the airport and merged into the heavy Miami afternoon traffic heading toward the Turnpike. She was a bit rusty since she hadn't driven for a while. Nobody needed a car in Boston. But soon she got used to driving in the heavy Miami traffic. Her GPS led her to the entrance ramp of "Turnpike South". Just as she merged onto the Turnpike, some first heavy drops smacked onto the car and a torrential downpour started as Sienna only knew them from Florida. Such a monsoon rain was unusual for March but the weather had been crazy lately. She only had a few years of experience driving in such a downpour but not in a convertible with a soft top so she felt insecure driving through the monsoon. The rain battered against the windshield and the heavy drops were noisy on the soft top. Traffic that was usually moving at 70 mph, slowed down to about 30 mph and, even going this slowly, Sienna could barely see anything. The windshield wipers weren't even fast enough on the highest setting. Rush hour traffic slowly crawled south, past Homestead and Florida City through the southernmost part of the Everglades National Park. The southernmost leg of Highway 1, Overseas Highway, began with Mile Markers showing how many miles Sienna was away from Key West. Turtle Key stretched from approximately Mile Marker 47 - 60 and was considered the heart of the Florida Keys.

*****

Sienna was finally past the "18 mile stretch", the notorious strip between Homestead and the Keys that was basically nothing and had seen many accidents with people falling asleep or driving too fast and losing control. Endless swamp and mangroves on both sides of the road were fenced in with eight feet tall chain link fences, with barbwire on top, to keep alligators and other wildlife from crossing the road.

The Mustang crossed over the Jewfish Creek Bridge heading into Key Largo. The rain stopped, the clouds broke open and the sun appeared, creating a big rainbow all the way across the horizon above the shallow turquoise-green water. On one side the Atlantic Ocean and on the other the Gulf of Mexico, a tropical paradise with little islands and fishing boats as far as the eye could reach. As Sienna drove over the 65 feet high bridge with water on both sides, she felt like a bird skimming over the water.

Sienna took the beautiful scenery in with a smile, but she also had tears in her eyes. She had missed this gorgeous area she had grown up in, but wished she were returning under more pleasant circumstances.

Sienna passed a few strip malls with a Winn-Dixie grocery store on the Gulf side, along with countless t-shirt, sandals, seashell outlets, diving schools and boat charters. She remembered that somewhere here was a little hole in the wall coffee place with the best Cuban coffee ever. First she drove past some bigger hotels and resorts with beautiful sandy beaches and swaying palm trees, boat storage facilities, marinas. She was amazed at how many new hotels and resorts had been added to the landscape since the last time she was there.

Then she discovered the sign pointing to John Pennecamp Coral Reef Park on the Ocean side where she had started diving lessons with Ricky the summer before she had left but never finished. She remembered the unreal feeling of breathing under water with an oxygen tank and like she was flying in between coral reefs and thousands of fishes.

Sienna snapped out of her daydream and memories about diving as she suddenly spotted her parents' former favorite restaurant "The Fish House". It was on the opposite side of the four-lane road, so she couldn't stop right now. She remembered going there with her parents and sister on Sundays and for special occasions.

She almost drove past the little hole in the wall Latin café she had been looking for that was painted in a faded turquoise and belonged to two of her old friends' Cuban parents and had been there forever. Sienna, Camilla and their friends had often stopped here for breakfast after a forbidden late night of partying in Miami since it was open 24/7.

She quickly took a right into the gravel parking lot and walked up to the building. "Buenas tardes," said Sienna, making sure to roll the R in "tardes" properly, as she walked inside the small café that was currently between lunch and dinner and essentially empty, also realizing she hadn't spoken Spanish in years. Spanish was almost a second language in Miami and the Keys. Only a lonely fisherman was having an early dinner in a corner in the back, enjoying his beer and grub after a long day fishing out on the ocean.

The older, heavyset Cuban lady behind the counter, who was currently counting the money in the register, looked up briefly, nodded and replied with a brief "Hola". She was tired and waiting for her son to take over for the evening shift. But then she hesitated, looked up again and took a closer look at Sienna. Her kind round face lit up and a smile spread across her face.

"Sienna? Que pasa? Is that you?"

"Hey, Maria," replied Sienna. She recognized the strict Cuban patron immediately who had been running the café for at least forty years now with her husband Juan after escaping Cuba on a boat and barely making it to Key West, penniless but alive. Her sons Miguel and Pablo had gone to High School in Turtle Key with Sienna and Camilla since they lived further south, closer to Turtle Key. Maria came around the counter and gave Sienna a big motherly hug.

"Sienna," she said with her loud, vivacious voice and thick Cuban accent, "I'm so sorry about what happened to your sister and Ricky. Is that why you came?"

"Thanks, Maria. Yup. It looks like I have to take care of the kids now and figure out what's going to happen with the Sea Turtle Sanctuary."

Maria was wringing her hands as her eyes welled up with tears.

"Oh, those poor little niños. Madre de dios. It happened right in front of the Dolphin Research Center, so tragic. There was nothing they could do for them. Let me know if I can help. I mean it, mi amore."

"Gracias, Maria. I might need that." She tried to change the conversation to a happier subject. "How are the boys? How many grandkids do you have now?"

"Ocho. Everyone's fine. Miguel is a hotshot plastic surgeon in Coconut Grove, but Pablo is here and runs the place with me now," Maria replied proudly and reached behind the counter to pick up a few photos from underneath the cash register. But then she realized that Sienna was probably hungry and thirsty and interrupted herself.

"I'm sorry, mi niña linda. I'm so selfish. Let me get you something to drink first. Are you hungry?"

Sienna shook her head. "No, I'd just love a Cuban coffee, how about a cafecito." She smiled. "As soon as I started thinking about it, I couldn't forget about it and thought of the good old days stopping here after partying in Miami."

Maria frowned and grinned. She didn't like those memories of worrying about her boys and their friends partying or going to concerts in Miami and Key West. But they had no choice, there was no nightlife whatsoever in the mid-Keys. She rushed behind the counter and prepared a fresh cup of Cuban espresso with granulated brown sugar and handed it to Sienna.

"Sit, my dear," said Maria worried. "How about an empanada or some tres leches?"

"Next time, Maria. Gracias. I really want to get to the Turtle Sanctuary before dark. I'm already running late."

"Okay, I understand, mi angel. It's so good to see you!" And she hugged her again.

Sienna sipped from the little espresso cup, set it down on the counter and was on her way. She merged back into the heavy rush-hour traffic on the Overseas Highway heading south and turned the radio on. Just by coincidence the chorus of the same song that she and her friends had listened to almost twenty years ago, "Livin' la Vida Loca" by Ricky Martin, came blaring out of the speakers:

Sienna tapped her fingers to the rhythm of the music. Suddenly, as she was heading out of Key Largo, She saw a sign for the "Blond Giraffe Key Lime Pie Factory" on the right and was barely able to break and take a right into the parking lot. She couldn't pass the home of the best Key Lime Pie in the world without stopping. One of her good friends from way back when, Tania, had entered her homemade key lime pie in Key West's pie contest 18 years ago, won and then a few years later opened up the Key Lime Pie Factory which became a huge success. Sienna stepped into the store. Tania immediately recognized her, came rushing around the counter and gave her a big bear hug.

"I'm so happy to see you, Sienna!" At first they beamed at each other but then they both got teary eyes because they both knew why Sienna was here.

"I'm so sorry about Camilla and Ricky," said Tania.

"Yeah, sorry that I didn't get in touch before this sad occasion but I've been following you on social media," replied Sienna.

"I understand," replied Tania who knew the whole story.

"Wow, this place looks great!" exclaimed Sienna, looking around the store with various Key lime pies in a glass case, candy, cookies, gifts, candles and other key lime specialties.

"Come and take a look at the garden," said Tania. She walked ahead of Sienna and showed her a beautiful open-air café with rows of hundreds of padlocks of love where people had "locked their love with the ones closest to their hearts."

"This is gorgeous. I'll have to come back so that we can catch up."

"Yes, please call me. I can also come down to Turtle Key and we can have lunch or so. Let me pack up a key lime pie for you to go. Is Meringue still your favorite?"

"Yes, I can't believe you remember," replied Sienna smiling.

She took the thermal container with the key lime pie inside and they hugged each other, promising they'd talk soon.

Sienna's picturesque drive continued and soon she passed the sign announcing Islamorada, which meant Village of Islands. As soon as her eyes spotted the giant lobster on the right at the entrance of Islamorada, she smiled again briefly. This giant Florida Keys Spiny Lobster - nicknamed Betsy - was an old Islamorada landmark. She was made of fiberglass and measured 30 feet tall and 40 feet wide and resided in a parking lot of the Rain Barrel Artisans Village, a tropical garden oasis lined with a collection of specialty shops, galleries and boutiques. Sienna and her friends had stopped there many times for silly photo opportunities and refreshments. She suddenly wondered if she'd still find her old photo albums in her old room in the cottage.

*****

As she continued her drive, Sienna passed several beautiful resorts where there used to be nothing but mangroves and the big sign pointing out "Theater of the Sea", a big entertainment and learning center all around creatures of the ocean from dolphins to sea turtles, sharks, sting rays and sea lions. Again, rinky-dink strip malls full of little shell, sandal and t-shirt "outlets" as well as dive shops lined both sides of the road, with palm trees, some residences and the ocean on the one side and the Gulf on the other right behind them. It seemed that tons and tons of condos had been built here too in the past 15 years. The march of progress hadn't stopped anywhere.

*****

Sienna had opened the top of her convertible and the balmy early evening wind blew through her beautiful reddish hair. She turned the radio back on. The warm sun tingled on her skin and felt so good – something she had really missed, especially after the long and dreary New England winter. She crossed a few more bridges, channels and Keys, again with beautiful turquoise water on both sides, passed the beautiful resort Hawks Cay on the ocean side on Duck Key and finally arrived on Grassy Key.

Sienna turned the music down as she passed the Dolphin Research Center on the Gulf. The dolphin statue that had been there since the "Flipper" days smiled down on her. The Dolphin Research Center had gotten its new name in the 80s after previously having been called "Flipper's Sea School". Sienna shuddered thinking that right here was where her sister and Ricky had died about two weeks ago. She could see the thick black skid marks in the road.

She turned the radio off and her eyes filled up with tears as she continued her drive into Turtle Key but she tried to shake off the gloomy thoughts.

*****

Sienna got distracted as she discovered the sign leading to Coco Plum Beach on the Ocean side, her favorite beach in the world where she and her friends used to party and make bonfires with wooden pallets they "borrowed" from the back parking lot of Winn Dixie. Another spot that was full of memories of her and Ricky. She wished she could have stopped for a swim but now she just wanted to get to the cottage. She passed the airport on the Gulf side, which she had kind of forgotten about too. Ricky's father used to be a member of the pilot's club and he and Ricky had taken Sienna on a few beautiful flights in his small Cessna. She remembered the gorgeous views from the plane and sighed. She had slowly blocked all of these beautiful memories out of her mind...

*****

Even after all this time, Sienna had no trouble finding her old home and the Sea Turtle Sanctuary. The lump in her throat became bigger and bigger as she pulled into the Turtle Sanctuary with her family's residence, a pretty pink two-story cottage on stilts, right behind it. The stilts had been added and the cottage rebuilt after the devastating damage from hurricane Andrew in 1992. She remembered everything, including evacuating and hunkering down in the hurricane shelter at Stanley Switlik Elementary School as if it were yesterday. Those were some not so happy memories of growing up in the Keys - grabbing some important belongings, stuffing the cat in his cat carrier and leaving everything else behind...

The hospital and its faded pink buildings were set back from the street in back of a parking lot that was big enough for about thirty cars, but right now the parking lot was pretty much empty. Everything was exactly the same as 17 years ago except that the paint now had a patina showing how the buildings had aged. The palm trees and other plants around them had grown twice as tall.

The Sea Turtle Sanctuary was already closed but there was always an emergency staff to take care of the turtles day and night.

Sienna didn't bother checking in at the rescue. She grabbed her suitcase, carry-on, purse and the thermal bag with the key lime pie and walked straight up to the quaint cottage on stilts in the back where she and her sister Camilla had grown up.

Chapter 6

Flashback

30 years ago, 1988, Turtle Key, Florida Keys

Six-year old Sienna and her eight-year old sister Camilla - Camilla with strawberry blonde hair and Sienna's a darker red - jumped out of the school bus that had stopped at the bus stop on Overseas Highway in front of the Sea Turtle Sanctuary. They had backpacks on their backs. The bus had its stop signs extended and lights flashing. All of the cars headed south had stopped, waiting patiently for the school bus to continue on its way.

A tall blonde au pair from Sweden, Agnetha, in short cut offs and a t-shirt, stood at the bus stop waiting for them. She greeted the girls with a big toothy smile, trying to give them hugs as they ran past her. They stopped for a split second, acknowledging Agnetha, but Camilla was on a mission and Sienna followed her.

"No, girls," yelled Agnetha after them, "your mom and dad have to concentrate. There's no news yet."

"We want to see the turtle that was reported this morning!" they both yelled simultaneously and ran into the entrance of the Sea Turtle Sanctuary, but young employee Bridget, stepping out of the reception area, stopped them sternly and explained:

"Guys, stop and listen to me for a second. Your mom and dad are still in surgery. It's a loggerhead and they named it Olivia. They have to concentrate and can't be bothered right now. They're still untangling all the fishing line from poor Olivia's neck and flippers and had to sedate her so she holds still. So you have to be super patient and wait until they're done."

"But we wanna watch and see Olivia," whined Camilla and Sienna chimed in. "Yeah, can't we watch through the window?"

"It's rather boring and they really have to concentrate," replied Bridget. "Why don't you guys go and get your homework done and I promise I'll call as soon as Olivia wakes up and Agnetha can walk you over."

The big loggerhead turtle weighing over 100 pounds had been discovered by a group of snorkelers the same morning floating around John Pennecamp National Park in Key Largo and was picked up by employees of the Sea Turtle Sanctuary after the Coast Guard had been informed. The loggerhead had yards and yards of fishing twine wrapped around its neck and front flippers and was in a very obvious state of distress.

Camilla and Sienna whined but complied. They knew that Bridget wouldn't back off. She was very strict and never caved. The turtles always came first. Camilla used to joke that turtles were protected but kids weren't. With hanging heads, they trotted to the cottage in the back, followed by Agnetha who tried to cheer them up.

"Girls, I'll make you some grilled cheese sandwiches for lunch and then I'll take you to Coco Plum Beach as soon as you're done with your homework."

"The turtles are always more important…" exclaimed a whiny Camilla, Sienna nodded but she was distracted easier as she looked out at the beautiful sparkling Gulf behind the cottage. Right now she was more interested in lunch, finishing her homework, and she loved Agnetha's idea of going to the beach for a swim or just jumping into the cool refreshing water from the dock.

Chapter 7

Back to present time

Sienna stood at the bottom of the stairs leading up to the front door of the pretty pink two-story cottage on stilts that could have used a new coat of paint. It was surrounded by all sorts of tropical "weeds", even a few big planters with pretty variegated ginger and lobster claw in them were full of weeds taller than the potted plants. Nobody seemed to be in charge or care for gardening around here. But Sienna could also tell that money was probably tight. All profits had always gone to the turtles and that obviously hadn't changed with the younger couple Camilla and Ricky in charge. Sienna looked around and discovered many new or rebuilt homes in the area that she hadn't seen before and had now been built according to hurricane code after some devastating storms had swept through the Keys.

*****

Sienna stood there, thinking about the episode with Olivia the turtle, which had been typical for their childhood. *Funny that I still remember Olivia's name*, she thought. The turtles had always been Number One. She and Camilla had always been number two. At least that's how it had felt for Sienna. Not only during the week but also on weekends and even vacations. There were always emergencies when their parents were paged and had to leave immediately to organize a turtle rescue, and the girls were always left with the current au pair. They had had countless au pairs since their early childhood replacing their constantly working parents, and they had always felt more bonded with them than with their parents. But often, the frustrated au pairs had quit and departed early, because they were overworked and never had time off. Sometimes, in between au pairs, the two sisters had been on their own, growing up early with a lot of responsibility, coming home to an empty house as latchkey kids, making their own snacks and doing their homework until their mom and dad came home.

That was why Sienna never wanted to take over the Sea Turtle Sanctuary and became a lawyer instead. She had always been surprised that Camilla had voluntarily and happily taken over the family's business. Sienna just didn't have this gene in her that made the rest of the family obsessed with turtles. She liked them and found them really fascinating but not enough to spend her entire life with them. Although, if things with Ricky and her had worked out, she might have thought differently...

*****

Sienna walked up the stairs and knocked at the front door, but the house was quiet and there was no answer. It was dinnertime, so she wondered where they could be.

She knew that Bianca was taking care of the kids until she arrived, so maybe they were next door.

She looked around for a key, and the first thing she saw was a weathered painted rock with a butterfly on it in a planter next to the entrance. She became a bit melancholy because she recognized the rock she had painted in elementary school years ago. She lifted it a few inches and – bingo! – The key was there. Just like old times. She let herself in, left her suitcases in the foyer, put the key lime pie into the fridge in the kitchen and walked down the hallway through the living room to the porch in the back of the house that had always had the most beautiful view onto the Gulf of Mexico. Of course all of the plants in the back had also grown about ten feet taller in the meantime, so the trees and palms were now gigantic, and the whole backyard made a very overgrown jungle-like impression. The view was almost gone, but there was still an opening in the middle and Sienna could see the old path they always used to run down to the dock. The overgrown atmosphere was actually nice because it gave the backyard a touch of privacy. She felt like going out back and walking down her old path to the dock and to the walkway behind the house leading to both the Sea Turtle Sanctuary and Bianca's house, but then she suddenly heard the front door opening and cheerful voices coming from the kitchen. Bianca had arrived with the kids and several of her grandchildren, who now ran through the house, said hi to Sienna briefly, ran down the back staircase and disappeared in the backyard. The beautiful Puerto Rican woman with curly blonde hair and brown eyes in her late fifties walked toward Sienna with big steps and took her in her arms.

"I'm so sorry, my dear. And sorry for bringing the whole gang up here. They could have just run through the yard but they were all curious and had to see you."

Sienna hugged her back. Bianca, aka "Auntie" Bianca, had always been like a second mother to her. They had been neighbors forever, and Bianca had always been the crafty housewife and mother who baked and cooked all day and threw great birthday parties. Sienna had always wished she had a mother like that, too. Bianca had three daughters and a son of her own, and Sienna and Camilla had always been over at her house to bake and play with her kids and hear Bianca tell one of her really cool stories when their parents were busy. It seemed like a lifetime ago and even a different life to Sienna as her eyes filled up with tears again.

"Thanks so much for taking care of the kids, Auntie. Gee whiz, how many grandkids did you say you have now?"

"Almost enough for our own basketball team," Bianca replied with a smile. Then she turned around and called down the hallway with a voice that accepted no backtalk: "Leo, Lindsey, Lilly! Come back and say hello to your Aunt Sienna!" The three kids had quietly snuck into their rooms and now came back out, with hanging heads and gloomy faces. The last thing they wanted to do was to be taken care of by an aunt they didn't even know and who probably wanted to make them move to Boston and go to a boarding school or a school where they had to wear uniforms. They had only met Sienna briefly once at their grandparents' funerals a couple of years ago and already back then she hadn't come across as someone who liked kids. Bianca re-introduced them. "Sienna, this is Leo, this is Lindsey and this is little Lilly." Awkwardly, they all shook hands and Sienna said: "I'm really sorry about what happened to your parents, guys. But I'm here now, okay?" They nodded with gloomy faces.

"May we be excused now?" asked Lindsey, the older girl into the silence that followed. Her voice sounded extremely annoyed.

Sienna just nodded. She was overwhelmed by the situation and had no idea how to handle these kids that were very obviously traumatized and sad.

"Sure, go on back to your rooms. Have you guys all done your homework?" asked Bianca in an upbeat manner.

They all nodded and went back down the hallway. Quietly, Bianca said: "The best thing to do is to treat them as normal as possible. They need their routine. They've been back in school after staying home for a week and all of them still have to catch up on their homework. Lilly is in elementary school, Lindsey in middle school and Leo in high school. All three school busses stop right in front of the Sea Turtle Sanctuary, just like when you went to school. Leo has his learner's permit and has actually been practicing with his mom and dad. Maybe I can help you with that and take him out a few times. He's a bit anxious because he's getting his license later than most of his friends. It was hard for Ricky and Camilla to find time for that. But I think he's already a pretty good driver."

She paused and looked at Sienna who seemed overwhelmed and just kept nodding. "Do you want to sit down, my love? I know this is all a lot for you. Just take your time to figure things out. We already had dinner at my house, and I brought you some chili. Sorry, nothing fancy, but with all these kids I have to make easy meals. I also went shopping and stocked up the fridge with some groceries. There's coffee, milk, some bagels, eggs, cream cheese and some fruit. At least you'll have enough for breakfast."

"You're awesome, Bianca," said Sienna. "Thanks for helping so much."

"That's what I'm here for," Bianca replied. "Please ask me for anything you need. Seriously, when the grandkids aren't around, I'm bored to death. I started working in a flower shop down the road in the mornings, but I'll tell you about it later. Orchids, one of our specialties, have become a bit of an obsession for me." She smiled. "I'll give you some privacy, you must be exhausted from the flight. You remember where your old room is? Or you could probably use the master bedroom now... Oh, and by the way, Lilly isn't speaking. She might just need some time. But you might have to consult the school psychologist. We can talk about it more after you've settled in."

Sienna nodded. Bianca continued: "Do you mind if I walk out back? We always walk that way. I'll gather the kids and we'll walk back toward my dock. You should go out too, it looks like the sunset tonight is going to be terrific."

She gave Sienna another quick hug, left through the sliding glass door in the back, walked across the lanai and down a staircase leading into the backyard. Then she disappeared down the enchanted looking path and was gone, the group of children following her like the Pied Piper.

Sienna finally had some time to look around now. The house was a MESS, especially with her Obsessive Compulsive Disorder. Clutter and dirt made her nervous and unhappy. There were dust bunnies everywhere, the dining-room table between the eat-in kitchen and the family room along with the kitchen counter were full of clutter and unopened mail, countless pillows were in front of the couch and not ON it and a few blankets had been bunched up on the couch. A tray with dirty dishes and a half-eaten sandwich was standing on the coffee table. Out of the corner of her eye, Sienna discovered a cockroach scurrying across the floor. She jumped on it and squished it. Disgustedly, she got some paper towels and cleaning supplies, picked up the cockroach remains and cleaned the floor and her shoe. She was absolutely beside herself but remembered that this was nothing unusual in Florida. She was going to have to call an exterminator tomorrow. It looked like someone had been sleeping and eating on the couch for days without cleaning up. Sienna quickly dumped the leftover sandwich in the garbage and wiped off the table. For a moment, she just stood there, wondering whether she should hire someone to clean this mess or do it herself, but then she tore herself away for something more pleasant and stepped out onto the back porch. She listened to the sound of the surf hitting against the dock that was so gentle down here year round, except during hurricane season, and the noisy evening concert of the cicadas. From time to time she heard an owl hooting. She remembered the screech owl egg she and Camilla had found in a hollow half-rotten tree trunk and taken to the Dolphin Research Center that also took care of other animals. The egg had actually hatched and as soon as the fledgling was big enough, the center had called them to pick it up again and they had released it back into their yard. Sienna wondered if its descendants still lived here and looked for the old tree trunk, but it seemed to be gone – it had probably disintegrated throughout the years.

She could see the sky through the trees. It was already dipped in all shades of red, pink and purple. She slowly walked down the narrow overgrown path, looking around at the old familiar sights and listening to the old familiar sounds. A few lizards scurried away in front of her and she smiled, remembering how she and Camilla used to rescue them from their old black and white cat Oscar who loved catching and playing with them.

They had always made up stories about how Oscar, the former stray, had escaped from Hemingway's mansion in Key West and came all the way up to Turtle Key, since he happened to be polydactyl, six-toed, just like the famous Hemingway cats.

After a few hundred yards, Sienna stepped out of the thick wooded area and arrived at three long wooden docks with boats tied to them, facing the Gulf of Mexico, just as

the last piece of the sun was sinking into the sea that was as smooth as glass.
The beautiful light lit up Sienna's face. She walked to the far end of the closest dock that belonged to the Flores family and sat down, taking in everything, her hair blowing out of her face in the breeze. There was a brief green flash and the reflection of the sky in the calm dark water was breathtaking. A great white heron standing in the shallow water at the far end of the property near the mangroves caught Sienna's attention. It quickly snatched something with its long orange bill. With a fish firmly in its possession, the beautiful bird spread out its big white wings, elegantly took flight and disappeared.

*****

Sienna took a deep breath. She had forgotten how beautiful it was here. She looked down into the water where she could see some smaller fish darting back and forth and remembered something, looked a bit further under the dock and smiled. Some Florida lobsters were hanging out among the rocks. She smiled but was surprised. They had always hung out there but not during lobster season and, as far as she could remember, that was still until the end of March, which meant nobody had been bothering them. She looked at two further docks and a boat ramp north of her that belonged to the Sea Turtle Sanctuary and Bianca's dock with a pretty little boat tied to it. There were no natural beaches on the Gulf side and most everyone had a dock in their backyard as well as a boat. This had always been the locals' way of getting around in the Keys. It was slowly getting dark. Sienna got up, walked off of the dock and back down the path toward the cottage. She was ready to use the flashlight on her phone but then she realized that little solar lights along the path illuminated the way. It looked beautiful but Sienna was glad when she arrived back in the yard with all the nightly rustling in the little wooded area between Gulf and backyard, especially after she saw a big iguana scurrying across the path. She remembered seeing one or two iguanas before she had left the Keys. The large species of lizards reached up to nearly five feet in length, had been brought here from Central, South America and the Caribbean as pets and released by irresponsible owners. They had multiplied and become invasive around the late 90s. Even though she knew they were rather harmless, Sienna couldn't imagine one of these monstrosities scurrying across her bare feet in chanx, the slang for flip flops used in the Keys.

Chapter 8

The next morning after all three kids had left for school Sienna felt like she had been hit by a truck and needed a nap. She had no idea that it was so exhausting to get three kids ready for school and wondered how people worked and had kids at the same time. Her usually organized and calm mornings which began with an hour of yoga and her favorite coffee, then reading news and choosing which one of her business outfits she was going to wear, was anything but organized and calm. Bianca had told her what time the school busses departed, but Sienna didn't really know how long the kids needed to get ready for school, so she just woke them all up an hour before their departure time. It would have been okay to get them all out at the same time, but all three went to different schools and pick-up times stretched from 6:45 for Leo who went to high school, to 8:15 for Lilly who went to elementary school to 9:00 for Lindsey who went to middle school. It was an endless drag and seemed to take all morning. When Sienna stuck her head into Leo's room at 5:45 and called him, he jerked up with tousled hair, glared at her for a second with sleep in his eyes and turned around, not hiding his anger.

"I don't get up until 6:25," he grumbled, pulling the blanket back over his head and moaning loudly. Shocked about making such a mistake on her first morning, Sienna closed the door and waited on standby with eggs that were going to be cold by the time Leo was ready – he obviously wouldn't even have time to eat if he only gave himself fifteen minutes until he had to catch the bus. At 6:40 Leo stormed down the stairs, made a quick stop in the kitchen to grab a cereal bar and a banana and was out of the door with a brief "morning", replying to Sienna's greeting. Sienna rolled her eyes and thought to herself: *well at least he took something nutritious to school.*

Lilly was the next one Sienna had to wake up. She knocked at her door. There was no answer. Sienna carefully opened the door and found little Lilly in her bed, sobbing quietly. Sienna walked through the messy room over to the bed trying not to step on toys and clothes and sat down, trying to comfort Lilly caressing her head, but Lilly backed off and made Sienna feel terribly awkward. She really didn't know what to do and say in a situation like this and knew that saying "I'm sorry" again and again wouldn't do much to soothe Lilly's pain.

"Is there anything I can do for you?" she asked carefully. Lilly pushed her lower lip forward, just shook her head, turned around and pulled the blanket back over her head. Sienna got back up, walked back toward the door and said:

"I have eggs and bacon ready if you want to eat something."

About fifteen minutes later, Lilly came downstairs fully dressed, sat down at the kitchen table and ate a huge portion of eggs with bacon and toast and had a big glass of orange juice. She still didn't talk but Sienna felt a wave of pride that at least Lilly was having a hearty breakfast.

"Do you take lunch to school?" asked Sienna. Lilly shook her head and was out the door before Sienna could even ask her if she was usually walked to the bus stop. It seemed dangerous for a girl in her age to be standing on such a busy road like US1 by herself, so Sienna followed her and caught up with Lilly in front of the Turtle Sanctuary. Two other moms with children were waiting at the bus stop and gave a friendly nod to Sienna as the bus arrived and the three children got in. Sienna walked back to the house, quite flabbergasted about how mature and grown up this five year old already was, but then she remembered herself and her sister at that age. They had also been quite mature with working parents and this was probably the same situation. She wondered if Camilla had been as much a workaholic as their mom and once again she regretted not getting back in touch earlier.

*****

Lindsey was already up doing some homework that she had forgotten the night before when Sienna knocked at her door to wake her up and nodded from her desk. She was wearing earphones and obviously listening to something and just looked back at her laptop without responding to Sienna's question about what she wanted for breakfast. Sienna walked up to her, trying to get her attention. Finally Lindsey took her earphones out of her ears and looked at Sienna, huffing and puffing.

"I really need to concentrate, Aunt Sienna. Now I lost my train of thought," she said impatiently.

"Sorry, Lindsey, I just wanted to ask what you want for breakfast."

Lindsey replied in a bossy tone: "I can't eat in the morning. But can you please make me a PB&J sandwich with the white bread that's in the bread box, a sliced apple with a little bit of lemon juice - but it has to be one of the really crispy apples - a bottle of water and a cereal bar."

Sienna swallowed. Wow, this young lady was very particular. *I sure hope Bianca bought the really crispy apples! I guess I won't be keeping up the daily special request program for too long,* she thought to herself. *I think this young lady will start making her own lunch very soon.* But she kept her mouth shut to keep the peace, went downstairs and started working on Lindsey's lunch. After a while, Lindsey came hopping down the stairs, grabbed her lunch box, said: "Thank you and bye" and was out the door. *At least she said Thank You,* thought Sienna to herself. The door opened back up and Lindsey stuck her head inside the kitchen. "Oh, Aunt Sienna, I have cheerleading right after school today, so I stay there and you have to pick me up at 6 pm. Is that okay?"

"Sure. See you at six." Sienna was happy that Lindsey was keeping some normalcy in her life and continuing her after school activities. She poured herself another cup of coffee, walked back to the lanai and sat down in front of her laptop, exhausted.

Chapter 9

Half an hour later, after returning some work emails and ignoring some flirtatious text messages from Craig, Sienna got up, grabbed her coffee cup, carried it over to the kitchen and did the dishes. She continued to clean up the kitchen that, in her opinion, looked like a bomb had hit it even though it really wasn't that bad. The whole house needed a deep cleaning and she was going to start with that today after going grocery shopping. But first she stepped out to the front, walked down the stairs and made her way over to the Turtle Sanctuary. She might as well go and say hello since she was obviously the boss now until they all figured out what to do.

In the Sea Turtle Sanctuary it was business as usual, despite the two hospital directors now being gone. The turtles didn't care. They had to be taken care of and kept on their daily routine, and the loads of incoming injured and sick turtles hadn't stopped. As a matter of fact, there was currently a very unusual record-breaking deep freeze in Texas and thousands of cold stunned sea turtles had been housed and kept warm in convention centers and other public buildings in South Padre Island, Texas despite widespread power outages.

Sea Turtles become cold stunned when water temperatures go below 60 degrees Fahrenheit. The cold-blooded animals become sluggish and lethargic when their body temperatures plunge. Since all of the locations in Texas needed help and all turtle rescue organizations in the south were at capacity, some of these turtles had been transported to the Sea Turtle Sanctuary in Turtle Key. They were just arriving in a truck and being loaded into the intake area. It was all hands on deck and to Sienna's big surprise she was put right to work by hospital manager Bridget, a petite wiry woman in her late fifties who had lived in the Keys her entire life. Her brunette hair with a few gray strands was pulled back in a tight ponytail and she was wearing khaki shorts and a Sea Turtle Sanctuary t-shirt. She seemed to be the boss of the entire operation as she barked orders out to several people, keeping everyone on task, yet working harder than anyone else.

"Jamie, you take this one, bring him back to Bay 1, Cynthia, grab on to the other side, he's too heavy for just one person," she said. She picked up a big sea turtle weighing in at least 70 pounds by the side of its shell and lifted it onto a cart, assisted by Cynthia, a young college student who was interning at the hospital. Cynthia pushed the cart to a second bay where the turtle was marked and named. A chart was started and then it was taken to one of the treatment rooms, where a veterinarian and a technician examined it.

Suddenly, Bridget realized that Sienna was standing there watching and stopped in her tracks.

"Hey, there, sweetie," she said in an endearing manner as she walked up to Sienna and gave her a quick hug. Her eyes filled up with tears. She had known Sienna since she was a little girl.

"I'm so sorry about Camilla and Ricky," she said. But there was no time for sentiments right now. "Can you stay and help a little?" Bridget asked, desperate for helpers. "You could assist with the intake paperwork and Diana over there," she said pointing at a young girl in Bay 2 with a clipboard in her hand, "could do something else. I need more people to help unload the turtles so that the truck can leave. It needs to depart for Texas today and get back by tomorrow night with a short stop in Miami. And the intake is quite complicated because not only do we have to keep the sexes apart but we also have to quarantine them. We have to make sure that they have no other contagious diseases. So, we're running out of space."

Even though Sienna really had other things to do on her first morning in the Keys, she saw that she was desperately needed and couldn't refuse.

"Sure," she said and walked up to Diana who handed her the clipboard. This was something she had already done as a teenager after school and on weekends, so it was like riding a bike – it came back naturally.

A couple of hours later, the last sea turtles had been unloaded from the truck, marked, had a chart started and had been taken to one of the treatment rooms to be examined. The two veterinarians Mark and Bella and some assistants were still busy examining them and determining whether they could go in a pool for healthy turtles or if they needed special attention and treatment.

Sienna looked at the time on her phone. She gasped. It was almost time to pick up Lilly from the bus and she hadn't even been grocery shopping. Like everyone else, she hadn't stopped for lunch and just now realized how hungry she was.

Bridget walked up to her and gave her another quick hug as she thanked her profusely. "You fit right back in, Sienna! It's so good to see you, even if the circumstances are horrible. I'm going back to help there, but you should probably go and have something to eat now. I'm sure you have a lot to organize."

Sienna nodded. "You look great, Bridget. It's good to see you. Yeah, it's a bit of a challenge going from being single to suddenly having three kids... "

Bridget nodded and asked: "Can you come back in tomorrow morning so that I can introduce you to everyone and fill you in on with what's going on here? I was planning on doing that today, but then this happened..." She pointed at the truck out front that was just departing. "We only got a couple of hours notice about this truck full of turtles being on its way here. It was supposed to go to the Center in Juno Beach but they are at capacity."

"Wow," replied Sienna. "Yeah, I'll be over tomorrow as soon as the kids are in school."

"Okay, thanks again. See ya," said Bridget, patted Sienna's back and walked through Bay 1 into a treatment room.

*****

Sienna walked through the back area of the Sea Turtle Sanctuary, opened and closed a gate, walked up the stairs and entered the cottage. She looked in the fridge and pantry for something to eat. There were some fresh groceries that Bianca had obviously bought, but everything else was unhealthy junk food like chips, candy, frozen pizzas and TV dinners that made Sienna, who usually ate super healthy, cringe. She warmed up some of the leftover chili in the microwave and looked at the clock on the wall. She might have time to run to the grocery story before Lilly came home and needed to be picked up from the bus stop but then she remembered that she also had an appointment with the attorney about Camilla and Ricky's last wills and testaments. Leo, who came home first, would obviously be able to fend for himself.

Sienna's phone rang. It was Bianca.

"Hey, Bianca, I'm so glad you called."

"Hi, my friend. I just wanted to check in. I work at the orchid nursery down the road in the morning and just came home and was wondering if you need anything, have any questions or just wanted to get together for a coffee."

"I was just about to call you too, Bianca. I don't know if you heard of the big shipment of turtles that came in today, but I went to the Sea Turtle Sanctuary to say hello this morning and they were so desperate for help that they put me right to work until 2ish. Now I really have to run to the store and I forgot that I have the appointment with the attorney about Camilla and Ricky's last wills and testaments. I don't even think they made one. Do you think you could meet Lilly at the bus stop if I'm not back on time?"

"Of course. Just take your time and I'll plan on it. Would you mind bringing me a gallon of 2% milk? My grandkids use about a gallon a day for their cereal."

"Sure! Thanks."

"And Sienna? Since your day got kind of busy, why don't you come over for dinner with the kids? We can talk a little more. I'm making burritos. All kids like those and they're easy."

"That would be really helpful. You're awesome, Bianca. I have to pick Lindsey up at six. She has cheerleading. It's the same middle school it used to be, isn't it?

Bianca laughed. "Yes, it is. You'll remember and get reacquainted with everything in no time. It's Turtle Key Middle High School. Leo goes there too, he's just in the high school section."

"That's what I thought, thanks. I'll see you tonight. Is 6:30ish okay?"

"Perfect," replied Bianca. "I can't wait to see you."

*****

Sienna left the cottage and tried to sneak upfront to the parking lot without running into too many people from the Sea Turtle Sanctuary and getting distracted. There was a path on the side of the facility leading up to the road, but people in the back at the exterior basins could see who was coming and going. It gave the cottage a bit of safety but not too much privacy. Just as Sienna was walking past a gate on the side of the hospital's property, a tall man rushed out of the gate and bumped into her so hard that Sienna almost fell backwards. It literally took her breath away. Not only the hard bump but also the man. He was at least 6'3" and very athletic, wearing board shorts with a flower motif and a "Sea Turtle Sanctuary" t-shirt, had thick brunette hair, the most beautiful speckled brown eyes she had ever seen behind a pair of round John Lennon glasses and a thick trimmed beard with an attractive smattering of grey. *What is it with men bumping into me and almost knocking me over or pouring coffee over me,* she thought to herself.

The man was obviously in a rush and apologized profusely.

"I'm so sorry," said the stranger who was obviously an employee of the Sea Turtle Sanctuary. "Did I hurt you? Is there anything I can do?"

Sienna needed a minute to get her wits' about her and held her right arm that was throbbing a little from the impact of this 200-pound guy's body. "It's okay, please just watch where you're going next time," she replied, slightly annoyed.

"Really sorry, I'm late picking up my daughter from school. I'm Mark Baldwin, one of the veterinarians here at the rescue. You must be Camilla's sister Sienna? I've heard a lot about you. I'm so sorry for your loss. And thanks for helping out this morning. Sorry that we didn't get introduced. Everyone was so busy."

Sienna just nodded.

"I hope I can make it up to you," he said with a smile. "Gotta go, sorry, I'm really late."

And he was gone. Sienna followed him up to the parking lot and saw his older white pick-up truck drive away in a cloud of dust and merge onto Overseas Highway. *Wow, that guy is crazy,* she thought to herself. But she was already hoping she'd see him again tomorrow during her meeting with Bridget in the hospital. She repeated his name quietly: "Mark Baldwin. What a nice name..."

*****

Sienna followed the pickup, merged onto US1 heading south and drove a few miles to a little strip mall where the attorney was located who took care of most of the locals' legal matters. The office was in a separate newer building on stilts at the end of the strip mall. Sienna stepped up to the front door, which had an old brass sign on it that read: "William A. LeFleur Esquire, Attorney at Law". Unlike the exterior, the interior looked old and dusty, like in an old attorney's office in a movie. The young blonde receptionist in tight jeans, a white blouse and cheap high-heels, chewing gum non-stop, led Sienna into Mr. LeFleur's office. Dark wooden bookshelves covered the walls, an old weathered leather couch with some matching armchairs and a coffee table filled one side of the room, a big old ornamental wooden desk, that barely fit into the corner, was situated on the other side of the room. The entire office smelled like pipe tobacco and Sienna wondered if she would smell like that too after the appointment. Mr. LeFleur, an older Southern gentleman originally from New

Orleans, sporting a blue baggy seersucker suit and tie, white curly hair and a long mustache that he liked to twirl, jumped up and came around the desk to shake Sienna's hand.

"I'm sorry for your loss, Miss Sienna. I remember you when you were this small," he said with a thick southern drawl, holding his hand up to his hip, showing how small Sienna used to be. "Why don't we sit on the couch, it's more comfortable."

Unlike Sienna's presumption that there would be no last wills and testaments, Camilla and Ricky had set one up a couple of years ago, right after Sienna and Camilla's parents had passed away. Considering the messy paperwork and piles of unopened bills in the house, Sienna was surprised that Camilla and Ricky had taken care of this important detail. Mr. LaFleur read the two pages out loud to her, confirming that she was to be the legal guardian of the children, the executor of the wills and CEO of the Sea Turtle Sanctuary. Of course she hadn't expected anything else since she was the last living relative of both Camilla and Ricky, but hearing it now from an official source gave her a bit of anxiety.

"Please sign here," requested Mr. LaFleur and pointed at a line at the bottom of a document, "this is just to confirm that you've received all the information and that I read the Last Wills and Testaments to you. You still have the right to decline this inheritance. If you do so, you will have to sign a disclaimer within nine months after your sister and brother-in-law's death."

Sienna signed the confirmation that she had received a copy of each will and testament, thanked Mr. LaFleur, nodded at the receptionist who was just sitting there, texting on her phone, left the office and stepped back out into the sunshine. She briefly smelled her hair that indeed had the odor of pipe tobacco now, carefully crossed to the ocean side in her car, made a quick stop at the grocery store, grabbed some items and was headed back north within a few minutes.

Chapter 10

In the evening, Sienna walked over to Bianca's house with Lilly and Lindsey. Leo had gone to a friend's house for dinner, so he didn't join them. The shortest way to Bianca's house was along the Gulf, so they walked down the path and arrived at the dock just as the sun was setting again. What a beautiful sight! It was low tide and the water was noticeably lower than the previous day, only halfway up the dock. A few crabs were rushing along sideways and quickly disappeared into holes in the sand. A few seagulls were slowly walking along the edge of the water, picking crabs, insects and other edible things they could find.

Sienna walked up to the dock, stepped down into the sand, which during high tide was usually covered with water, and picked up a pretty pink conch shell that was almost entirely intact, tried showing it to Lilly and Lindsey, but Lilly looked down and Lindsey crossed her arms and said: "We find those all the time and it's actually forbidden to collect them. They're protected."

Excuse me, thought Sienna. *I'm just doing my best...* She remembered seeing signs that it was indeed forbidden to collect queen conch shells and threw it far out into the water, full of frustration.

She was really not that much into kids but these kids made it extremely difficult... *I guess I have to cut them some slack,* she thought. She looked across the shallow, ankle-deep water around the docks and suddenly her eyes filled up with tears again.

Flashback

19 years ago, 2000, Turtle Key, Florida Keys

Eighteen-year old Sienna walking down the path toward the Gulf, listening to Ricky Martin on her discman. Suddenly she discovered someone sitting on the dock in her and Ricky's special spot and walked closer. It looked like Ricky and she started walking faster toward him. Maybe everything would turn out to be a mistake and he still loved her. She just needed to talk to him. Sienna realized that it was Ricky but he wasn't alone. He was with Camilla in *their* special spot, kissing her. Quickly, Sienna turned around and ran back the other way, feeling as if she was running in slow motion, tears running down her cheeks. She ran back down the path and all the way up to her room where she threw herself on her bed, sobbing broken-hearted.

*****

Back to Present Time

Sienna shook her head slightly as if trying to shake off these memories that made her even more upset than she already was. Ricky wasn't alive anymore. Nor was Camilla. She'd never see either of them again. But even though it was such a long time ago, she still couldn't believe that Ricky had let Camilla steal him from Sienna.

Sienna really thought she was over it, but sometimes she tortured herself, wondering again and again what she had done wrong. Should she have fought for Ricky? Would things be different if she had stayed? They probably wouldn't. At least this way she had her career and her life away from all this...

She took one more look at the dock stretching out into the Gulf that held so many memories. Camilla left college without graduating, gave birth to Leo a few months later and got married to Ricky. Sienna talked to her parents and Camilla less and less until finally they barely heard from each other. Life in Turtle Key was busy with the Sea Turtle Sanctuary and three small children and life in Boston was busy as a junior lawyer.

Sienna wondered if she should have forgiven them and tried to stay in touch, but it wasn't like they ever asked her for forgiveness.

*****

Sienna gazed at the beautiful sky with the setting sun above the Gulf. Then she walked up the path leading to

Bianca's house. Several wooden pergolas had been set up along the path, full with blooming orchids.

"Yup, my new obsession," said Bianca who was standing right there in one of the pergolas. Sienna could hear the pride in her voice as she walked toward her and gave her a hug. "I started working at this flower shop down the road that also sells orchids and have become obsessed. I basically leave my entire pay there but have also met a ton of friends in the orchid society meetings."

"They're beautiful," said Sienna, admiring some fluffy pink Cattleyas in bloom right in the front of the first pergola.

"You'll have to give me a tour when we get a chance."

"Sure, I'd love to," replied Bianca. "I was starting to worry about you. Lindsey said you were right behind them, but they arrived a while ago," said Bianca with a smile as they walked up to the house, which was also on stilts. They walked up the stairs onto the lanai that was also full of orchids.

"Sorry. The sunset was so beautiful, I stopped to watch it," replied Sienna. "I had almost forgotten how beautiful it is here."

"It never gets old," replied Bianca with a smile. "I feel very blessed to live here. The kids have already started with dinner," she said, pointing at the big table as they walked into the family room where a bunch of kids including Lilly and Lindsey were sitting, making their own burritos with chicken, rice, beans, Mexican cheese, guacamole, salsa, veggies and salad. "We call this our private Chipotle," she said, smiling. As she noticed Sienna's hesitation, she asked: "Would you like me to make you a burrito? I'm an expert."

Sienna nodded, smiling. "Yes, please, I haven't done that in ages."

Lindsey interrupted: "Bianca, can you roll my burrito?"

"Sure," replied Bianca, stepped next to Lindsey, folded the left and right side onto the loaded tortilla, then the bottom side, then she flipped the entire tortilla including contents over to the top of the plate, patted it a bit into shape and a perfect burrito was ready to be eaten.

"Thank you, Bianca," said Lindsey beaming. She took the giant burrito into her two hands and took a big bite.

Sienna noticed how different the kids seemed to be in the company of others, not as sad and quiet.

Bianca, always the helpful hostess, turned toward Lilly, rolled her filled tortilla shell into a perfect burrito as well. Lilly still didn't talk as Bianca held a monologue asking what Lilly wanted on her burrito while Lilly just nodded and shook her head. Then she took a new plate, put an empty tortilla on it and started making a burrito for Sienna.

"I'll never be able to eat that much," said Sienna smiling.

"You wait and see. I made us margaritas," Bianca said proudly as she and Sienna stepped out onto the lanai and set their plates down onto a little table in between two armchairs. She walked back inside, returned with a little pitcher and two margarita glasses and poured the lime-green colored drink into the glasses.

They both lifted their drinks and Bianca said: "Salud!"

"Salud," replied Sienna, "thanks for everything, Bianca, this looks wonderful." They both drank, Sienna smiled and said: "This is really good. What kind of tequila do you use?"

"Whatever's currently on sale," she replied grinning. "My favorite is Casamigos though, it's really smooth. You know, the tequila company co-founded by George Clooney."

"No, I didn't know that!" said Sienna who usually never drank tequila and took another sip. Then they just sat there for a while, enjoying their burritos and enjoying the beautiful view into the backyard and, further in the back, the Gulf.

"Unfortunately, I have to bring up the Celebration of Life," said Bianca into the silence. "I'm dreading it myself, but we have to get it done. I told you that we have it scheduled for the day after tomorrow at 10 am, correct?

Sienna nodded. "Yes, I wish I could have helped you with this. Sorry that you had to do all the planning by yourself."

"It's okay, I feel like I belong to the family as well. You can count on me."

Sienna nodded thankfully. "I really appreciate it."

"Your parents are in Key West at the cemetery and, as you know, that's totally overcrowded. Camilla and Ricky were cremated and their ashes will be spread in the ocean in front of our properties. That's actually what they requested. Before that we will have a memorial in the chapel, held by Pastor Van Doren, then a boat parade with the spreading of the ashes and after that lunch here. I'm having my friend Jeannie cater it. She's a chef at The Jumping Dolphin and does a really good job."

"That sounds beautiful," replied Sienna.

"Yes, I think it'll be nice. So, everything is organized. Do you think you would like to say a few words? Other than that you just have to show up with the kids."

Sienna hadn't even thought about holding a speech. But what would she say?

"I know you and Camilla didn't part on good terms, so I respect your decision, whatever it is."

"Do you know if anyone else is holding a speech?" asked Sienna after a brief pause.

"I think Bridget is. She was not only their closest coworker but also Camilla's best friend. And you know Ricky was also estranged from his parents and the only child, so there won't be much family at the service. Mostly Sea Turtle Sanctuary staff and some other locals."

"Let me see if I can come up with something, but of course I barely spoke with them for 17 years, so I can only talk about memories from our childhood..." Sienna replied.

"That would be nice, I think."

They just sat there for a while eating, when Bianca interrupted the silence and asked:

"So, she's still not talking, is she?"

Bianca didn't have to say whom she was talking about, but she nodded over at the dining-room table where Lindsey and Lilly were still sitting with some of her grandchildren.

"Nope. They are all not talking to me very much," replied Sienna frustrated. "I'm just not used to dealing with kids."

"Just treat them like grown-ups," replied Bianca. "I've done okay with that. They want all the privileges, so they can behave like grown-ups as well. My kids always had their chores and jobs and had to do them without constantly being reminded. The grandkids too. And they all do fine with that."

Sienna nodded smiling. "You've always been great with kids, Bianca. I'll have to get used to it, but that's great advice. Thanks."

"Let's just keep an eye on Lilly. The school psychologist will probably get in touch with you sooner than later. I wonder how her grades are. You might have to get in touch with the teachers anyhow to keep an eye on their progress. There's a website with their progress reports that parents can sign into and remain up to date. You need to get the log in information from the kids or their teachers. If you don't have time for meetings yet, just call the school offices and get their email addresses and communicate with them via email. Or ask the kids if they have their email addresses somewhere."

"That's a great idea, thanks."

*****

After a while and drinking another margarita, Sienna thanked Bianca for dinner and the drinks with a hug and walked back down the path past the pergolas toward the Gulf. The girls had already gone home a while ago to do their homework. Sienna felt a little tipsy and had to pay attention to not stumble over a root or branch and fall. The full moon was out and illuminated the docks and surrounding area so brightly that she didn't have to use her phone's flashlight. The Gulf was so calm and the waves very quiet, but she could hear them as they gently lapped against the docks. She heard the slight rustling of the leaves as the palm fronds above her swayed in the wind.

To the left, where Bianca's property ended, she saw the silhouette of a bird, maybe a pelican, sitting in the branches of a mangrove tree bathed in an eerie light. Mangroves belonged to the tropical coastal vegetation that lined more than 1,800 miles of shoreline within the Florida Keys National Marine Sanctuary and where most of the animals found protection. Sienna was surprised to see the pelican. They weren't usually out this late, and she wondered if something was wrong with him, but then her phone suddenly bleeped with an incoming text message and the bird was gone.

It was Craig.

"How is everything going down there? I miss you..."

Sienna couldn't believe that Craig was still texting her and pretending that everything was okay after she had broken up with him. She was glad that she didn't get more involved and had ended things, but how long was this messaging going to continue and what was going to happen when and if she returned to Boston and had to work with him again? She felt she couldn't totally ignore him since she was going to have to see him again, so she replied in a neutral manner, trying not to engage too much:

"Good, it's beautiful here, but unfortunately I just had to talk about the Celebration of Life which is coming up..."

"Not good, so sorry."

"Well, you are sorely missed, especially by me," he added with a heart emoji.

No reply from her.

"Can't wait for you to come back home."

"Lots to sort out here...." She replied. "Will let you go. Got to put the kids to bed."

Then he sent a kiss emoji, which she ignored.

Sienna's normal life in Boston felt so far away right now and Craig's behavior was really bothering her. She felt her eyes well up with tears but she quickly looked up into the sky and blinked a few times. Nowhere was the sky as wide and beautiful as in the Keys. It soothed her soul as she took a few deep breaths and just looked up at the Moon and out over the endless Gulf.

Then she continued walking along the water toward the Sea Turtle Sanctuary and suddenly discovered a small tent in the area where the area in front of the Gulf met the overgrown backyard of the cottage, fifty yards past the path that Sienna was about to turn onto. A scrawny middle-aged man with a ponytail and a long beard wearing a worn plaid shirt had made a little campfire and was sitting in front of it but was sitting with his back to her and couldn't see Sienna. Sienna wasn't so sure whether he was allowed to camp there and didn't want to say anything or attract his attention. She just quickly snuck up the path, hoping he wouldn't notice her and locked the screened in porch door along with the door of the living room leading onto the porch, a bit uneasy that a stranger was camping in her backyard.

Chapter 11

The next morning after all three kids had left for school, it was time for Sienna to go over to the Sea Turtle Sanctuary and have her meeting with Bridget and some of the other staff members.

She took a last sip of coffee, rinsed all of the dishes, put them into the dishwasher, started it and took a quick satisfied look at the kitchen and the dining area which looked a lot cleaner than it had looked the day she arrived. Then she grabbed her cell phone and her purse and walked over to the side entrance leading to the back area of the Sea Turtle Sanctuary with several round above ground 30,000 gallon holding tanks, all covered with shade cloth. This was the rehabilitation center section of the facility with various turtles swimming in the tanks. The most impressive section was the massive 100,000-gallon saltwater pool that housed sea turtles that were permanently disabled and couldn't be released back into the wild.

Sienna took a quick peek into one of the tanks containing many sea turtles, but she continued to the back entrance where she bumped into Bridget who was also on her way to the meeting room.

"Hey! How are ya?" said Bridget in an upbeat manner. "I'm on my way to our meeting, I think everyone else is there already. Do you want to grab a coffee on the way?"

"I'm okay, how are you?" replied Sienna. "Sure, I'd love a coffee."

They stopped at a little kitchenette in the hallway with tiled floors leading away from the loading dock and Bridget grabbed two cups out of a cupboard and a poured two cups of coffee.

"Milk and sugar?" Bridget asked.

"Only milk, please," replied Sienna and Bridget opened a little fridge, took out a quart of milk, opened and smelled it grinning, then she handed it to Sienna.

"Not many people here use milk, so I wanted to make sure it's still good," Bridget said smiling.

Sienna, who had already poured the milk into her coffee, looked into her cup with a disgusted look, but the coffee was fine. Suddenly, Sienna remembered something.

"Oh, Bridget, I wanted to ask you something. Do you know what the law is regarding camping in the mangroves or on Florida beaches? Are all beaches and other waterfront areas still public and everyone can hang out where they want to, even if it's in front of a private residence? I'm asking because there was a guy camping on the Gulf last night. It was a bit creepy, he was almost right in our backyard."

"Hmmm, I think the beaches are still public. But I don't think camping is allowed at all. There are "wanderers" around from time to time. You should keep an eye on whether he comes back or not and make sure to lock all your doors. If he doesn't leave, I'd report him. Or d'ya know what? Tell Pastor Van Doren about him. He takes care of a lot of "wanderers."

Sienna nodded and said: "Thanks."

The two ladies walked into a conference room at the end of the hallway where most of the Sea Turtle Sanctuary staff was already waiting, except two employees that were on their way to pick up a turtle in the ambulance since an emergency call had come in a few minutes ago. Dreamy veterinarian Mark Baldwin with his John Lennon glasses, wearing a veterinarian coat and a green smoothie in front of him, was sitting between fellow veterinarian Dolores Sanchez (40) and technician Ashley Bradley (26). He found Sienna rather intriguing. Their eyes met briefly, she felt the tension and had to look away quickly to make a professional impression and not blush.

Bridget started the meeting by introducing Sienna.

"Good morning, everyone. Some of you have already met Sienna Brantley, formerly Anderson, Camilla's younger sister, who has basically "inherited" all of us due to the sad circumstances. She used to work here as a teenager with her parents so she knows a bit about our operation. But we are all going to have to help her because, even though not much has changed, it's been 17 years since she was here the last time."

Everyone "applauded" with knocks on the table and Sienna nodded to the group.

Bridget continued: "As we all know, we have been in the red for quite a long while now, so I think we might want to come up with new fundraising opportunities. Remember the "Adopt a Turtle" fundraiser where people could virtually adopt a turtle and then pay an annual or monthly contribution for them? That was a success..."

Everyone mumbled. Some agreed, most of the administrative staff didn't like the idea because it caused a lot of additional paperwork, but they knew it was for the good of the rescue.

"Well, enough of that for now. This is just a meeting for you all to meet Sienna and for her to be informed about the situation we are in right now. Sienna basically has to figure out what she is going to do. She can either assume the position of President/CEO of the organization and become one of us or put one of us in charge and just stay in touch remotely. She still has her job as a lawyer in Boston, but she has good qualifications to run our organization.

We will remain a non-profit organization no matter what and will rely on donations as usual." She continued, looking at Sienna: "But we also have to inform Sienna that the company won't be able to pay our salaries in just a couple of months and money is quickly dwindling." She explained further: "As you know, our only sources of income are the gift shop, the tours and donations. But our expenses are sky-high. And none of us can afford to work for free. We all have bills to pay..."

That was it. Just like most meetings at the Sea Turtle Sanctuary, it was interrupted by an emergency. They were permanently understaffed and all hands were needed. The ambulance pulled into the loading dock and Kurt, one of the interns who usually drove the ambulance, informed the staff via walkie-talkie that he and Anna, another vet technician, had picked up two turtles, both showing extreme symptoms of fibropapillomatosis, the aggressive herpes-like virus that causes the growth of tumors. The two veterinarians as well as Bridget and Ashley jumped up and made their way back to the loading dock. Bridget asked Sienna:

"Can you come? It might be interesting for you to watch. Maybe you and I can continue our meeting afterwards? I'd also like to give you a tour. By the way, your old buddy Olivia is still here. We were never able to release her..."

"Sure. I'll come along," replied Sienna and smiled in anticipation of seeing Olivia the turtle again. She jumped up out of her chair and followed them.

*****

When Sienna and Bridget arrived at the loading dock, one of the massive loggerhead turtles had already been lifted onto a metal table in one of the three intake bays that led to the examination rooms. They had already determined that she was a female, that the person who found her had named her Lucille and they started a chart. The turtle was weighed and measured.

"How do you know she's a female?" asked Sienna as she heard Anna, the tech, calling her Lucille.

"No external differences in sex are seen until the turtle becomes an adult," explained Bridget. "The most obvious difference is that the adult males have thicker tails, shorter plastrons and lower shells than the females. All of us here can kind of tell right away in the meantime."

She pointed out a big tumor on Lucille's flippers and some smaller ones on her mouth.

"See this? This is fibropapillomatosis, or short FP, the disease that gives sea turtles giant cauliflower-like tumors on their eyes, mouths and flippers. It's a viral disease that can kill them, caused amongst other things by agricultural runoff and biotoxin producing algae. We have big problems with that type of pollution down here in the Keys, and it gets even worse in summer when the water is warmer. Remember Red Tide every summer when you were a kid?"

Sienna nodded sadly. "I remember lots of turtles already had FP back then. How is it treated again?" She was truly interested.

"First of all, she has to regain some of her strength," replied Mark Baldwin with his deep pleasant voice that made Sienna's heart beat faster, as he stepped up with a rolling cart to take Lucille into the examination room. "Initial treatment consists of supportive care and antimicrobial therapy which is basically an agent that kills microorganisms or stops their growth. But after that we'll perform surgery with CO2 laser."

He looked into Sienna's beautiful green eyes and had a hard time pulling himself away but remained professional and asked Anna: "Can you please give me a hand?"

"Sure."

Together they lifted the heavy loggerhead turtle onto the cart and wheeled her into the adjoining treatment room, followed by Bridget and Sienna.

"Sienna, have you met our vet Mark Baldwin yet?" asked Bridget. "I actually wanted to have everyone introduce themselves in the meeting but then..." She pointed at Lucille.

"Yes," Sienna and Mark locked eyes again and even Bridget could feel the tension between them. "We literally bumped into each other yesterday," Sienna replied.

Mark grinned slightly and looked down at Lucille the turtle and started examining her, assisted by Anna, who had pulled up a little medical cart. He asked Anna some questions about where and how Lucille had been found as he gave her a first quick examination and then came up with a treatment plan for her.

As soon as they were done, Bridget asked: "Do you guys want to go and have lunch or have one of the interns pick up some takeout? I'm starving."

Even though Sienna would have loved to spend some more time with Mark, she still had too much to do before the Celebration of Life tomorrow and declined.

"I still have a meeting with Pastor Van Doren and a ton of stuff to prepare for tomorrow," she said sighing. "Are you guys coming?"

"Oh, sorry Sweetie, I forgot about that. Yeah, most of us are coming. All of us were very close to Camilla and Ricky. We'll only have a skeleton emergency staff stay at the hospital tomorrow."

Mark and Anna nodded as well and said simultaneously:

"We'll be there too."

Sienna nodded, said: "Thanks, I'll see you guys tomorrow," turned around and started walking back toward the cottage. She couldn't help it and looked around one more time and caught Mark gazing at her as their eyes met again.

*****

Another text message from Craig came in. Sienna frowned. What was up with that? While she was in Boston he had been so noncommittal at first and now that she was out of reach and she had broken up with him, he kept messaging her. She shook her head. She really didn't know what to think of him and ignored his message again.

Chapter 12

The next day Camilla and Ricky's "Celebration of Life" took place in a little chapel of a funeral home in Turtle Key. Sienna had brought a black suit for the ceremony but she realized that the whole event with the burial at sea and boat parade was going to be much more casual and she put out a "skort", a white polo shirt and a pair of casual shoes that would be comfortable on a boat.

It was a bit more difficult with the kids since Lindsey had already ordered a beautiful black lacey dress for the event and was determined to wear it even though Sienna thought it would be totally out of place. But who cared. Nobody really. Sienna searched Lilly and Leo's closets and found some plain shorts and collared shirts. She went into Lindsey's room and realized that Lindsey still had her nice dress in a box.

"You should hang the dress on a hanger until tomorrow," said Sienna as her OCD eyes spotted some wrinkles in the pretty lacey fabric.

Lindsey just rolled her eyes again but took Sienna's advice, which Sienna acknowledged, a bit satisfied.

*****

The day of the service all three kids missed school and, as they came down for breakfast, Sienna tried to prepare them for this hard day. As usual, she tried to be a good aunt to the kids and make up for lost time but failed miserably.

"Kids, it will be tough seeing your mom and dad's urns and ashes and dealing with all the people..."

Lindsey interrupted her and stated matter-of-factly. "We've been to funerals and services like this and we know what's going to happen."

Leo just grabbed an egg bagel on a plate and some orange juice and was back upstairs in thirty seconds. Lilly sat at the counter, pushing her eggs back and forth with a gloomy face.

Sienna gave her a quick hug and said: "We'll get this over with, right?" Lilly just nodded, staring into thin air, avoiding eye contact, as usual.

*****

A quick beautiful service took place in the little chapel of the funeral home in Turtle Key, held by Pastor Edward Van Doren, who had married Camilla and Ricky eighteen years ago. He was an older tall Dutch gentleman with thinning hair and watery blue eyes who had started coming to the Keys over thirty years ago on dive trips, then eventually stayed and had dedicated a big part of his life to feeding and working with the homeless, which were a major issue in the Keys. When he wasn't seen in the soup kitchen with his wife or in church holding a sermon, he was found kayaking the mangroves on the ocean side, pursuing his hobby, bird photography. Sienna was surprised about how many people showed up to the service, but Turtle Key was a tightly knit community and the Sea Turtle Sanctuary that Sienna and Camilla's parents had started had always been a popular pillar of Turtle Key and the surrounding Keys.

Everyone from the Sea Turtle Sanctuary and their families attended, except two technicians on emergency call, Bianca and her big family, some other neighbors and even local shop owners who had closed their stores for the morning out of respect for Camilla and Ricky - like Bianca's good friend Louisa who owned a coffee shop next to Bianca's flower store. Maria from the Cuban café and Tania from Blond Giraffe Key Lime Pie Factory and their spouses had come as well. Some people gave beautiful speeches and told touching and funny stories from memory - one of the craziest being that Camilla's water broke and she went into labor with Lilly on the beach during a turtle rescue and was taken to the hospital in the turtle ambulance. This memory and others made people smile and stop crying for a moment. Lilly, who was sitting next to Sienna, looked up at her with a rare smile. For a second, their eyes met and Sienna caressed Lilly's hair, but then Lilly's face became sad again and she looked away.

Camilla and Ricky had been there for the turtles day and night just like their parents before them. Sienna realized it was meant to be that Camilla and Ricky got together and not her and Ricky. They seemed to have led a happy life together while she was happy with the life she had created in Boston.

Bridget, Camilla's best friend, had prepared a slide show, mainly of their work at the Sea Turtle Sanctuary, but also of some school events and kids' birthday parties, private outings at the beach and on their boat. Their life had revolved around the ocean, which they loved and had tried to protect as well as they could. Camilla and Ricky had even requested that in lieu of flowers people donate money to the Sea Turtle Sanctuary.

Sienna looked around the little chapel. People were happy and talked about their mutual memories. This was really a celebration of life and not a sad funeral. Even the kids didn't seem as sad anymore, surrounded by their family and friends they had known their entire lives.

Sienna, who until now still hadn't figured out what to say, suddenly knew. She had written down a few "funeral quotes" and looked at her notes as she stepped up to a pulpit in front of the rows of benches. She suddenly knew which quote to choose. She cleared her throat and nodded at the rows of people looking at her.

"What you leave behind is not what is engraved in stone monuments, but what is woven into the lives of others," Sienna started her speech and paused for a few seconds to let this quote sink in. "Camilla and Ricky have left us so much. They left such beautiful children and they have left us all with so many wonderful memories." She waved her open hand from Lilly to Lindsey and then to Leo.

"They left a whole community of friends that will never stop remembering them and the Sea Turtle Sanctuary where their work will live on forever."

Everyone was touched by the way Sienna had managed to complete the wonderful service. People got up and slowly left the rows of the little chapel and met in the front to drive home, get their boats and then meet in the Gulf in back of the Turtle Hospital for the spreading of the ashes and the boat parade.

Half an hour later at the dock, Pastor Van Doren climbed into the Flores family's boat with Leo, Lilly and Bridget who captained the boat. Sienna and Lindsey, holding the two urns, followed carefully. Bridget slowly steered the boat away from the docks out of the no-wake zone, followed by two boats full of Bianca's family members, and two boats with members of the Turtle Hospital including Dolores, Ashley, Mark and his daughter Sidney. Approximately twelve other boats with friends and business acquaintances from all over the Keys were already waiting out in the Gulf. They were escorted by two Coast Guard boats, one leading the boat parade on, the other bringing up the rear. The parade, which was quite a sight, went up to the Seven Mile Bridge and then circled back around to the Turtle hospital where all the boats formed a big circle. Fortunately, it was a very calm day on the water and the sun shone down on the group. Pastor Van Doren said a few more comforting words. Sienna handed the urn she had been holding to Leo and he, Lindsey and Lilly took turns slowly pouring their parents' ashes into the water. Two of Bianca's nephews and Bianca surprised everyone:

They had brought guitars and played some beautiful songs, accompanied by Bianca, singing in a beautiful soprano that Sienna suddenly remembered hearing when she was a little girl.

Sienna, almost in tears, had to clear her throat and looked down at Lilly. She looked up at Sienna with her serious big blue eyes and Sienna instinctively took her hand. For the first time, Lilly grabbed Sienna's hand and held it tightly. They looked at each other briefly, and, for a second, Lilly reminded Sienna a bit of herself as a five year old. Sienna couldn't hold her tears any longer and just let them flow.

Bianca, as well as many other people in the other boats, had brought various flowers, which they now all threw into the Gulf. The sight was beautiful and for a while everyone just sat in their boats, reflecting on their memories of Camilla and Ricky. Pastor Van Doren said a few last words and the ceremony was over. The boat with

Sienna and the kids just sat there, bobbing slightly up and down, while people slowly drove up and saluted them one more time, expressing their sympathy.

There was going to be a small lunch at Bianca's house now. Most people left, but the closest friends made their way back to the three docks by the turtle hospital. As Sienna, Bridget and the kids climbed out of the boat, Mark with a little girl holding his hand walked up to Sienna and the kids.

As Mark shook the kids' hands, Sienna examined him and the little girl who was obviously his daughter and about the same age as Lilly. He was at least 6'3" tall and had the thickest dark beard and hair she had ever seen. He looked incredibly distinguished with the gray smattering in his dark hair. His beautiful speckled brown eyes were behind a pair of aviator sunglasses but Sienna could still see that he was secretly examining her. His presence made her feel tense and awkward, and she quickly looked at his daughter who had the same thick dark brown hair and beautiful brown eyes and shook her hand.

"Thanks for being here," said Sienna to Mark, Sidney and Bridget. "Are you guys staying for lunch?"

"I'm coming," replied Bridget, "but Mark has to drop off Sidney with his ex-wife."

Sienna nodded, hiding her disappointment and looked into the group, feeling a bit guilty - not only about having these feelings right after her sister and brother-in-law's funeral but also happily taking note of the fact that Mark seemed to be divorced...

"Well, thanks for coming, sorry you can't make it for lunch."

He raised his sunglasses, looked at her through his long thick lashes, smiled at her and said: "So sorry for your loss," and was gone.

Chapter 13

Sienna looked at Leo, Lindsey and Lilly as they quietly walked up to Bianca's house. Three beautiful kids. They had all behaved so well during the ceremony. Sienna was very impressed with them.

What was she going to do about them with her busy life in Boston? Move to a bigger place and have them live with her? Send them to boarding school? Could she afford that? They probably had some insurance money coming and maybe some savings from their parents but would that be enough? She'd have to look for important paperwork in the house. Would they be happy if she tore them away from their roots in the Keys? Were they happy here?

Her thoughts were interrupted as they arrived at the top of the stairs and stepped into Bianca's kitchen, followed by Bridget, Pastor Van Doren and some other people who were attending the luncheon. Bianca had hired a catering company for the special event so everything was already set up when they stepped into the house. Everyone gathered around the buffet in the kitchen and dining-area, filled their plates with fresh calamari, mahi-mahi and grouper, rice or potato salad, fresh salad and rolls as an option to make sandwiches. And there was key lime pie and brownies for dessert. The kids ate a little but disappeared down the path leading to the Gulf after a while as the adults sat down on the lanai, still talking about Ricky and Camilla and about how much they had done for the community, how badly they would be missed.

*****

About two hours later, the last guests left and Sienna and Bianca were alone. Sienna cleaned up, throwing paper plates, cups and utensils into a big trash bag, while Bianca brewed some coffee. Sienna was tired and just felt like hanging out with Bianca and not going anywhere, as Bianca told her about her fun job in the orchid nursery and proposed they tour her extensive orchid collection in the backyard.

Suddenly, the doorbell rang. Bianca and Sienna stopped what they were doing and looked at each other.

"Maybe someone forgot something," said Bianca, walked up to the front door and opened it.

It was a female police officer with Leo.

"Oh, hi, Detective Baldwin, what's going on? Leo?" asked Bianca.

"Hey there, Bianca." Detective Baldwin, a beautiful Columbian female officer, and Leo stepped into the foyer and then the kitchen. "I'm looking for Leo's legal guardian. Nobody was home at the Flores residence," she said with a deep stern voice, Her eyes looked around the room and stopped on Sienna. "Is that you, by any chance?"

Sienna's heart sank to her knees. She hoped nothing bad had happened after just getting the service for Ricky and Camilla over with. She rushed up and stopped in front of Detective Baldwin and Leo. "Yes, Sienna Brantley. I'm Leo's legal guardian. Is everything okay?" She looked at Leo who was almost in tears.

"What happened, Leo?"

"Leo was just stopped by one of our police patrols near Sombrero Beach, driving without a valid driver's license. Actually he was also speeding," said Detective Baldwin for him. "Driving without a valid license is a misdemeanor in Florida. A conviction carries a fine up to $500 and a maximum of 60 days in jail," said Detective Baldwin sternly, but then her expression became softer. "Some of my Coast Guard friends and colleagues escorted your boat parade this morning. Since we know what you're going through, Leo, losing your parents and all, and I am a mom myself, I will let you get away with a warning this time. But don't do this again."

Leo, Sienna and Bianca collectively took deep sighs of relief and thanked the detective profusely. She remained serious and didn't even crack a smile.

"Thanks for bringing him home, Detective," said Bianca. "Can I offer you anything, maybe some coffee and pie?"

"That's very nice of you, Bianca, but no thanks. I actually have Sidney this week and I was supposed to be off two hours ago. It's been one of these days."

Bianca and Sienna nodded.

"Well, thank you very much, Detective, and it's nice to meet you," said Sienna and shook the detective's hand.

"Nice to meet you too. Oh, and you'll have to go and pick up the van at Sombrero Beach. That's where it's parked." Sienna nodded and thanked her again.

As soon as Detective Baldwin had left, Sienna unloaded her frustration on Leo. "Gosh, Leo, do you know in how much trouble you could have gotten us both into? I could have even faced jail time for letting you have those van keys."

"Sorry", he said, head hanging as he sat down on a chair at the kitchen table and stared into thin air.

"Well, just don't do it again, okay? I know you're going through a tough time," Sienna replied. "We're lucky that Detective Baldwin let us get away with a warning."

Bianca walked over to Leo and gave him a hug.

"It won't happen again, right, Leo?"

"No. Can I go home now?" Leo asked quietly.

"Of course, but please don't go anywhere for about half an hour. I'll finish helping Bianca with the clean up real quick and then we'll go get the van. Bianca, I hate to ask you this, but would you mind helping us when we're done? You could drive us over to Sombrero Beach and Leo and I drive back together?"

"Sure," said Bianca and Leo was on his way.

The cleanup was basically done, so Bianca poured herself and Sienna a quick cup of coffee. They walked over to the comfortable couch on the lanai and sat down. Sienna was physically and mentally exhausted after the service and episode with Leo and Detective Baldwin but the strong coffee and talking to her friend helped.

"I'm surprised she let you get away with a warning. Isabel is usually a bitch and will do anything for her career," Bianca said. "Did you know she's Mark's ex-wife?"

"Oh, wow," replied Sienna, "I had no idea. It didn't click when I heard her last name. She's gorgeous."

"Yes, she is... But you can imagine that things haven't been going well between the police office and the Turtle Sanctuary since they broke up. The Turtle Sanctuary really relies on the support of the police. Lots of people call the police regarding sick turtles because they don't know about the Sea Turtle Sanctuary or how to reach them. Due to Isabel being angry with Mark, some turtles haven't gotten the help they needed on time. He's the one who broke up and she's not too happy about it... although supposedly she's the one who cheated on him."

"Oh darn and he's so hot," replied Sienna dreamily, staring into thin air. Bianca looked at her surprised. She didn't know whether Sienna was joking or not. She wasn't usually so outspoken.

Chapter 14

When Lindsey's classroom teacher Ms. Smith called Sienna the next morning and informed her that Lindsey had been sent to the principal for responding to her questions with rude sarcastic remarks and she then received an email from Lilly's teacher Ms. Fisch requesting a conference about Lilly's silence, Sienna knew she was in trouble and these kids needed more attention and psychological guidance than she could give them.

Sienna ended the call and sat down. She called Bianca to ask if she could pick Lilly up from the bus while she went to meet Lindsey's teacher in the afternoon. She sat there, staring into thin air. Things were so complicated and she needed to make some decisions.

After moping around for a little while, she shook her gloomy feelings off, looked out of the window at the beautiful palm trees swaying in the breeze and decided to go for a swim. Physical activity always helped her when she didn't feel good. She recalled being a good swimmer in high school and how much she had enjoyed it. She walked over to the master bedroom, changed into her bathing suit, grabbed a towel and her phone, slipped into her flip flops at the back door and left the house. Then she jumped into her car and drove a few miles on US1 north to her favorite beach, Coco Plum Beach, where she and her friends had hung out many times in middle and high school.

She took a right down a small road leading her through a residential neighborhood, which hadn't been there 17 years ago but then she saw the dirt road she remembered from way back when and the beautiful beach spread out in front of her. There was layer of sea grass along the shore but it didn't bother her. She was immediately happy that she had decided to get out for a while. It was a beautiful sunny day but also breezy and not as hot and muggy as it would be in summertime. Sienna dropped her towel into the sand, took her flip flops off and slowly stepped over the sea grass and into the water that was colder than she had expected, but shallow and crystal clear. The visibility was so good that she could see her feet in the water and some little fishes scurrying away. The water was very shallow but soon Sienna reached thigh deep water. She stretched her arms out, pushed herself off and dove down beneath the surface. It was a wonderful refreshing feeling. She opened her eyes briefly, admiring the beautiful underwater world, but the salt stung and she shut her eyes tightly again. Coming back up, she swam a few strokes, turned around, floated on her back and just relaxed for a while, floating parallel to the shore. She knew it wasn't a good idea to swim too far out because there were too many speedboats out there. She held her face into the sun and blinked a few times to get the salty water out of her eyes.

She was about to wipe her eyes with her hand, when she suddenly got splashed by the strong set of arms of a swimmer paddling straight into her. Sienna reacted quickly: She turned around and dove down again, straight underneath him, avoiding being kicked by his legs. The swimmer realized that he was mowing someone over, stopped and took his goggles off as Sienna came up, coughing and gasping for air. They were both hip deep in the water, standing about 3 feet apart from each other, staring at each other speechlessly. Sienna, still gasping, recognized that it was Mark, the veterinarian from the Sea Turtle Sanctuary. He was quite a bit taller than her and all she could see at first were his broad shoulders and muscular chest and arms. He ran his fingers through his dark thick hair as he took his goggles off and realized whom he had almost bumped into again. He swallowed because he felt terrible but absolutely didn't mind what he saw. Sienna was even gorgeous coming out of the ocean gasping and coughing with her red hair tied back to a ponytail and her athletic body.

"Oh, no," he stuttered embarrassed, "Sienna, I'm so sorry, I really didn't expect anyone else here at this time of day. I always come and get in a workout first when I start later in the morning, I live right up the road..."

Sienna still couldn't reply, but now she wasn't sure if she was speechless from almost being mowed over in the ocean or from the fact that he was so extremely handsome he took her breath away.

"I hope it doesn't become a regular thing, us bumping into each other like this all the time," she said grinning, trying to sound stern but thought: *although I wouldn't mind...*

"Sorry", he said truly remorseful. *She must think I'm a moron,* he thought.

Treading through the shallow water next to each other, they made their way back to the shore, carefully stepping over the sea grass. Mark's towel was about twenty yards down the beach. He went and put it around his shoulders but walked back over to where Sienna was drying herself off. She pretended to be looking out at the ocean but had followed every move he made out of the corner of her eyes. She felt the same tension that she had felt the first time she had laid eyes on him. They were both drawn to each other in a way that only happened once in a lifetime.

At first, there was an awkward silence as he stepped back up to her with his towel around his shoulders, the water droplets on his tanned shoulders glistening in the sun, but then they both started talking at the same time and burst out in laughter. The tension was gone. They sat down on their towels and talked nonstop until Mark suddenly remembered that he had to go to work, looked at his phone and jumped up, embarrassed that he had forgotten the time like this. Sienna stood up as well, picked up her towel and looked up at him as he said: "Sorry, I have to go. I'm late for work now – I seriously enjoyed talking to you."

"Me too," she replied. "I hope we can do it again..."

He leaned down and was just going to give her a quick peck on the cheek when she turned her head around a bit more and their lips met. At first it felt awkward and he wanted to pull back and apologize, but then he realized that she was kissing him back and their kiss became more and more passionate. Mark had to tear himself away so that it wouldn't lead to more. He just said quietly: "I've got to go," and was gone. She stood there, watching him leave and put her fingers on her mouth, savoring the feeling of his soft lips on hers and his taste in her mouth, wishing for more.

*****

Sienna still had her meeting with Lindsey's teacher later in the afternoon and had to get some work done before that, so she couldn't remain in her daydream about Mark any longer, even though she just wanted to stay on the beach remembering every single word of their conversation and every moment of their kiss.

She walked down the beach, into the parking lot, wrapped her towel around her waist to not get the car too wet, hopped into the car and quickly drove home.

When Sienna arrived back at the Sea Turtle Sanctuary, she pulled her sundress over before she scurried down the path toward the cottage, hoping nobody would see her with her hair all wet and tangled, looking out for Mark even though he was probably not there yet.

She jumped in the shower, still thinking about Mark's kiss. Suddenly her phone beeped again with an incoming text message from Craig and it felt like all of her troubles were back. She ignored the text message like she had mostly the past few days and spent the next few hours answering emails and tidying up the house. Then she ate a quick bite and hurried to get ready for the meeting with Lindsey's teacher.

As Sienna walked down the walkway toward the parking lot past the Sea Turtle Sanctuary, she couldn't help it but check again to see whether she saw HIM somewhere. He was, indeed, standing at one of the big outside water basins, checking on a turtle, looking very sexy with his speckled eyes behind his John Lennon glasses, writing some comments into the turtle's chart. He heard Sienna's heels clicking on the sidewalk and looked up. Their eyes met and they both smiled. Her heart skipped a beat. She was falling for this handsome veterinarian...

*****

Walking up to the light blue three-story building of Turtle Key Middle High School that hadn't changed a bit in all these years, Sienna had flashbacks of walking through the hallways or spending her lunch break on the big patio on the side of the main building with her group of friends, always on the lookout for Ricky in the high school section. Ever since he moved to Turtle Key, she had always had a crush on him and everything revolved around him. Thankfully, Sienna's grades had been very good and nobody had ever realized that she spent more time daydreaming about him than she did studying.

She walked into the office and informed the receptionist that she had an appointment with Mrs. Smith, Lindsey's teacher.

"Unfortunately, Lindsey's behavior has been anything but acceptable since her parents' death," Mrs. Smith explained. "And of course we're giving her the benefit of the doubt right now, but maybe she should stay at home for awhile. Her current behavior is unacceptable and her attention is basically non-existent. There are homeschooling options after such a traumatic experience..."

"But don't you think it's better for her to have the normalcy of attending school and being around the other kids?" asked Sienna. "She'd just sit in her room, constantly be reminded of her parents death and probably become depressed at some point. I don't think she'd study much on her own."

Mrs. Smith and Sienna were sitting in one of the conference rooms of Turtle Key Middle High School. Sienna knew that Mrs. Smith truly cared but she also felt that it would be an easy fix for the school to have Lindsey home school and she automatically turned into the lawyer she was. She didn't think it was the right thing for Lindsey to home school by herself and that she needed the social interaction with her classmates. Sienna didn't know much about kids, but she knew that a depressed teenage girl sitting alone in her room was certainly not going to concentrate on studying...

"Is there a school psychologist she could speak with? Or could we speak with him or her together?" asked Sienna.

"We have a guidance counselor who is fully aware of the situation and pretty experienced with that type of problem. The school psychologist works for several schools in Monroe County and only comes here once a week, but I'll see if you and Lindsey can get an appointment with her," replied Mrs. Smith. "Maybe you can talk to Mrs. Martin, our guidance counselor, first. Actually, let me see if she's still in her office." She picked up her phone's receiver, dialed a few numbers and waited. Someone answered. "Linda, do you have a moment to come and talk to Lindsey Flores' legal guardian, Sienna Brantley, and me about Lindsey? Yes, Lindsey, whose parents had the accident. Okay, thanks."

She put the receiver back and said: "She'll be right here."

Just a couple of minutes later, guidance counselor Linda Martin stepped into the office and Mrs. Smith explained the situation. Mrs. Martin greeted Sienna and replied right away: "I'd say we let Lindsey decide what she wants to do. Only she can decide if she's ready to be back in school or not."

The school bell rang and Mrs. Smith called the substitute who was currently teaching her class.

"Maria, can you please send Lindsey Flores to the front office?" she requested.

A few minutes later, Lindsey stepped into the conference room. She hadn't been aware of the meeting and almost walked backwards out of the room when she saw Mrs. Martin, Mrs. Smith and Sienna sitting there. Her previously happy face turned into a frown.

"Hi Lindsey, please sit down," said Mrs. Martin.

Lindsey sat down on the corner of a chair, looking uncomfortable.

"Unfortunately, we had to call your Aunt Sienna because of your poor behavior toward Mrs. Smith lately," explained Mrs. Martin. "We understand that you are upset about what happened to your parents but rude behavior is unacceptable, as I'm sure you know. Do you think it's okay for you to be back in school already or would you rather still home school for a while?"

"Why? Does the school want to get rid of me?" asked Lindsey in an offensive tone.

"Of course not, Lindsey, we all want what's best for you. We would like you to stay and I'm sure your friends do too, but we want to make sure that you're ready. When someone has a death in the family, it's normal to mourn and be out of school for a while," replied Mrs. Smith quickly.

"We think maybe you'd like to speak with the school psychologist Mrs. Banner about the situation?"

"Why do you guys even care? I'll probably have to move to Boston anyhow," Lindsey replied again in a hostile manner, nodding toward Sienna but not looking at her.

Sienna was caught off guard and didn't quite know how to reply since she didn't know what she was going to do with the kids herself. She caught herself quickly and replied slowly and insecurely: "That's a possibility. Unfortunately my job is up there and you guys might be stuck with me now."

Lindsey jumped up and ran out of the room, slamming the door. Mrs. Smith and Mrs. Martin looked at Sienna who felt like she had to rush after Lindsey but didn't want to leave the meeting in the same abrupt manner.

"Well, that's something that has to be settled, I guess," said Mrs. Martin. "She obviously has terrible anxiety about her uncertain future?"

"Do you mind if I text her real quick?" asked Sienna and texted Lindsey: "Please meet me at the car in five minutes."

"Yes, unfortunately this is a shock for everyone. I'm their only relative now and I do live and work in Boston," replied Sienna.

"Have you talked to the kids about it yet?"

"No, we really haven't had a chance to breathe. I just arrived a few days ago and yesterday was the service for Camilla and Ricky. It's been really busy. I'm single, work as a lawyer, usually about 60 hours a week, and I have no idea how to raise kids."

"Why don't you try to explain your situation to the kids and get yourself some more time to make a decision? Are the other two having any problems?" Mrs. Martin thought for a moment and asked: "Leo goes to our high school, doesn't he?"

"Yes," answered Sienna, "the other two certainly are having problems as well," without going further into detail.

"Do you have any friends you can speak with?"

"Not many... Well, there are a couple, I guess," she replied, thinking of Bianca and Bridget.

"Well, please let us know if you think you'd like to speak with the school psychologist regarding the kids, but you might need a different type of counseling..." said Mrs. Martin, shaking her head empathetically. "I'm so sorry about this situation."

Sienna thanked them, shook their hands and left, feeling a bit better than before. At least they seemed to genuinely care and she knew that she'd be able to contact them again for advice if she needed to. She stepped out of the building and walked over to the parking lot, happy to see Lindsey next to the red Mustang.

"Would you like to drive with the top down?" Sienna asked and Lindsey nodded, cracking a little smile. Without talking, they drove down US1, enjoying the ride and the afternoon breeze. Sienna had a spontaneous idea.

"What's your favorite food?" she asked.

"Pad Thai," replied Lindsey.

"Are you serious?" answered Sienna, "mine too! Is there a good Thai restaurant somewhere close by?"

"Yeah, in the same plaza as Publix."

"Oh, that's coming right up. It's early, but shall we get it now? Do the others like it too?"

"Yeah, Leo likes the thick noodles, pad see ew, and Lilly likes massaman curry. I'm starving."

Sienna had a better idea. "Well, instead of getting take-out, why don't we go pick them up and go there right now? The house is only five minutes down the road. Can you call Leo and check if he's home? I'll call Bianca to get Lilly ready."

"Okay."

*****

About 20 minutes later, they were all sitting in a booth at the local Thai Restaurant, which had always been the Flores family's favorite. The restaurant was empty this time of day, the food came out quickly and they all ate with gusto. Sienna could tell that even Lilly, who still wasn't talking, was pleased, quietly inhaling a giant portion of her favorite dish. The waitress knew the kids, brought them some special hard candies in colorful wrappers and the atmosphere was more relaxed than usual. Sienna didn't talk much, watching the children, hoping Lilly would forget about the situation and just say something. But she didn't. Lindsey had become used to being her voice and had ordered for her and answered all questions that were posed to Lilly.

After the table had been cleared, they sat there for a while, everyone was tired and full. Sienna seized the opportunity to have a talk with them as Mrs. Martin had suggested.

"Guys, I've been wanting to talk to you. You know, I don't want to rip you out of your surroundings and take you to Boston. This is a surprise and as sad for me as it is for you. Well, it is worse for you since it was your parents. But I don't know what to do myself. I just wanted to say, we'll figure out what's the best for everyone, okay?"

They all nodded. Maybe they did understand a tiny bit that Sienna was in an awkward position as well because Lindsey said:

"Thanks, Aunt Sienna."

It always seemed hot and cold with Lindsey but Sienna took what she could get and nodded appreciatively.

"So," Sienna didn't want to ruin the nice atmosphere they had had during dinner and had another good idea, "is the soft serve ice cream place a few houses down from the Turtle Sanctuary still there?"

Everyone's faces lit up.

"Yes!" said Leo and Lindsey. Sienna was sure that Lilly was about to say something. But just almost. Sienna jumped up and said: "Then let's go!"

Things with the kids seemed a little more upbeat after this fun afternoon.

Chapter 15

Sienna had so much on her mind that she suffered from insomnia that night. Tossing and turning, she couldn't stop thinking about Mark and the unusual attraction she felt for him. She had butterflies in her stomach like she hadn't had since she was a teenager in love with Ricky. She had never had such strong feelings for her ex-husband Jake, who she had met in law school, during their short and not very happy marriage. This "rebound marriage" had ended in a divorce just two years later.

However, things with Mark and his wife seemed much too complicated and things for her weren't currently easy either. She looked at the clock on her nightstand. It was 2 am, but her brain couldn't stop churning. There were too many other things that kept going through her mind, the kids... she had truly enjoyed dinner last night and felt that they were all getting used to each other. Whatever she did, it truly wasn't going to be easy. Should she give up her career with an international firm in Boston to work for some small-town lawyer in the Keys who probably had nothing but divorces, car accidents and other liability cases – or estate planning like Mr. LaFleur – had she worked so hard all these years to end up with a job like that? Maybe she could work in South Miami - Homestead, Kendall or Coral Gables – lots of people probably commuted to Miami – or Key West.

Then Craig. He kept texting her and even though she had told him several times that they were not together anymore. Her feelings for him were definitely gone and she found his texting annoying and childish. He needed to realize that their relationship was over and she wondered when he would finally accept it. Thinking of his possible reactions and seeing him again scared her. He didn't seem like the type of guy who accepted it when other people called the shots.

Sienna looked at the clock again. It was 3 am now. The ticking drove her crazy. She got up, wrapped the clock in a towel in the bathroom and closed the door. She still couldn't sleep, was wide awake, so she got up, put her flowing silk bathrobe on, walked out onto the lanai and sat down on the rattan couch. No wonder that she couldn't sleep, the moon wasn't full anymore, but the waning crescent in the clear sky was shining bright and seemed unusually big. Sienna looked up into the sky and listened to the nightly sounds. An eastern screech owl was calling, the cicadas were chirping loudly, the pitch of the amphibian chorus was so high that it almost sounded like yelling children, but these sounds were so old and familiar to Sienna that they relaxed her and she finally slipped into a much needed sleep.

*****

The next morning, Sienna jerked out of her sleep. Lilly was shaking her. She had slept on the short overstuffed rattan couch on the lanai for the rest of the night and her back hurt accordingly. Leo had already left, but Lilly was obviously hungry and wanted breakfast. She didn't talk, as usual, but Sienna was already that much in tune with her. Lilly woke up hungry and needed a big breakfast in the morning but usually didn't eat anything for lunch.

Today was the meeting with Lilly's teacher, Ms. Fisch, about her continued non-speaking. But first Sienna had to get Lindsey off to school and make another attempt to have another get together with Bridget at the Sea Turtle Sanctuary to get into the swing of things and talk about the financial disaster the hospital was in. Sienna rolled her eyes. They were probably going to get interrupted again because of some emergency, which seemed to be the norm. It was very sad that, mostly due to the environment, the number of sick and needy turtles was infinite and never-ending. Turtles were the "canaries in the coal mine" of the Keys, showing symptoms and diseases before anything else did.

Sienna got Leo and then Lilly off to school and then she jumped into the shower before she had to send Lindsey off. Lindsey's behavior toward Sienna had improved a bit since their meeting with Mrs. Smith and Mrs. Martin and the nice dinner but she was so moody that it was hit and miss. Sienna never knew how Lindsey would act from one day to the next. Today she was grumpy and barely spoke with Sienna at all. Sienna remembered being thirteen and tried not to take anything personally, she knew that in addition to Lindsey losing her parents, her hormones were raging too...

As soon as Lindsey had left, Sienna got ready to go over to the Sea Turtle Sanctuary. Of course, she became nervous thinking she might run into Mark and wondered how their encounter would be. Sienna picked outfit after outfit and nothing seemed good enough as she turned back and forth in front of a full-length mirror. Finally, she chose a light green shift dress that accentuated her red hair and green eyes but still looked casual and not dressed up.

Her heart was racing as she stepped into the Sea Turtle Sanctuary. Mark was really affecting her, she felt like a teenager, in love for the first time. Was she seriously so nervous about their next encounter? She told herself that she was a professional businesswoman in her mid thirties - but that didn't seem to help.

She was actually a bit upset when Bridget stepped up to the reception desk, led her to Camilla's old office and they did NOT run into Mark. Bridget gave her a double take. "You look nice today," she said grinning. She obviously DID realize that Sienna had put a lot of effort into getting dressed today.

"Mark is coming later today, he had something going on with his daughter this morning," she said.

"What do you mean?" asked Sienna, trying not to grin, having a hard time looking Bridget in the eyes.

"Oh, come on, do you really think I didn't notice the tension between you two the other day? He's the nicest guy and you'd make an awesome couple! But be careful, his ex-wife is a real bitch and she is not very supportive to the Sea Turtle Sanctuary as it is. And guess what makes things even worse," asked Bridget after a brief pause. "Her father is the director of the bank where we have all our bank accounts and our credits. So we rely on his sympathy. He's the one who makes the final decision when we're really in the red again and need another loan..."

Sienna nodded speechlessly but then she asked desperately:

"Aren't they divorced?" admitting she had feelings for Mark.

"Yeah, but she seems to regret it. She cheated on him and he's the one who wanted the divorce." Bridget looked at Sienna, thoughtfully. "Aren't you planning on going back to Boston anyhow, Sienna? Is there a future for you two?" Sienna squirmed as the subject was brought up again.

"I seriously don't know what to do, Bridget. Of course I have my whole life in Boston. And my career. But can I really rip these kids out of their surroundings and make them move to Boston? I can't sleep, Bridget, because I don't know what to do."

"Yeah, honestly, I don't know what I'd do in your situation either. Well, I can only say one thing and I think I speak for the whole Sea Turtle Sanctuary: We'd all be ecstatic if you stayed. Everyone loves you, especially the older staff like me," she said grinning.

Then Bridget walked over to a sideboard, picked up a pile of thick file folders, bringing them over to the big desk that they now sat down at. She opened the first folder and handed Sienna a piece of paper that looked like a bank statement. At the bottom of the page, a number was circled with a red sharpie. Sienna swallowed as she read the number. It didn't look too good: - 75,459.—

There was a brief silence in the office and Sienna and Bridget could have heard a pin drop.

"Wow. That's how much the hospital is in debt?" Sienna asked shocked.

"Yup. I think there's another small account that's still in the black, but that's barely enough to pay the employees next month and buy the bare-bone necessities for the turtles. Then we have a car payment for the ambulance, insurance, gas, utilities and all that stuff. It doesn't look good."

She opened up a second file folder and handed the top sheet to Sienna. This one looked a bit better, approximately $35,000 without the minus symbol in front of it, but Bridget explained: "That's about what our expenses for one month are. Camilla and Ricky were a great office manager and vet but not very good at running a business."

Sienna was speechless and absolutely discouraged.

Of course she had some savings, but was she going to have to use up her lifetime savings for her retirement to save the Sea Turtle Sanctuary and the mess her sister and brother in law had left behind? Would there be any insurance money for the kids from the truck driver's company? Did Camilla and Ricky have any savings?

If yes, that couldn't be used for the Sea Turtle Sanctuary either – it had to be used for the kids and their education. Sienna would have to meet with their bank manager - obviously Mark's ex-wife's father - and check into all assets and probably go through all of their paperwork in the house and even their computer files. She felt like she'd be intruding on their privacy, but there was no such thing when death was involved. The thought was depressing but she was used to dealing with such unpleasant business matters and had learned to turn off her emotions.

Bridget's phone bleeped with an incoming text message. She read it and looked at Sienna.

"I have to go and take care of something. There's a reporter who's writing an article about us, which is actually good for exposure," she said and got up. "I'll be about half an hour, let me know if you need me later."

Sienna nodded and started going through the paperwork on her own. It was very discouraging because it was nothing but unpaid bills, reminders and negative bank statements. She opened a few drawers, which were full of unfiled old paperwork and even unopened letters – someone had obviously just crammed it in to get it out of sight. Sienna looked around her sister's office, which before that had been her mother's and was still decorated with the same old inexpensive plywood office furniture. Nothing had changed here in thirty years. Sienna had been here many times to visit her mother in her office. The same old framed photos of Camilla, Sienna and their parents dressed up and always taken by the same photography studio in Key Largo decorated the walls. They hadn't been dusted in a while and looked old and almost antique. Old big conch shells that Camilla or Sienna had found on the beach were used as paperweights. Some very special and unique ones as well as her grandmother's old collection of pink conch pearls were displayed in a glass case that had the words "Conch Republic" engraved in the top part of the wooden frame. "Conch Republic", a name originated in 1982 originally only for Key West as it declared itself a micro nation but then expanded to all of the Keys, was also what their mom had lovingly called her office. She used to say in the morning before she went to work in a joking manner: "I'll be in my Conch Republic if you need me." Sienna had to smile as she stepped up to the glass case and observed the many beautiful shells and conch pearls in different shades of pink that were possibly valuable. Before their mother, their grandmother whose husband had been a fisherman in the Keys and had often brought his wife the biggest most beautiful conch shells home from his fishing trips as far as to the Bahamas, had found a few of these pink conch pearls and collected them, obviously not realizing their immense value. Conch pearls usually occurred in the warm tropical waters of the Caribbean, from the Yucatan all the way up to Bermuda but some seemed to have made their way to the Keys. One conch pearl was found in every 10,000 - 15,000 shells.

Suddenly, Sienna remembered an incident when she and Camilla had obviously found an unusually large pink conch pearl in a queen conch at Coco Plum Beach. They had proudly given it to their mother and she, distracted as usual, had just put it in her pocket, deep in her thoughts.

*****

Flashback

30 years ago, 1988, Turtle Key, Florida Keys

Six-year old Sienna and her eight-year old sister Camilla, both wearing sensible shorts and t-shirts, skipping along the shallow clear water at Coco Plum Beach. They were both full of freckles and their lighter and darker red hair was shining in the sun. Their parents and some other adults were in an anchored boat in the distance, obviously taking care of a turtle that they had just rescued. The girls were bored and had run off to play. They had grown up here, were good swimmers and were used to being alone on the beach.

Suddenly, Camilla bent down and picked up a giant queen conch out of the shallow water. It was perfectly intact. Sienna stepped up and they both examined the beautifully iridescent pink sheen of the spiral shell and felt its smooth surface. Camilla held it up to her ear, trying to hear the sound of the ocean waves. Then she handed it to Sienna who did the same. Suddenly, something fell out of the shell and dropped into the ankle-deep water.

"Get it!" yelled Camilla and tried to grab the little rock or ball floating in the water as it slowly drifted away, with the next wave slowly coming up.

Sienna quickly bent down and grabbed the perfectly oval dark pink ball. It looked like an oval marble and had a beautiful sheen to it, but they had no idea what they had just found.

"We can use it later to play marbles," said Sienna as she held it up to the light and examined it, "but it probably won't work, it's not round enough."

"Why don't you keep the marble and I'll keep the shell," said Camilla, thinking she was getting the better deal, and

Sienna nodded. Soon they were distracted by another interesting object on the beach and Sienna stuck the "marble" in her pocket.

Later, when their parents came to get them, Sienna realized that she still had the marble in her pocket and handed it to her mom.

"Mom, look what we found. It's a present for you!"

"Oh, thanks, honey, what a pretty little marble, it looks almost like one of Grandma's old conch pearls. I'll put it into the glass case with them," she replied and stuck it in her pocket, not even giving it a second thought.

*****

Back to present time

Sienna suddenly realized that what she and Camilla had found over thirty years ago at Coco Plum Beach must have been a gigantic pink conch pearl. Feverishly, she started looking for the pearl but, even though there were others in the display box, she couldn't find it. It was at least four times bigger than the others.

Somewhere Sienna had read about the 45-carat conch pearl set into a necklace by New York jeweler Harry Winston in the 1980s and modeled by Liz Taylor around 1990, which was extremely valuable but now untraceable. She took all of the pearls out of the display box and put them into a little black velvet bag with a drawstring that she found in a drawer in Camilla's desk, containing even more pearls, all of them adding up to a total of twelve pearls. After examining them one more time, she carefully stashed the bag in her purse. She was flabbergasted. These pearls seemed to be floating all over the place and nobody here had a clue how expensive and rare they were. She concluded she should go and have them appraised.

*****

After a while, Sienna realized how hungry she was and that it was already past lunch time. She grabbed her purse and rushed down the hallway. Just as she was rounding the corner close to the exit, she bumped into Mark again.

"Wow, you certainly must be stalking me," she said, grinning.

He grinned as well. "No, I'm just drawn to you like a moth to the flame," he replied with a smile. "Animal magnetism."

He looked around briefly to check if anyone was coming down the hallway, but then he took her in his arms, pressed her against the wall and started kissing her passionately. She was blown away and kissed him back, enjoying every second of this forbidden hallway kiss. Suddenly Bridget stood behind them, clearing her throat.

"Um, guys, you might want to take this somewhere else," she said grinning.

Mark and Sienna staggered apart, embarrassed like teen-agers caught red-handed.

"Mark, can you meet me in dock one?" asked Bridget as she continued walking down the hallway.

"I need to see you. Tonight?" Mark whispered quickly before he followed Bridget.

Sienna just nodded, again a bit dizzy from the passion of their kiss. Her heart was pounding in her chest and the butterflies in her stomach were out of control as she walked back toward the cottage.

*****

In the afternoon, Sienna had her meeting with Ms. Fisch, Lilly's kindergarten teacher at the local elementary school. Sienna was impressed by how friendly and well prepared Ms. Fisch was and how much psychological research she seemed to have done.

"Children are resilient," she said, "but when children don't speak, psychological problems or emotional stress, such as anxiety, may be involved which clearly is the case here. She needs to feel safe and loved. How is your relationship with her?"

"We've gotten a bit closer in the past few days but we barely know each other," replied Sienna, "I live and work in Boston and really had no contact with the family until now."

"It might be a good idea for Lilly to speak with a child psychologist," said Ms. Fisch. "But I assume there might also just be some spontaneous event when she forgets thinking about her traumatic experience and just talks. Why don't you think about it and I'll give you some recommendations."

Sienna hesitated and looked at Ms. Fisch. She said: "You know, I've been thinking I know your name from somewhere and now it suddenly clicked. "Did your mother teach high school back then and your father community college? I remember having your mother during senior year and I think your father taught my sister in community college."

"What a small world," replied Ms. Fisch and her face lit up. "You're right, we're a family of teachers. I think I remember you and your sister too. Your sister graduated with my brother. I'm a few years older than you."

They both smiled thinking about old times and chatted about the past, some mutual friends and memories. Again Sienna left feeling a bit better than before, because she could tell that everyone here knew each other and genuinely cared.

The bell had rung and she had to pick up Lilly. On the way back to the cottage, they ran into Bianca who was walking her dogs, two mutts, Golden and Sam. Golden looked a bit like a golden Retriever, therefore the name, but Sam was unidentifiable, he could have been a mix of a Basset Hound and a Labrador because his legs were extremely short. Lilly was happy to see them and let them lick her face, but Sienna was a bit more careful and petted the dogs with the tip of her fingers. She wasn't really a dog person but didn't want to insult Bianca.

"How's it going?" asked Bianca as Lilly ran ahead toward the cottage.

"I just met Lilly's teacher Ms. Fisch. We talked about her silence and she proposed seeing a psychologist. She really seemed to know what she was talking about..."

Bianca became angry that Sienna still didn't get it. "There's no counseling for a problem like this. It's called common sense. You put yourself behind and the kids first. You're their legal guardian now. They need you. Does the law firm need you? Have they been ringing the phone off of the hook or did they make you a partner?"

That last comment really bothered Sienna but Bianca wasn't done with her rant.

"If you stay, it doesn't mean you have to stop working. Things could always be worked out. I could watch the kids and you work in Miami or Key West, for example... And what about you and Mark? You need to figure things out, Sienna, and then Lilly, Lindsey and Leo will be fine too."

Bianca marched away with her dogs, huffing and puffing, talking to herself in Spanish about young people nowadays. Sienna watched her, subdued. She knew Bianca was right. How nice would it be to always know where you belong, like Bianca, she thought.

Mark, who had somehow snuck Sienna's phone number from the Sea Turtle Sanctuary's receptionist Andrea, texted her in the late afternoon, asking if she could meet him for dinner. Of course, today of all days, Sienna was feeling guilty because of what Bianca had said but then she thought real parents go on dates too and changed her mind because she really wanted to see Mark. She could even ask one of Bianca's older granddaughters or Bianca to check on the kids tonight.

After calling Bianca, she texted Mark back:

"Meet you at The Jumping Dolphin at eight."

He texted back: "Can't wait. I'll make a reservation."

Chapter 16

The Jumping Dolphin Waterfront Restaurant on the ocean side was one of Turtle Key's most renowned restaurants, built in the late seventies and still run by its original owners. The food and service were excellent and the place was very laid back like most restaurants in the Keys. The small entrance made it look like a little rinky-dink hole in the wall bar, but it opened up to a big dining room and the beautiful interior was a nice surprise, decorated with the old original wooden bar and lots of memorabilia, paintings all over the walls and dark wood table and chairs. There were a few tables on a little waterfront patio on a dock along the restaurant's exterior wall where the hostess led Mark and Sienna as they checked in at 8 pm. Locals at the bar greeted Mark, high fived him and looked curiously at Sienna as they walked by. It was a slow Tuesday evening and they realized to their satisfaction that they were the only guests on the patio tonight.

The waning crescent of the moon stood high in the clear sky, lots of stars were visible and the calm water lapped gently against the dock. The tall palm trees in front of the property swayed in the gentle breeze and the amphibious creatures in the mangroves surrounding the dock were busy playing their nightly concerto.

Sienna, dressed beautifully yet casually in a dark green shift dress that accentuated her beautiful red hair and her athletic figure, sandals in the same color with a small heel, and Mark in a pair of nice khakis and a pink button-up shirt with casual leather shoes matching his belt, followed the hostess to their table right on the water. Mark couldn't take his eyes off of Sienna as he followed her across the patio and then pulled a chair up for her as she sat down. She looked stunning.

The hostess left two menus and said: "Your waitress tonight is Julia, she'll be right with you to take your drink order."

There were a few first moments of silence and Sienna's OCD kicked in as she started rearranging and straightening a few items on the table. Mark noticed that she was nervous and gently placed his hand on hers. She looked into his beautiful speckled eyes behind the John Lennon glasses and wished he were closer so she could kiss him.

In that instance, server Julia walked up. She greeted them and poured two glasses of ice water.

"Hey, guys, oh hi, Mark," she said as she recognized Mark.

"Hi, Julia, this is Sienna, Camilla's younger sister. Julia grew up here too, Sienna. You might actually know each other from school," replied Mark.

"Which year did you graduate?" asked Sienna, examining Julia's face. "I do think I remember you. Were you in the class of 2000?"

"Yes, I was!" said Julia, full of excitement. "It's so good to see you, Sienna. I'm so sorry about your sister and Ricky." She paused for a second because she knew that Ricky had been Sienna's boyfriend back then, but didn't want to go there.

"Thanks, Julia," said Sienna. Her face became sad and serious for a moment but then she tried to change the subject to something more pleasant.

"Didn't we go to the Ricky Martin concert together back then?"

"Yes, that's still one of the best concerts I've ever seen."

"I wasn't supposed to go and really got in trouble when my parents found out," replied Sienna, laughing. "Weren't you and I both grounded for a while afterwards?"

"Yeah, but I still don't regret it!" Julia said grinning. "So, do you guys know what you'd like to drink?"

Mark asked Sienna: " Would you like to take a look at the drink menu?"

"I'll have a Mojito, please."

"And for me a Mai Tai, please," said Mark.

"Okay, I'll get them out here as quickly as I can. Also, our special today is locally caught grilled grouper with homemade rice pilaf and mango/pineapple salsa. But you can have it prepared any other way too. I really like it blackened. And of course, as you know, our sushi is outstanding."

"Thanks, give us a minute, we'll take another look at the menu," replied Mark.

"Sure, I'll go and put in the drink order, oh, and we also got some really fresh Florida lobster in today if you're in the mood for that. It's still lobster season for a couple of weeks," said Julia.

They both nodded and thanked her.

"Oh, and by the way, keep an eye on the water," Julia said pointing down. "Some guests saw the manatees today that hang out here sometimes."

Mark and Sienna looked down into the water.

Julia walked across the patio and back into the main dining room where she punched the drinks into a computer.

Mark and Sienna made their choices, set the menus aside and admired the beautiful sky. There was a moment of silence but then they quickly started talking at the same time. They had to laugh, looked deep into each other's eyes and Mark again placed his hand on hers on the table. Sienna felt the butterflies fluttering in her stomach again as Julia returned with the drinks and set them down on the table. Mark and Siena lifted their cocktails and Mark proposed a toast:

"To us."

He didn't say anything about her having to make up her mind whether she'd stay or not and that's what she liked about him. Things were so easy and he didn't pressure her. They could basically just sit there and gaze at each other but then there was also so much to talk about. They ordered and it wasn't long before Julia brought out the food. They tried each other's meals, truly enjoyed the food and felt as if they had known each other forever.

Suddenly, they heard a boat speeding up to the dock behind the patio. It was a smaller 23 ft. center console speedboat with the words "Coast Guard" written on its side. A handsome officer jumped onto the dock and tied the rope to a cleat in the front and back. The other officer in the boat didn't belong to the Coast Guard. She seemed to be a regular police officer. To Mark and Sienna's surprise it was Isabel, Mark's ex-wife.

The Coast Guard officer held his hand out and helped her on land. Laughing she jumped onto the dock and walked up to the patio, followed by her accompaniment. She had her usual tight dark braid hanging down her back, which made her look starker than she was. Her face froze into a grimace as she saw Mark and Sienna sitting there, finishing their romantic dinner. Walking past them, she barely nodded at Mark, but if looks could kill, Sienna would have dropped dead to the ground...

"Boy, that sure was a dirty look," remarked Sienna.

"Should I be worried? She certainly didn't look like she didn't care that you're going out with someone else."

"Well, we are officially divorced, I don't know what's wrong with her. When we were together, she couldn't get away from me soon enough," he replied.

"Well, you are quite the catch," said Sienna grinning as she looked in his dreamy dark brown eyes again. "Anyone would regret not keeping you around."

They both leaned forward and kissed each other gently on the lips. Isabel, who had stopped at the outside bar with her friend, was looking at them again. Her expression was more than angry as she saw her ex-husband kissing the lawyer from Boston. Sienna noticed that they were being watched and proposed:

"We're kind of done anyhow. Shall we have a nightcap somewhere else?"

Mark looked at her with a smile of relief. "Absolutely."

The next time Julia came outside, they requested the check and were out of the restaurant in no time. Thank goodness they could walk to the front straight off of the dock, so they didn't have to go through the restaurant and encounter Isabel again, who was now sitting inside with her date.

Mark took Sienna's hand and, laughing like two teenagers, they ran to the front parking lot where they stopped in front of Mark's car. They didn't notice Isabel watching them again as she stared out of the window, gloomily.

Mark took Sienna in his arms and kissed her again. They ended their kiss but stood there, just gazing into each other's eyes. Mark said: "Well, Sidney and the babysitter are at my house, and I guess your three are at your house or could come home any second if they're at Bianca's..."

Sienna looked at her watch. The kids should be home by now with Bianca's oldest granddaughter watching them, except Leo who might still be out with his buddies. She had an idea. "How about grabbing a bottle of wine at Publix and then hanging out at Coco Plum Beach?"

Mark nodded. “Great idea. That’s right where I live. Unfortunately my ex-wife lives right down the road too, but we know she’s not home, I guess.” They both giggled, feeling sneaky and adventurous.

They both got in their cars, drove down the road to Publix where they grabbed a bottle of Merlot, an inexpensive corkscrew and a set of plastic glasses. Sienna had a small blanket in her trunk and got it out as they arrived at the beach. They both took their shoes off and walked hand in hand through the warm sand to a protected spot close to the mangroves.

The small crescent of the moon was still bright enough to keep them from needing the flashlights on their phones. Sienna spread the little plaid blanket out in the sand. They sat down, Mark opened the wine and poured it into the cheap plastic glasses. Then they toasted, had a first little sip and looked out at the dark ocean. Sienna looked up and saw a shooting star. “Look!” she said, pointing up into the sky. He looked up briefly, but then he took her wine glass, stuck both of them into the sand twisting them a little and started kissing her, more and more passionately. Their arms held each other while Mark’s hand gently pulled Sienna’s shirt over her head as their bodies slowly slid down onto the blanket and the two shadows became one…

Chapter 17

Mark Baldwin, in a pair of gym shorts and a t-shirt, stepped into his small yet tasteful oceanfront condo close to Coco Plum Beach after walking his daughter Sidney to the school bus the next morning. He stretched, yawning and poured himself a second cup of coffee in the sunny little galley kitchen. He hadn't felt this good in a while. He was falling in love with Sienna and couldn't stop thinking of the way they had made love last night in the moonlight.

Suddenly, there was an assertive knock on the door. Mark stepped forward and opened the door. He wasn't expecting anyone, but for a brief second he hoped it might be Sienna.

His jaw and his mood dropped when he realized it was his ex-wife Isabel standing in front of his door, trying to look casual with her long thick hair open, but obviously dressed up in her sexiest low cut top, a pair of leggings and cute sneakers. Unfortunately, she lived in walking distance and still stopped by whenever she felt like it.

"Can I come in?"

"Sure." He opened the door further and stepped back to let Isabel come in.

Isabel had come with the best intentions to be nice and make up with him, but as it so often happened the past few years, her anger and unhappiness surfaced and once again turned the formerly beautiful woman into a fire-spewing dragon.

"So, is that what you do during the nights you have Sidney? Spend valuable one on one time with her or go out with this *perra* while Sidney sits at home with a babysitter?" she attacked him. "I guess you don't need joint custody then if you're already looking for a new family?"

"What are you talking about, Isabel?" Mark felt his blood pressure rise and he immediately went on the defense. "This is the first time I've had a date in two years, since you cheated on me with your hot coworker and left me. So blame only yourself."

The fiery Columbian suddenly changed her entire attitude, walked up to him, batting her long dark eyelashes at him and tried to put her arms around him but he backed off. "Mark, that was a one-time mistake. Forgive me. You know I love you. Remember the night four weeks ago?"

"That was also a mistake, Isabel. We've grown apart. I'm not putting up with your mood swings and drama anymore."

"I'm came to tell you I'm pregnant," she said as her eyes filled with tears. "That night four weeks ago, it was so passionate, we are meant to be back together. Sidney is going to have a little sister or brother."

She turned around and left, her hair flowing behind her, dramatic as usual, but not before she had seen Mark's horrified expression.

Mark stood there, speechless, feeling as if he were an actor in a soap opera.

They had been out four weeks ago to talk about some issues with Sidney who was failing in some of her classes. He drank a bit too much and they ended up in bed, something he absolutely regretted the next day. Isabel was not good for him. She was toxic and made him unhappy. At the end of their relationship, they had fought almost every evening and slept in different rooms. He knew things weren't going to change. But what if she was really pregnant? Could he make Isabel have the child by herself? Sidney would be so disappointed.

He slowly got in the shower and then got dressed for work, in his thoughts. His mood was a bit different than earlier this morning...

Chapter 18

After Lindsey had left for school, Sienna made her way over to the Sea Turtle Sanctuary to have another meeting with Bridget about some fundraising activities and to continue organizing and cleaning the office. Her heart was pounding in her chest as she thought of Mark and their passionate lovemaking last night on the beach. She had never felt like this with Craig, possibly with anyone. Reminded of Craig, she made a plan to call him later in the evening and tell him to stop texting her. For her things had ended a while ago but obviously not for him.

Mark was nowhere in sight as Sienna opened the gate, entered the back exterior area and walked past the turtle basins. She stepped into the building and walked toward Camilla's former office, peeking into the two intake bays and the exam rooms, but Mark was nowhere to be seen.

"Mark requested to accompany the rescue team today if you're looking for him," said Bridget, suddenly behind Sienna, grinning.

Sienna turned around, startled and blushed. "Um, yeah, thanks," she stammered.

"You guys have really hit it off, haven't you?" asked Bridget smiling. "I'm happy for you. He's a great guy."

"Yeah," Sienna just replied dreamily, not wanting to give away too many details as they walked side by side toward Camilla's office that now was Sienna's.

"Oh, before I forget: We're releasing Tammy, the turtle in basin two, by the docks later this afternoon. Do you want to come with the kids? It's always a big deal, even the local press is coming."

Sienna snapped out of her daydream about Mark.

"Sure! And if the kids don't want to join me, I'll come by myself," she replied, hoping Mark would be there.

They both sat down at the desk in the office, Bridget across from Sienna. Bridget started showing and explaining some fundraising ideas to Sienna. "So, let's get back to the idea of an Open House where people can adopt a turtle again and make a monthly contribution to their care," when suddenly her phone beeped, informing her of an emergency situation. This usually meant that someone had called in a turtle in distress and a rescue was required. Bridget rolled her eyes as she got up.

"Sorry, we're just never going to have a meeting without being interrupted."

Sienna nodded. "It's okay. I kind of understand what's going on. Just copy me on all e-mails you think I should know about."

Bridget nodded and left the office, dialing Mark's phone number to coordinate the new rescue.

*****

Sienna continued organizing the piles and piles of paperwork in the office into three categories: junk mail, important paperwork and unpaid bills. She sighed as she opened yet another drawer that someone had just shoved unopened mail and other documents into. She took letter by letter and threw them into two different filing trays or the garbage can. The amount of unpaid bills was terrifying. How could Camilla, Ricky and even Bridget have run a business like this? Sienna wondered how the Sea Turtle Sanctuary was even still able to order the basic necessities like food and medicine, but she assumed that Bridget was keeping an eye on at least those invoices.

Sienna picked up the last few documents in the last drawer and discovered a stack of hidden old photos underneath. This crazy messy office sure held a lot of surprises. Curiously, Sienna picked up the photos and went through them. Some were not that old and seemed to be pictures of some rare family weekends when the kids were smaller, Lindsey in a stroller in Key West, Leo as a toddler on the beach, Lilly sitting on her dad's shoulders in a nice hotel pool. Sienna smiled wistfully as she looked through the nice memories of what seemed to be a happy family. Then she found an old photo album in the back: Ricky's childhood. Formal photos of what looked like Ricky's baptism, a beautiful dressed up mother and a dad in a suit and tie in church with two godparents and Ricky in a long white baptism gown, the same beautiful mother with Ricky in a stroller, a dad with Ricky in front of a small Cessna at the airport in Key West, even one of her, Sienna, and Ricky in front of a plane at the Turtle Key airport, the mother with Ricky at the pool. The photos made Sienna sigh and think about old times. Sienna knew that Ricky had been very wealthy growing up in Coral Gables but that he also hadn't spoken with his family in years. His father wasn't happy that he had become an idealistic marine biologist and veterinarian against their wishes instead of taking over their lucrative law firm in Miami.

How ironic, Sienna thought. The daughter-in-law they originally should have gotten is a lawyer now. How would I have loved to take over that law firm. She took at closer look at the mother and father and started wondering whether these grandparents were still alive and where they were...

She put down the photo album and started typing names into the computer's search engine: Flores Law Firm in Coral Gables, Richard Flores. The big law firm in Coral Gables wasn't that hard to find – Ricky's father had retired years ago but was still a namesake partner and advisor of the firm Richard Flores Esq. and Associates.

Sienna dialed the phone number and a receptionist answered.

"I'm sorry, I can't give you any personal information about Mr. and Mrs. Flores," she said in an impersonal but professional manner.

"I have three orphans here that might be their grandchildren," said Sienna urgently, "It's really important."

"You know I'd get fired if I gave you that information," replied the receptionist. "Feel free to make an appointment with Mr. or Mrs. Sardinia, the new owners, or send them an email."

"Could you take my information and try to get it to them?" Sienna asked.

"Sure," replied the receptionist a bit annoyed and wrote Sienna's phone number down but Sienna didn't get her hopes up. She'd have to continue her research on her own.

*****

Just as Sienna ended the call, she heard a lot of commotion in the front area of the hospital and walked out of the office to see if it was Mark returning with the rescued turtle. He was busy unloading the most gigantic loggerhead sea turtle Sienna had ever seen, assisted by Jamie and Bridget. It was so heavy, probably almost 120 lbs., they had to lift it with three people. As they heaved it onto the table in Bay 1, Sienna could already recognize from afar that the sea turtle had a barnacle infestation. Mark was explaining to Cynthia: "Barnacle cover can be a sign of general bad health of turtles. Usually they have some other issue first and then become covered with other organisms such as barnacles or algae because their immune system is weakened. Turtles can recover from such infestations, but you have to remove them really carefully with surgical scissors otherwise you can cause damage to the turtle's shell. Some people pop them off with knives but that's too dangerous. You might also get some off by soaking the turtle in sweet water for a while. That kills the barnacles."

He carefully spread out the turtle's flippers and showed the others: "See, guys, he even has some embedded in the skin of his flippers." He realized that Sienna had stepped up, briefly stopped in his tracks and said: "Hey, Sienna," but that was it. She was a bit taken aback but he was busy after all.

Mark continued: "We're going to take him into Exam 1 and give him a full examination first." He pushed the cart out of the bay and into the closest exam room where he immediately started giving him a thorough check up.

"The guy who called him in named him Gus after his dad, by the way. Nice fitting name for such an old guy." He looked up and smiled at Sienna one more time in a rather noncommittal manner before he concentrated on the turtle again, but she realized it wasn't a good time and went back to her office.

Sienna chalked Mark's behavior up to the other coworkers being around, but when she found out that he had left at 2:30, obviously to pick up his daughter Sidney from school, without contacting her she started wondering and texted him, as she was walking to the bus stop to pick up Lilly:

"Didn't see you at the rescue anymore, is everything okay?"

He replied: "Busy, had to pick up Sidney early today but almost back at Turtle Sanctuary to be there for Tammy's release. Will you be there with the kids?"

Sienna had forgotten about Tammy's release later in the afternoon. Releasing a sea turtle back into the ocean was always a big joyous event.

She replied: "Will try to be there."

The school bus stopped in front of her and Sienna was distracted. Lilly climbed down the steps that were steep for her. As usual, she smiled at Sienna but didn't say a word.

"Did you have a nice day today?" asked Sienna, trying to coax Lilly to talk, but she just nodded. Sienna remembered their nice evening at the Thai restaurant and ice cream parlor afterwards and asked:

"Shall we go out tonight again and maybe have pizza or so this time?"

Again, Lilly just smiled and nodded. They walked toward the cottage. Sienna's heart sank to her knees when she saw a man in an expensive fashionably wrinkly white linen suit standing at the top of the stairs by the front door. Even from the back she recognized his stature and posture. It was Craig. He looked like he had watched an episode of Miami Vice to get dressed for his Keys vacation.

*****

Craig heard Sienna and Lilly walk up the stairs and turned around. He smiled and tried to give Sienna a kiss as she walked up but she turned her head away so that he could only kiss her cheek.

At first Sienna was absolutely speechless, but then she stammered: "What are you doing here, Craig?" as Lilly got the key out of its usual hiding spot underneath the rock in the planter and unlocked the door.

"I have a couple of days off, so I thought I'd surprise you," he said, obviously very proud of himself and his idea.

"I've never been to the Keys. I'm in a really nice resort right down the road." He looked down at Lilly. "May I be introduced to this beautiful young lady?" he said in his most charming manner, smiling at Lilly. "I'm Craig Wilson, Sienna's friend from Boston." He stretched out his hand to shake Lilly's but she didn't react.

"She doesn't talk," said Sienna.

Lilly nodded at him briefly but then she unlocked the door, disappeared inside and ran to her room.

Craig didn't really react to what Sienna said about Lilly but continued talking about his drive from Miami. He had very much enjoyed it and was in a great mood. "Did you know that there's a Key named Craig Key? They must have named it after me," he said grinning.

"You can't just show up like this, Craig," said Sienna, "there's so much going on with the kids and the Sea Turtle Sanctuary and really, I've been telling you, we are not together anymore!"

"Well, why don't I give you some time, go back to the resort and hang out by the pool. You can join me for dinner tonight. I thought you'd be excited to see me."

"I actually already promised the kids I'd take them out for dinner tonight."

"Why don't you bring them and they can hang out by the pool. It's really super."

"That's not a good idea, Craig. I really don't know what you think you're going to achieve here…"

He interrupted her the second time. "Shush, my darling. It's so good to see you." Sienna was now really upset. It was so typical of Craig to overrun her like that and not even let her complete her sentences. She needed to talk to him but not here and now.

"I've already promised to take the kids out tonight. How about I meet you afterwards in the bar of your resort. Where are you staying?"

"Coconut Key Beach Resort, it's just a few miles south of here on Knights Key."

Sienna held her breath for a second. She had heard that Coconut Key Beach Resort was one of the most expensive and exclusive resorts in the middle Keys.

She was willing to meet him later to get rid of him now and agreed. "Okay, I'll be there at 8 o'clock."

"Great, I can't wait to show you my suite," he said in a flirtatious manner. He tried to kiss her again but she backed off and then squeezed past him into the cottage, turned around and said "see you later," as she closed the door. Still pretending not to notice (or was he really that oblivious?) that Sienna wasn't happy to see him at all, Craig said: "Cheerio" and walked down the path past the Sea Turtle Sanctuary where Mark, who had already returned, was working with Tammy the turtle, watched by his daughter Sidney. Mark noticed him and looked up curiously, wondering, who the guy coming from Sienna's cottage was, wearing the Miami Vice outfit. Their eyes met for a split-second as they nodded at each other.

*****

As Sienna watched Craig leave, she pressed her forehead against the kitchen door and moaned. How could Craig just show up here? Under normal circumstances it wouldn't be necessary, but obviously Sienna had to tell Craig again and in person that they were not together anymore. She was dreading tonight and it put her stomach in knots but she had to get it over with.

Suddenly, Sienna felt someone hugging her legs from behind. It was Lilly who could tell that Sienna was upset. Sienna held her breath in awe, turned around, kneeled down and took Lilly in her arms with tears in her eyes. Lilly still wasn't speaking but she was slowly warming up to Sienna. Sienna felt something in her heart that had never been there before. She cared for this little girl more than she had ever imagined and just wanted her to be happy.

As Lilly sat at the kitchen table doing her homework and Sienna was making a snack for her, Sienna suddenly had an idea. She interrupted what she was doing, looked for the little velvet bag in her purse, poured the little pink conch pearls onto her hand and showed them to Lilly.

"Lilly, have you ever seen any of these before?"

Lilly shook her head. But then Sienna turned around and she drew a big pink pearl on a shelf in a children's room on an empty sheet of paper. Sienna was already back at the stove, making the grilled cheese sandwich and didn't pay attention to what Lilly was drawing.

*****

Around 4 pm, Bridget sent a text message to Sienna that they were starting to transport Tammy the turtle outback toward the dock area behind the Sea Turtle Sanctuary and the cottage. A paved driveway led down all the way along the cottage's backyard and ended on the Sea Turtle Sanctuary's dock where also its boat was anchored. Lindsey was at a friend's house working on a group assignment but Lilly was home, so, even though she was still doing her homework, Sienna interrupted her.

"The people from the Sea Turtle Sanctuary are releasing a turtle right now down at the dock. Would you like to join me and watch? Mark's daughter Sidney will be there too."

Lilly nodded vehemently and they both walked back to the lanai, put their chanx on, that stood there rowed up neatly, and walked down the path to the dock.

As they were walking, Sienna texted Bianca asking if she'd be interested in coming as well. A whole group of people including several employees of the Sea Turtle Sanctuary were already standing on the side of the dock, waiting for Tammy the turtle who was being pushed in a big low wheel barrel with a plastic bin in it that looked like it had a slide on the one side.

Bianca and two of her granddaughters came running up and Bianca gave Sienna a hug. "How exciting when one of the turtles has recovered and can be released!"

The entire event was like a party and the local press was there, documenting everything with photos.

Sienna watched Mark direct the entire operation. She loved watching him as he gave instructions in a calm and confident manner. Unlike Craig, he didn't seem to constantly have to pat himself on the shoulder. He took one last look at Tammy and then the container with the slide was carefully tipped forward into the shallow water. Slowly the turtle swam out and back into freedom. She slowly floated into deeper water and underneath the dock as the spectators all clapped furiously, so happy that Tammy was better and back to freedom.

Just like everyone else, Sienna turned around to leave and caught a glimpse of the guy, who had been previously camping and making fires down here, disappear into the thicket behind the cottage. She told Bianca who said:

"Yeah, there's a problem here in the Keys with people without homes. You should contact Pastor Van Doren. He might be able to come and tell this guy where he can camp. Right behind the cottage of a single woman with three kids might not be a good choice."

As soon as they were back in the cottage, Sienna looked up Pastor Van Doren's phone number and called him.

"Hmmm," he replied. "We are certainly having issues with more and more people without housing. It's late today, but I can certainly come to the Turtle Sanctuary tomorrow and have a word with this guy. There is currently a camp underneath the Boot Key Bridge and he can stay there. That bridge is almost directly across US1 from the Turtle Sanctuary and it's abandoned. It's an old drawbridge permanently stuck in the raised position. "

"Sounds like a great idea. He only seems to be there in the evening though. He must pack his stuff and hide it somewhere during the day. Is there any way you could come today, Pastor?"

"Okay, I'll be right over," replied the Pastor after a brief pause and sighed.

"I appreciate it, Pastor," replied Sienna.

*****

Pastor Van Doren told his wife that he had to put out a fire, put on a baseball cap and a pair of sunglasses, since he'd be driving into the evening sun, jumped into his old pick-up truck and took Overseas Highway south to the Sea Turtle Sanctuary. He parked his car and walked down the path on the side of the Sea Turtle Sanctuary and Sienna's backyard toward the docks. Wayne, the Vietnam veteran from Texas who had been hanging out in the Turtle Key area for almost a month now, had just returned, was hauling his tent and some other belongings from out of the woods. He was about to start setting up his small one-man tent as he saw a man walk onto the beach. At first he was alarmed and wanted to jump back into the woods, but then he recognized Pastor Van Doren.

"Hey, Wayne, howzit going?"

"Good. Hey, Pastor."

Pastor Van Doren cleared his throat. He didn't know how to say, without hurting Wayne's feelings too much, that he needed to camp elsewhere.

"Wayne, you know Camilla and Ricky from the Sea Turtle Sanctuary died, right?

"Yeah, I heard that. Very sad"

"There's a new lady living here in the house now, Camilla's sister. She's not used to what goes on here and would prefer if you didn't camp here, is that okay? You know, single lady with kids... makes her a little nervous."

"But Camilla and Ricky always lemme camp here. They knew I was a biology teacher before I went to Nam and know lots about turtles."

"Yeah, but they're gone."

"I watched out for them and I be watching out for the new lady too. They were so nice, always givin' me someth'n when I don't know where'da get my next meal."

"You can go down to the camp over by the Boot Key Bridge."

"I like bein' by myself. Too many people and trouble over there."

"Well, please think about it. Maybe I can find a better place for you," replied Pastor Van Doren.

He felt as if he were talking to a wall because Wayne wasn't going to leave as long as he felt obliged to the family. Pastor Van Doren left and walked to the other side of the dock. There was a little overgrown wooded area behind the mangroves, mainly pine trees and palmettos. He made his way into a part of the wooded area that was not so overgrown and found a smaller 8 x 10 ft. opening. It looked like this wooded area still belonged to the Sea Turtle Sanctuary property and not to the next neighbor's backyard. Then he walked back over to Wayne who was setting up his tent in the meantime.

"Hey Wayne, how about you camp on the other side of the dock, there's a pretty good protected area about twenty feet away from the path and you wouldn't be bothering anybody."

"Okay," Wayne replied, "but I'll still be watching out for the lady. I wanner to be safe."

*****

In the meantime, Sienna and the girls went out for dinner. They returned to the cottage after dinner at a nice local pizzeria. Sienna felt good about how the girls were slowly warming up to her. Lindsey had been pleasant tonight too. Sienna put the leftover pizza in the fridge for Leo who was out with some friends as usual and hadn't joined them. He was going to be the toughest one to get through to because he was never around and not interested in communicating with Sienna at all. Sienna made sure that the girls got into their pajamas, were done with their homework and then she started getting ready to meet Craig.

"I will only be about an hour, girls," she said as she said goodbye to the girls who were sitting in the living room, watching TV. "If something comes up, please text me and I'll either come right back or Bianca can come over. I'm just about a mile down the road. Please don't open the door for any strangers and leave the doors locked, okay?"

Lindsey and Lilly nodded. This was not the first time they had been left alone and Lindsey was a responsible

babysitter. Sienna grinned as she turned around and already heard Lindsey bossing her little sister around. She smiled, remembering how Camilla had talked to her and bossed her around when they were kids.
Suddenly, Sienna's phone bleeped. It was Mark.

"Sorry, got some news about something today I have to deal with. Will talk to you tomorrow."

"Okay, have a nice evening," she replied, "miss you."

"Miss you too."

The text made her feel better and gave her strength for what was to come tonight.

Chapter 19

Sienna arrived on Knights Key and took a left onto a dirt road that looked like it was leading straight into the mangroves and not to an exclusive resort. There were no signs or any indication of a resort. Talk about low profile, thought Sienna. She found a guard shack and a narrow road leading toward the ocean, let the security officer know that she was expected and slowly drove up to a beautiful ornamental metal gate that opened slowly and silently. She followed a winding narrow road through the mangroves, parked her car in a self-parking area and walked through the very well groomed tropical gardens of Coconut Key Beach Resort past some guest bungalows. She entered the very contemporary looking lobby from where she could already see the beautiful views of the Atlantic Ocean. To the right she saw the beginning of the iconic Seven Mile Bridge, spanning over the water between Knights Key and Little Duck Key.

The view made Sienna think about the past and how much the Keys had changed in the last 20 years. She and her friends used to go fishing here on Knights Key as teenagers. They had told their parents that they were sleeping at each other's houses and camped out here when there was nothing around but mangroves and an old RV resort. The beach she could now see from the lobby must have been all man-made.

Knights Key had also been the set of the James Bond movie "A License to Kill" in 1989 when Sienna was seven years old. She remembered the commotion of having the film crew and actors in town and how exciting it had been to watch some of the filming as a child. Everyone had been dying to possibly work as an extra. She smiled thinking of these memories. Camilla even used to say that she had seen Timothy Dalton and, even though Sienna never knew if this was true or not, she was so impressed that Camilla almost rose to celebrity status too. But that was just the typical admiration of a little sister for her big sister.

****

Sienna texted Craig that she was in the lobby, and a few minutes later he appeared. Again she found him a bit ridiculous. He looked as if he had stepped out of an episode of "Miami Vice" and was trying too hard to look cool and casual in his expensive wrinkly linen slacks with the matching blazer and Gucci sandals. Even though the resort was very upscale, all the other men were wearing shorts, t-shirts and flip flops. That was regular resort attire in the Keys. Craig walked up to Sienna smiling and led her through the property to another white Greek looking contemporary building which was one of the pool bars. He had obviously already made friends with the beautiful approximately 25-year old female bartender wearing a tank top and the shortest cutoffs Sienna had ever seen.

"Giselle kept me company all afternoon since you weren't around," he said, trying to make Sienna jealous but he didn't succeed. Sienna smiled at Giselle and ordered a drink.

"Hi, could you please bring me a Cosmo?"

"And I'll have another Bloody Mary," added Craig. "You can charge it to my room."

Giselle nodded and turned around to prepare the drinks, watched by Craig who couldn't take his eyes off of her as she stretched to grab a bottle and her entire midriff was exposed.

Sienna and Craig chit-chatted for a while about the beautiful resort and Craig told her about some of the very important cases he had been working on lately as a partner in the firm, emphasizing this several times. Sienna realized, once again, how Craig constantly needed attention and admiration, typical character traits of a narcissist. The bar was quickly filling up and as soon as they had their drinks, Sienna asked:

"Can we go somewhere where we have some more privacy?"

Craig thought Sienna wanted to be alone with him and applauded the idea of a more intimate atmosphere.

"Sure, I don't blame you," he said, looking around.

It was indeed getting crowded. He pointed at several empty Adirondack chairs down on the beach, past another beautiful white building that looked like it was a restaurant. "Let's go down there. It's much more romantic."

They grabbed their drinks and walked down to the beach.

The moon hung in the clear sky and cast a bluish light across the horizon. Some tiki torches had been set up along the shore and highlighted the tropical atmosphere with groups of tall palm trees growing everywhere on the superbly manicured property. Craig tried to make eye contact with Sienna and take her hand but she avoided it and pulled her hand away. She drank her drink much too fast as she tried to pluck up the courage to point out to Craig again that she had already broken up with him two weeks ago and what he was doing here was uninvited. Getting a little tipsy helped.

"Craig... I've been trying to tell you..."

He immediately interrupted her again. "Don't the stars look beautiful? Look, there's the Big Dipper."

"Craig, please let me finish my sentence. I'm really sorry and I'm especially sorry since you came all the way down here, but things didn't work out between us. I'm seriously considering staying here to take care of the kids and..."

"What do you mean, things didn't work out? We get along great. And you're not telling me you'd give up your job?" He laughed a fake laugh. "You're a workaholic. Just like me."

"I don't love you, Craig!"

He tried to take her hand again, this time almost forcefully, and they ended up wrestling with their hands in a non-gentle manner, him trying to hold hers, her trying to pull them away. She jumped up to create some distance between them, feeling a bit unsafe down here on the dark empty beach with him. His face was beet red and he just wasn't accepting what she had said.

Suddenly, her phone rang. She felt like she was being rescued by this phone call, but things went from bad to worse.

"Hello? Is this Sienna Brantley?"

Sienna held her hand up for Craig to back off who was breathing heavily.

"Yes, it is."

"Detective Baldwin with the Turtle Key Police Department speaking. Unfortunately, I have to inform you that we have taken Leo into custody. We caught him stealing alcohol with two other boys."

Sienna's face dropped. At the same time, Craig was standing in front of her, looking more mad than upset.

"Okay, Detective Baldwin. I'll be right there."

She ended the call and said hastily: "Craig, I'm sorry, my nephew Leo just got arrested for shoplifting. I have to head over to the police station right away."

He hesitated and stepped back, realizing that the police had just been on the phone.

Without waiting for his reply, Sienna started walking away from Craig and set her empty glass down on a table as she left the beach, heading back toward the lobby. Craig followed her into the lobby and out into the parking lot. But she was faster and got into her car before he could catch up with her and start arguing.

As she drove down the parking lot, exiting the resort in her red convertible, her hair blowing in the wind, he yelled after her angrily: "You're going to regret this!"

Chapter 20

This time, Leo was sitting in front of Detective Isabel Baldwin's desk, his elbows on his knees, chin in his hands. His eyes were red and puffy from crying but now his tears had dried up and he looked angry and distant. His parents would have treated this with a certain sense of humor but this serious Aunt Sienna, was probably going to stick him in a boarding school now to punish him.

Sienna stepped into the office following Detective Baldwin with a very serious expression on her face, but to Leo's big surprise she sat down next to him and tried to give him a hug. He sat there limp, looking down and didn't reciprocate.

"What's going on, Leo?" she said. "You know this can get you into so much trouble."

. "I just tagged along with my buddies," he tried to defend himself, "I don't even drink. It was kind of a dare."

Officer Baldwin examined Sienna, the woman who she had seen kissing her ex-husband, and once again she didn't like what she saw. She was a totally different type than herself and stunning in a very different way with her deep red hair and her light freckly skin, green eyes and athletic body.

Isabel tried to remain professional but she didn't intend on giving them a break this time around.

"I can't be as forgiving this time," said Detective Baldwin sternly, "since this is your second offense within a week. You should really be cited with two city ordinance violations. One for retail theft and one for minor in possession of alcohol."

Leo looked at her, shocked and Sienna looked up too.

"But, Detective, don't you think Leo deserves mitigating circumstances after all he's been through?"

"Oh, so everyone going through a hard time can become a criminal?"

"Give me a break," replied Sienna. "He's not a criminal after stealing alcohol as a teenager. That's a minor misdemeanor. And any judge will agree with me on that."

Isabel ignored Sienna and addressed Leo.

"You will have to attend a court date and speak to a prosecutor. I'm guessing you will end up having to do some hours of community service. So..." she sat down behind her desk and started typing something on her computer. "I'm going to write a report. You can leave now but will be ordered to attend a court hearing. Please wait here until I'm done with the paperwork and then you and your aunt as your legal guardian can sign it."

Sienna was fuming. She wondered whether Detective Baldwin was giving them an extra hard time because she had seen Sienna and Mark the other evening at The Jumping Dolphin, but she kept her mouth shut to not make matters worse.

*****

About fifteen minutes later, after signing Detective Baldwin's report, Sienna and Leo stepped out of the police station, got into the convertible and Sienna merged onto

Overseas Highway, which was empty and pitch black this time of night. They both remained silent, having to stomach what had happened this evening. Leo was ashamed of himself and very upset.

Sienna pulled into the parking lot of the Sea Turtle Sanctuary and closed the convertible's top with a button. It made a silent buzzing noise as it slowly covered the car. Sienna closed the latch in the top middle of the car and rolled up the windows. Before Leo could jump out and run up to his room, she stopped him with a motion and said:

"Leo, of course this shouldn't have happened and you will have to face some consequences, but remember: Your Aunt Sienna is a good defense lawyer. We'll handle this together, okay? Don't worry too much."

For the first time tonight, Leo's face lit up. He nodded and smiled a careful smile. "Thanks, Aunt Sienna."

Then he got out of the car, rushed down the path toward the cottage, grabbed the leftover pizza out of the fridge and disappeared into his room.

*****

Sienna stayed in her seat in the convertible for another minute, staring at the Sea Turtle Sanctuary across the parking lot. Tonight had been a bit much between dealing with Craig and then Leo. The tension she had been holding in all night just fell off of her. Tears began pouring out of her eyes and she sobbed uncontrollably for a few minutes. Then she dried her eyes, blew her nose and got out of her car. She needed a stiff drink.

Chapter 21

The next morning, Sienna woke up earlier than usual, bathed in sweat and breathing hard. She felt like she was having a panic attack but then she realized she had been having a nightmare. She was running down the road toward the Sea Turtle Sanctuary, followed by Craig with a gun in his hand. Finally she found refuge in the labyrinth of hallways and doors of the Sea Turtle Sanctuary, hid under the table in the conference room where Bridget, Mark and some other employees were currently holding a meeting but quickly hid her from Craig without even asking twice.

Sienna laid there for a while, thinking about last night's occurrences and how lucky she was that she hadn't gotten even deeper into the relationship with Craig. He was obviously a narcissist and she wondered whether he'd also become physically violent. Then her thoughts wandered to Leo who was showing signs of a troubled teenager and who probably needed some special attention. Sienna thought: *maybe I should carve out some time and give him some driving lessons, that way we could have some one on one time...*

She decided to go for an early morning swim, which would help clear her mind and make her feel better. She looked at her watch. There wasn't really enough time to drive to the beach, so she threw her bathing suit on, a beach dress on top of that, grabbed a towel and walked down to the dock. The sun wasn't even up yet but the Gulf was dipped in twilight and the sounds of nature calmed her nerves. The rhythmic back and forth of the tide had always made Sienna think it was the heartbeat of the Earth. Seagulls dove into the water, grabbing an early morning snack and landed to devour their prey. Sienna held her breath as she discovered a few Roseate Spoonbills at the end of the beach near the mangroves. They were usually found in fresh water but sometimes made their way to the Gulf.

She looked around, checking whether the guy without a home was there and wondered if Pastor Van Doren had spoken to him last night. He seemed to be gone. Sienna sighed relieved and pulled her dress over her head. She took her chanx off and carefully wrapped her phone into the dress, then set the dress and towel down on the dock. She slowly climbed down the ladder until her legs were immersed in water. It was high tide and the water was as deep as it could be this morning. She turned around, leaped forward and dove down with her arms stretched above her head. The salt water burnt her eyes that were irritated from crying but also temporarily washed away her troubles as she swam parallel to the shore, getting a good workout.

Finally, as she had reached the end of Bianca's dock, she turned around, swam back, climbed up the ladder, picked up her towel and dried off.

Sienna smiled as she recognized Bianca walking toward her, going for an early morning walk without dogs.

"Good morning, Bianca!"

"Good morning, wow you're good, already going for a swim this early."

"I needed to clear my head. Yesterday was an awful day, Bianca."

"What happened?"

"I told you about Craig in Boston, didn't I?"

Bianca nodded and looked worried.

"Well, he kept texting me and didn't seem to accept the fact that I broke up with him and yesterday he suddenly showed up. I told him again that it's over."

"Oh, boy," said Bianca, "how did he react?"

"To say the least: He was not too happy. He's the type who breaks up and not the opposite. And then, while I was talking to Craig at his hotel, Leo got arrested for shoplifting…"

"What? Oh no, that poor kid really needs some extra attention. If you want I'll talk to him. And let's discuss giving him some driving lessons. That'll give him something to do."

"I thought about that too. And it'll give you or me some one on one time to talk some sense into him."

"What is the penalty going to be? What did he steal?"

"Not sure yet, he has to attend a court hearing. The bad thing is he and his buddies stole a bottle of vodka. And, as you can imagine, Detective Baldwin was not too forgiving this time."

"Oh, boy, well at least his aunt is a criminal defense lawyer, but you probably can't represent him, right?"

"No, I'm not a member of the Florida Bar, but that's something to think about if I stayed here…"

Bianca listened up. "Oh, Sienna, are you at least considering it? I'd be so happy! Bianca stepped up to her and gave her a big hug. "It's so nice to have you here!"

Sienna nodded. "I still can't make up my mind, but it really would be the best for the kids, wouldn't it? And now, when I just think of working in the same company as Craig… That would be nauseating…"

"How hard would it be to take the Florida Bar? I can tell, the kids are getting attached to you…" said Bianca.

"Actually it's not hard at all. I can apply without even having to take the exam since I've worked five out of the last seven years."

Bianca nodded and looked at her watch.

"Well, I've got to go and get some grandkids to school and then to the flower shop. Please come and visit me, it's a really beautiful store, mainly orchids but also cut flowers, bouquets and some other plants."

Suddenly, they both froze. A pelican that had been sitting at the end of the dock flew up, plunged down into the water, surfacing with its throat pouch full of fish, throwing its head back to let the water drain out, swallowing the fish whole.

Sienna and Bianca looked at each other.

"It never gets old, does it?" said Bianca and gave Sienna another hug. "I'll talk to you later." She smiled and walked down the path leading to her house.

Sienna watched Bianca leave, she really appreciated the way the people in Turtle Key had made her feel at home after she had left so abruptly years ago. She thought of her organized life in Boston and how she'd probably lead a wealthy busy life for another thirty years without any surprises or unusual occurrences. In the Keys she'd face financial challenges and all sorts of problems but her life would be colorful and happy. She admitted to herself she felt like a different person now.

She still had a week of her vacation and time to figure things out. There were enough challenges ahead of her with the kids and the Sea Turtle Sanctuary – and with Mark and his ex-wife. Sienna took one last look at the Gulf and inhaled deeply. She hoped Craig would leave her alone now. She turned around and walked back up the path toward the cottage. It was time to wake up Leo...

******

After Sienna had gotten all three kids off to school, she walked over toward the Sea Turtle Sanctuary, but then decided spur of the moment to go and visit Bianca in her flower shop. It was in the next strip mall and just a short five-minute walk away. Bianca had told Sienna so much about it that she was curious and thought it would be nice to buy some flowers for the office.

As Sienna stepped into the store, a little bell rang and Bianca, who had been unpacking a shipment of beautiful Cattleyas, looked up. Sienna was totally surprised and impressed by this beautiful flower shop, which she hadn't expected in a typical strip mall in the Florida Keys. It was more like a European shop with buckets of various types of cut flowers that could be made into custom bouquets, but there were also premade bouquets for people who were in a rush. An entire back sunroom was full of various orchid genera in pots, on mounts on stands and beautiful Vandas hanging from display racks. There were also other potted tropical plants and a corner with gifts, books and cards. It was a place in which you could stay and relax for hours.

"I'm very impressed, Bianca," said Sienna, "this place is a haven. Can you recommend a pretty orchid for me that would survive in my office?"

"Most orchids you really want to keep outside because the a/c and dry air are really not that good for them, but here are some pretty Phaleonopsis that you could keep inside while they're blooming." She showed Sienna some beautiful cascading white Phaleonopsis and Sienna chose one she really liked.

"These are my favorites," she said. "I have them in Boston too."

"By the way, do you have a picture of Craig?" asked Bianca as Sienna was getting ready to pay at the register. "There was a stranger hanging out in the parking lot in his car earlier when I went to work. I wonder if it was him."

Sienna couldn't even find one photo of Craig on her phone, but then she looked up the law firm's website and a photo of Craig came up under "Partners".

"Yeah, I think that was him."

Sienna shuddered at the thought that he might not leave her alone now or even stalk her.

"Maybe you should call the police," said Bianca.

"I can't really call the police before he's done anything," said Sienna. "He's allowed to hang out wherever he wants. But it is kind of creepy."

Chapter 22

Suddenly Sienna's phone rang. It was Bridget.

"Sienna, we are taking the boat out to Sombrero Key. Someone called in an injured loggerhead turtle that might have been hit by a boat propeller. Do you want to join us? We leave from the dock in five to ten minutes."

Sienna hesitated for a second, but then she realized that Mark might be going and replied:

"I'd love to tag along but would we be back by three? That's when I have to pick up Lilly from the bus stop."

"Yes, it won't take that long and we probably have to get the turtle right back to the hospital to take care of him. It's no pleasure trip, unfortunately. But put your bathing suit on, just in case."

"Okay, I'm in Bianca's shop right now, I'll run back and change into something more appropriate for a boat. Meet you at the dock."

"Okay, we'll wait for you," replied Bridget.

Sienna quickly walked back up the road and turned onto the Sea Turtle Sanctuary's parking lot with access to both her and Bianca's cottage. She looked around to see if she could see Craig in one of the parked cars but if he was there earlier he wasn't there anymore. *Maybe it was someone else*, Sienna calmly told herself and rushed down the path toward the cottage. She quickly changed from her shift dress into her bathing suit, on top of that shorts, a t-shirt and a pair of sneakers that wouldn't be slippery on the boat. Before she left the house, she grabbed a bottle of water, a towel and a bottle of reef-safe sunscreen. She quickly stuffed everything into a beach bag and rushed down the path toward the Gulf and the docks.

Some of the Sea Turtle Sanctuary employees including Bridget and Mark were already in the bigger center console boat, preparing for departure. The motor was chugging rhythmically and the typical smell of a diesel engine wafted through the air. As soon as Sienna jumped into the boat, Jamie, on the dock, released the ropes from the cleats, threw them toward Ashley in the boat who caught them and stowed them away carefully. Bridget, who was driving the boat today, steered it slowly out of the no wake zone, pointing at a brown pelican, flying up out of the mangroves. As usual, Sienna's heart started pounding faster as she discovered Mark in a pair of orange board shorts, a white Sea Turtle Sanctuary t-shirt and a pair of teva sandals. He looked sexy with his aviator sunglasses, tan and dark beard as he smiled at Sienna with those perfect white teeth and made motions for her to take a seat next to him.

Just as Sienna sat down next to Mark, Bridget put the boat in full throttle and it sped across the calm Gulf. Mark pointed at a pod of dolphins jumping in and out of the water. Sienna nodded and watched the beautiful creatures until they were gone. She pulled her hair that was flying around and whipping her face into a ponytail. Despite the smell of the engine and the wind, she could smell Mark's cologne and felt the knots in her stomach again. He hadn't tried to touch or kiss her, maybe because of the others on board, but as the boat ride turned bumpy and they were pushed against each other, her thigh pressed against his, Sienna felt this unbelievable tension again.

The boat arrived at the Seven Mile Bridge and Bridget had to slow down again to safely drive through the bridge pilings underneath the famous overpass to the Atlantic Ocean side. They still had about five miles to go and Bridget sped up again. The bright red 142-foot iron lighthouse, Sombrero Light, sitting on a mostly submerged reef, was already visible as the boat quickly approached it. Since Mark and Sienna were the only ones in the boat's stern and everyone else was looking ahead, Mark finally put his arm around Sienna. She wanted to sink into those strong arms and kiss him and forget everything around her, but he looked at her with a serious expression, whispering into her ear: "I'm having some issues with my ex-wife. Can we meet for a drink tonight? Unfortunately, I have to get ready for the turtle now."

She nodded as he moved his arm away, got up and turned all business. Bridget slowed the boat down again as Mark made his way up to the bow. Everyone was on the lookout for the turtle. Some other boats were anchored around the lighthouse and the water was crowded with snorkelers and divers. They slowly drove up to the first boat, watching out for any swimmers or snorkelers in the water and asked if the passengers had heard about the injured turtle. The man who had called it in had already left and the turtle could have moved far away in the meantime.

"Yes!" said the younger father who was eating an early lunch with his wife and two kids. "We saw the turtle while we were snorkeling. He was floating around by the lighthouse about ten minutes ago. I don't think he could have gotten very far yet. He seemed lethargic."

The Sea Turtle Sanctuary's offshore 40 ft. boat was equipped with both dive and snorkel equipment since nobody ever knew what was going to be necessary. If the turtle was floating close to the surface, snorkel equipment would suffice, if it was floating deeper in the water, they were going to need to dive down with at least two people to bring it up. The boat very slowly made its way toward the lighthouse but at some point it became too crowded. Mark and Ashley put on their snorkeling gear and jumped into the water from a platform on the stern to swim to the lighthouse. The water was turquoise and crystal clear. Even from the boat, Sienna could see some big groupers, hogfish, parrotfish and other schools of smaller fish. Everyone kept looking out for the turtle.

"Sienna, why don't you go and swim with Mark and Ashley? You've always been a pretty good swimmer, haven't you?"

Even though the last time Sienna had been snorkeling was an eternity ago, she didn't think twice, stripped down to her bathing suit and Bridget handed her mask, fins and snorkel. She donned the snorkeling equipment, the fins last, and then she slowly slid into the turquoise-colored water from the platform in the back. The water was warm and she quickly got used to the snorkel and listening to the sound of her own breathing. The underwater world was breathtaking, the fish were plentiful and beautiful. She took in the views and searched for the turtle as she tried to catch up with Mark and Ashley. Suddenly, Sienna slowed down and looked beneath her. She heard a funny crunching sound and realized that there were some beautiful parrotfish underneath her, chewing on coral. She made a funny blubbering noise while laughing under water and had to come up for air because she started taking water into her mask and snorkel. She came up gasping for air and realized how close she was to Mark and Ashley. Suddenly and simultaneously they all saw the injured turtle. Coughing and pulling her mask off to get the salt water out of her eyes, but trying not to make too much of a scene, Sienna watched Mark and Ashley carefully examine the turtle. The turtle was floating slightly below the surface. It looked like one of its front flippers was badly injured. Mark and Ashley started gently pushing the turtle toward the boat, followed by Sienna. Finally, they arrived at the stern, where they attached a harness hanging from a small crane around the turtle's shell and entire torso and it was lifted onto the platform.

"Awww, poor guy, they got you really bad," said Bridget as Mark, Ashley and Sienna quickly climbed aboard and Mark started giving the turtle some first aid.

"Yeah, I don't know if we're going to be able to save that flipper," said Mark as he prepared an infusion of pain medication, assisted by Ashley and injected it. Then he cleaned the wound and carefully applied honey to it. Sienna watched him, surprised.

"Yeah, it's amazing. Regular honey is a natural topical antibiotic," Mark said with a smile, noticing Sienna's flabbergasted expression. "We'll have to wait and see how it heals. I really hope I don't have to amputate the flipper." He handed the jar of honey back to Ashley and said: "Now let's put him into a safe position so that Bridget can get us back quickly," and they both heaved the turtle into a big bin that Sienna hadn't noticed before.

Bridget slowly steered the boat away from Sombrero Reef and the other boats and people. Then she yelled: "Full speed ahead! Hang on, everybody," putting the boat into full throttle again. Everyone either sat down or hung on to the railing and in no time they were back at the Seven Mile Bridge.

Sienna noticed lots of wooded areas that looked damaged and asked: "Is that all still from Hurricane Irma?"

Mark replied: "Yeah, the storm surge was up to eight feet high. Some of the areas, especially trailer parks, still haven't recovered and are barely getting back to normal."

They drove underneath the Seven Mile Bridge and in a few minutes they could spot the Sea Turtle Sanctuary from the water and arrived safely back at the dock.

Sienna looked at her watch. She had just enough time to eat a quick lunch, take a shower and then pick Lilly up at the bus.

"Thanks, guys, I've got to go," she said, waving at the crew that was heaving the turtle onto a rolling cart on land.

"See you later," said Mark and pointed at his phone, meaning he'd call or text her later.

Chapter 23

When Sienna got back to the cottage, a beautiful arrangement with white orchids was standing at the front door. She realized that she had forgotten her orchid at Bianca's store – the same type of white Phaleonopsis that she had wanted to purchase was in the arrangement. She called Bianca to thank her and tried to pay for the orchids that looked expensive.

"Oh, that's not from me," said Bianca surprised. "The orchid you wanted to buy is still here. I was going to drop it off later."

Sienna looked for a card in between the leaves but she couldn't find anything. "I hope these are not from Craig," said Sienna with an ominous feeling. "Where else could they be from if not from your shop?"

"Hmmm..." said Bianca, thinking. "Maybe Mark sent them? Why don't you ask him? The closest orchid places are in Homestead though. Actually, there's another really nice nursery in Islamorada where we get a lot of our stuff too. Are there any ribbons or plastic wrap? There might be an indication of the nursery on those."

Sienna examined the entire arrangement but she couldn't find a name or anything that would have given away where the orchids had come from.

"Was Mark on the boat?" asked Bianca to distract Sienna.

Sienna told Bianca about her adventurous trip to Sombrero Reef.

"Yes, he acted a bit distant. I don't think his wife is too happy about seeing us at The Jumping Dolphin the other night."

"I wonder why," replied Bianca in her thoughts. "She seems to be happy with her new boyfriend, Jim from the Coast Guard. He's been coming and buying tons of flowers for her on a regular basis for the past two months."

"Well, that's good," replied Sienna and forgot about it right away since her phone rang. It was Mr. Chesterfield who had a question about a new case similar to a case Sienna had recently worked on with success.

Frowning, Sienna picked up the orchid arrangement and stepped inside the cottage.

"We all miss you, Sienna," said Mr. "C". "I was wondering if I could copy you on emails regarding this new case? Or are you too busy down there? It might be something you could take over when you're back in the office. We are having a situation right now. We are a bit short on lawyers for the many cases we have. You probably know that Craig had a family emergency and had to go to London for a while?"

"No, I didn't know that," she replied, a bit flabbergasted. That's what Craig had told the firm? "But sure, go ahead and copy me," she replied even though legal cases and Boston seemed so far away right now and she didn't know when she'd have time to read and answer emails. But she could hardly say no, since it wasn't unusual to do some work while on vacation for her and her colleagues.

They both ended the call and Sienna had an idea. Maybe there'd be a possibility to continue working remotely and it was a blessing in disguise that she hadn't become a partner...

She didn't have much time to think about it further since it was 2:45. She had to get in the shower, pick Lilly up at the bus stop and she had also promised Leo to practice driving with him.

Sienna looked at the orchid arrangement again that she had set down on the kitchen countertop. She didn't really want the orchids in the house if they were from Craig so she put them out on the lanai.

It was another busy afternoon and Sienna forgot about the orchids quickly as she first picked up Lilly and then made her a snack. Fifteen minutes later, she and Leo pulled out of the Sea Turtle Sanctuary's parking lot onto US1. Leo was in the driver's and Sienna in the passenger seat. Tomorrow morning, Sienna and Leo had an appointment with his lawyer about his court hearing next week. He was nervous about it and therefore made a few mistakes as he drove down the busy road. He forgot to turn on the indicator as he was switching lanes and a car had to break, honking at them. But Sienna wasn't a very good teacher either. She was way too nervous about having no control over the car and was scared that Leo would cause an accident. Her OCD seemed to make things worse. Leo used the brakes too late when driving up to stopped cars at a red light and was way too fast in general.

"Stop!" Sienna yelled as he was only a few hundred yards away from stopped cars at a traffic light and kept going a steady 40 miles per hour. He stepped on the brakes so abruptly, that they almost got rear-ended by the car behind them. "Well, I didn't mean THAT suddenly, Leo. You have to start slowing down when you see cars ahead of you standing at a traffic light."

"Well, I was going to slow down in a few seconds," he replied upset. "I wasn't doing anything wrong."

All in all the driving lesson didn't go too well and Sienna decided to ask Bianca if she'd continue teaching Leo.

"I'm sorry," said Sienna, "I wasn't a good teacher and passenger. Can I make it up by buying pizza tonight?" as they took a left back into the Sea Turtle Sanctuary's parking lot. Leo got out. He was grumpy and hadn't had a fun experience but appreciated Sienna's apology. He knew she was working hard with him and his sisters and that she hadn't had a clue about kids before she came here.

"Sure. It's okay," he said with a slight smile. "Maybe Bianca can take me out next time again."

"Yeah, I think she's a better teacher than me," replied Sienna. "Leo," she said as he walked away. He slowed down and turned around again. "But I have to say you're a pretty good driver already."

"Thanks." He rummaged through the fridge, couldn't find anything, grabbed a protein bar out of the pantry and disappeared in his room.

Later, when Sienna was sitting at the kitchen table with the girls and Leo, eating a slice of pizza, a sort of satisfied feeling overcame her. This was the first time Leo was eating with all of them. Usually, he grabbed something and went upstairs to eat by himself. Leo laughed with the girls and they all quarreled in a good-natured manner. A feeling of guilt overcame Sienna that she hadn't visited earlier and participated more in her nephew and nieces' lives. But it was what it was. She couldn't make up for lost time but could do her best from now on.

Her phone bleeped with an incoming text message from Mark. "Can you meet me at "Henry's" at eight?"

She replied: "Sure, see you there."

Chapter 24

At 8 pm sharp, Sienna pulled up to the parking lot in front of a rinky-dink hole in the wall bar named "Henry's Bar & Chowder House". The front didn't look particularly inviting, as a matter of fact, it looked like a concrete building with just a little door in the front and no sign. Sienna wondered if she was at the right place. But then Mark pulled up, led her straight to a back patio and she realized that this place wasn't very fancy but a hidden gem. The wooden patio with tables covered with thatched umbrellas was a tropical oasis surrounded by palm trees, hibiscus shrubs and plumerias with a beautiful view onto the Gulf of Mexico. A Beatles revival band was playing inside but it wasn't too noisy on the patio and they could still hold a conversation.

"The band is actually pretty good," Mark explained. "It's a bunch of locals, two of them are brothers. The guitar player and singer Alex is really talented. And his brother Paul is a great bass player."

Sienna nodded and listened. She actually enjoyed old Beatles music and began tapping her foot to the beat as they started playing "Octopus's Garden".

"What would you like to drink?" Mark asked as he got up to go inside and place an order. "I don't know if they are serving out here since we seem to be the only ones."

"I'll have a glass of Chardonnay," she replied. He nodded and said: "I'll be right back."

Sienna leaned back, listening to the music that reminded her of her snorkeling experience today and put her in a good mood. As Mark returned with two glasses of wine in his hand, she told him about the chomping parrot fish that made her laugh, flood her mask and get water up her nose.

He laughed and said: “We should take all of the kids out snorkeling one day to hear the parrotfish chomp on coral. I actually have my own little skiff.”

Sienna nodded. She loved that Mark was making plans with her and the kids.

He continued: “There’s a funny story that back in the fifties a famous local author supposedly wrote a book of manners to address this annoying fish habit he discovered while wading in the waters near his home. The book was published but sadly upon distribution it was discovered the ink was subject to “bleeding” in the salt waters. None that needed this lesson were ever able to read it. The crunching continues to this day.”

They both laughed. “What a funny story,” Sienna said. Life was so easy and fun with Mark. They clinked glasses, took a sip of wine and both looked out into the starry night. They could hear the rhythm of the Gulf in the distance.

“How’s the turtle with the injured flipper?” asked Sienna.

“His name is Charlie. The guy who called him in named him after his son. He seems to be doing okay so far. He’s on antibiotics so if there’s no infection, we might be able to save his flipper. I’d really hate to have to amputate it.”

Sienna cringed thinking about that and nodded. Mark seemed to be such a good vet and to genuinely care about his patients.

A female server came out and brought silverware wrapped in paper napkins, two small appetizer plates and an appetizer platter with something that looked like chicken nuggets with a dip, probably Ranch dressing and some carrot and celery sticks.

"Have you ever had gator?" Mark asked Sienna grinning as he thanked the server and introduced her to Sienna. "Thanks, Tina, this is Sienna, Camilla's sister from Boston."
All locals knew each other and were mostly very friendly.

"I'm sorry for your loss," said Tina. "Bridget and I are friends. My family and I are always at all of the Turtle Sanctuary's events."

Sienna nodded at the server Tina and said: "Hi, Tina. Nice to meet you - and thanks. No, I've never had gator," she continued looking at Mark, "and I think I might keep it that way. I actually refused as a kid when my parents tried to make me eat it a few times," Sienna responded, making a funny face about the thought of eating alligator meat.

"Oh, c'mon, it tastes like chicken! Please try it for me."

She didn't want to be a bad sport, picked up the smallest piece, dipped it into the ranch dressing and took a bite. It really tasted like grilled chicken but she told him grinning that one piece was enough for her.

He grinned and quickly devoured the rest of them.

"I'm starving. I haven't had dinner yet, how about you?" he asked.

"I already had pizza with the kids," she replied rolling her eyes. "They're destroying all my attempts to ever stay in shape.

"Yeah, that's tough with kids," he replied. "Sidney loves junk food too and constantly begs to go to McDonald's or Chick-fil-a. Thankfully the closest one is in Largo and her mom hates cooking so she gets her fix when she's with her. We share custody so she's there for one week and then at my place the next."

"That must be tough for her…"

"Yeah, it's always hard on kids, but she's handling it well."

He waved at Tina as she came out to check on them and ordered grilled grouper, rice and veggies. After Tina had walked away again, Mark paused for a second as he looked into Sienna's green eyes and took her hands into his across the table.

"I want to be honest with you about something…"

Sienna swallowed. It didn't sound like he was about to tell her something pleasant.

"I got drunk a few weeks ago and my ex-wife and I had a one-night stand. Don't even ask me how it happened because I can't stand her, although she can also pretend to be quite charming. I guess there's a reason I used to love her. But – what I wanted to be honest with you about is: She told me yesterday morning that she's pregnant."

Sienna's mouth dropped open. She pulled herself together to not seem too shocked. It was none of her business what he had done before they had met and she certainly had her own baggage with Craig.

"So, what are you going to do? Does she expect you to get back together with her because of that?"

"I really don't know. I don't even know if she's planning on having the child or if it's even really mine. She's been seeing someone on a regular basis, remember the Coast Guard officer we saw with her the other day?"

Sienna nodded. Something came to her mind. "Funny you should mention that, because Bianca just told me earlier today that your wife's boyfriend has been constantly buying flowers for her. I guess the one you just mentioned."

Mark nodded. "Yeah, he's the guy she cheated on me with before we broke up."

He didn't understand. Why would Isabel tell him she was pregnant by him if she was sleeping with someone else? Maybe she just didn't want him to be happy with Sienna.

"Let's not talk about Isabel anymore," he said as his food came out. He unwrapped his fork and knife and started eating.

Sienna's mood was pretty much ruined but she tried not to let it bother her. It wasn't his fault – or was he going to have sex with his ex every time he drank a bit too much? The last thing she wanted was more drama after just breaking up with Craig. "I'm not sure if I should let you sort this out first, Mark. And me too, to be completely honest with you…"

She decided that now was the perfect time to tell Mark about Craig as well.

"While we're spilling the beans about our past, I was kind of dating this guy in Boston before I had to come here…"

Mark looked at her, stopped eating and listened.

"I already knew up there that it had no future. He's British and guess I fell for his British accent and charm. We work for the same law firm and I've since determined he's a narcissist. I had to constantly tell him how great he was and he was incredibly controlling. So, before I left I broke up with him and told him to please not contact me anymore. But yesterday he suddenly showed up at the cottage."

"Oh, I think I saw him. Was he wearing a white linen suit with a Hawaii shirt and has brown hair?"

"Yes. I told him again last night that we are no longer dating and he became extremely angry. I'm really not happy that he just showed up here."

"Boy, do we both have some baggage," said Mark, staring at the Gulf. After a short pause, he looked back at Sienna with an honest expression on his face. "All I can say is that you blow me away, Sienna. I don't think I've ever felt this way about anyone before."

"I feel the same way," she replied. They lifted their glasses and clinked them again, losing themselves in each other's eyes.

*****

Mark and Sienna just sat there for a while, listening to some more Beatles songs and nature's concert that was coming directly out of the mangroves and from the Gulf. Despite the problems with Mark's ex-wife and Isabel, Sienna felt very much at ease with him. They could even be silent together without it feeling awkward. He pulled his chair next to hers so that he could see the band inside, put his arm around her shoulders and kissed her gently.

Sienna remembered her research on Ricky's parents and told Mark what she had found out. "I think they were quite wealthy. Back then the dad was a lawyer in Coral Gables. At first when I met Ricky they just had a weekend house here but eventually the mom and Ricky stayed here full time and the dad simply went to Coral Gables for important meetings. They owned a really nice oceanfront mansion," said Sienna out loud, but completely reliving the thoughts in her brain. "His father seemed okay when he started dating me, but when Ricky went to veterinary and not law school and my sister got pregnant, I think he totally cut Ricky off. He was supposed to take over his father's law firm one day and not run an unprofitable turtle rescue and save the world…"

Mark nodded. He had heard the gossip about Ricky's wealthy upbringing and knew what an idealist he had been. He thought for a while. "I never made the connection but there is a Flores Foundation for Children in Need in Key West and I think I've heard that they live fulltime in a cottage right by the upscale hotel Casa Bella. Flores is a common name, but I think it might be them. I've heard something like that. You should try to contact them. It would be great for the kids to have grandparents."

The band stopped playing and started dismantling and packing their equipment, Tina came outside and asked whether they wanted another drink. "Last call, y'all, we close at 11 on weekdays."

Shocked, Sienna looked at her watch. It was hard to believe that they had already been sitting there for almost three hours. They closed out their tab and walked across the parking lot to their cars. As they stood next to their vehicles and kissed each other, Mark asked: "Sidney's at Isabel's, do you want to come over for a night cap?"

“I really can’t,” she replied regretfully. “Today was such a long day and tomorrow morning I have to meet with Leo’s lawyer to get ready for his court hearing next week. I told you about that, didn’t I?”

Mark nodded.

Sienna continued: “I have to be on top of it - I can’t represent him but I can advise his lawyer, so I still have to read up on similar cases before tomorrow morning.”

As Sienna pulled into the parking lot of the Sea Turtle Sanctuary five minutes later, she thought she saw someone sitting in a car parked there, idling, but when she looked again the car was empty. Was she being paranoid and seeing things…?

Chapter 25

The appointment with Leo's lawyer, Timothy Berg in Key Largo who specialized in juvenile law, was quick, cut and dry. He agreed that Leo should get mitigating circumstances because of his parents' death and supported Sienna's idea that Detective Baldwin was probably being unreasonably harsh with Leo due to personal reasons. It was subject to the local police station's discretion whether cases like this were forwarded to court and it didn't seem right.

"Of course we can't mention this part to the judge but the part about Leo's parents might suffice," said Mr. Berg. "The worst I expect are a few hours of community service. But often the court will only give the juvenile a lecture or stern warning about shoplifting and the trouble that can come with further violations. They might also order counseling if the violation was caused by psychological trauma, as in Leo's case."

Sienna and Leo nodded, thanked him and left the office. Since the appointment had been so fast and Leo wasn't going to school today, they now had a few hours before Sienna had to be back to pick up Lilly. Sienna thought it would be a great opportunity to spend some one on one time with Leo, and as they walked to the car she asked:

"Shall we go and have lunch somewhere? Or is there anything else you'd like to do? "

He looked down, hemming and hawing. He didn't really want to tell Sienna what was going on but then he included her, blushing a little:

"I really have to do my homework now because I'm meeting my girlfriend after school. So can we just go home?"

Sienna smiled. She was not only happy about him being so responsible but also because he was telling her such a personal thing.

"Oh, I didn't know you have a girlfriend! What's her name?"

"Alana."

"Nice name. I'd love to meet her," said Sienna.

They had arrived at the car and Sienna proposed: "I know I'm a lousy teacher but do you want to drive to get some more practice? You need some more hours for your driving log."

Leo nodded, got into the driver's seat, started the car and slowly merged onto US1, signaling properly and double-checking in his side and rear mirrors.

Sienna watched him do everything properly benevolently and said: "Good job." Then she continued: "And I'm also very proud of you for being so responsible about your homework. Can I give you some money to take Alana somewhere? Maybe get a pizza or ice cream?"

"That would be great. Thanks, Aunt Sienna. I hope you're not upset that I don't want to do anything right now."

"No, that's okay. Trust me, I have enough to clean and organize in the house. You know I'm kind of a neat freak," she said grinning.

"I actually like how clean the house is now. My mom hated cleaning… Aunt Sienna, I'm still sorry about the vodka my buddies and I stole," Leo said. "It was really just kind of a dare."

"Well, I guess you'll never do it again, right?"

He nodded. They were silent for a while. Then he asked:

"Are you going to make us move to Boston, Aunt Sienna?"

Sienna took a while to answer, since she really still didn't know what to say.

"I don't know what to do myself, Leo. I really like it down here, but my job is up there. I only have about one more week and then my company expects me to be back at work."

He nodded gloomily, thinking about his girl friend. It seemed that every time he was happy with someone they were taken away from him.

"But I promise, I won't force you to move to Boston if you don't want to. We'll figure something out," said Sienna even though she had no idea what that was.

It took about an hour to drive back from Key Largo to Turtle Key. They arrived back at the Sea Turtle Sanctuary. Leo turned the right signal on, slowed down and took a right into the parking lot.

"Great job driving today, Leo," said Sienna.

He nodded, pleased with himself. "I can take my test for my official permit in three weeks. Can you make an appointment?"

"Sure," she replied as they both walked up to the cottage.

To Sienna's surprise, the front door wasn't locked even though she was certain she had locked it when they left. The key was under the old weathered rock in the planter as usual. Someone had left another beautiful white orchid, this time on the kitchen counter where some of the drawers in the kitchen had been pulled open and someone had rummaged through them. Sienna's face froze but she didn't say anything to Leo and she didn't want to seem paranoid. Maybe this was the one from Bianca, and Bianca had put it here and forgotten to lock the door? And maybe one of the kids had looked for something?

*****

As soon as Leo was upstairs, Sienna grabbed her phone and dialed Bianca's number, looking around the cottage a bit nervously.

"Hi, this is Bianca."

"Hey, Bianca, I just came back to the cottage and there's another white orchid in the kitchen and the front door wasn't locked. Did you happen to come and leave it here?"

"Nope. It's still standing here. I've been really busy all day. That's starting to sound a bit creepy though..."

"Yeah, I'm starting to get worried. And now that person is coming into the house! And it looks like someone rifled through the kitchen drawers. I have to say, I'm a little freaked out."

"Should you call the police?"

"I'm not sure, let me think about it."

"Okay, there's a customer here, I've got to go. Talk to you later."

"Okay, thanks."

Sienna ended the call, frowning. If this was Craig, did she have to be worried about her and the kids' safety? She realized that when he had shown up at the cottage the very first time, Lilly had pulled the house key out from underneath the rock in the planter and he had seen that. So he'd know how to get into the house. Was he really in London like Mr. C. had told her or was he still here in the Keys? Should she call the police? Too bad that Mark and his ex-wife didn't get along. She'd be able to investigate whether Craig had a rental car in town or Miami. Would they take her seriously if she reported that two orchids had been put in her house? Probably not. That would sound quite silly. She decided to keep it to herself for now.

*****

Meanwhile, Mark had to pick up his daughter Sidney at his ex-wife Isabel's house. It was his turn to take Sidney. He rang the doorbell and Isabel opened, wearing a pair of tiny hot pants and a small tank top. She was wearing her long hair open and red lipstick. Obviously, she was trying to make an impression but it didn't do much for Mark. Too much had happened between them and Isabel had shown him again and again that he couldn't trust her and she didn't care about anyone but herself and maybe her daughter.

Mark didn't want to come inside but she said: "Sidney's down at Coco Plum Beach with a few friends and some moms. Can you go and get her while I pack her stuff? They're at the usual spot."

It was typical, that Sidney was never ready when he came to pick her up. Isabel had to show him that she didn't care whether he had to wait or not. Today he was actually glad that Sidney wasn't in ear's reach because he wanted to speak to Isabel privately.

"Listen, Isabel. How come you're telling me that you're pregnant if you've been dating Joe for three or four months already?

He caught her off-guard with that question and she didn't know what to say for a second. "Women just know something like that. Intuition," she replied.

"Well, that's not going to get us back together, Isabel," he said. "You know we're not good for each other."

She batted her long dark eyelashes as her eyes filled with tears. "What is Sidney going to think about that? How can you do that to her? We should be a family again."

"Well, we can do a paternity test when the baby's here. Sidney will understand if we stay separated. I actually think she's doing so much better without the constant fighting around her," he said. He abruptly turned around, left her standing there and walked down the road toward Coco Plum Beach that the people in the neighborhood all frequented.
Isabel watched him leave, her hands clenched in fists.

"I'll show you and that *puta* from Boston," she said quietly under her breath.

Chapter 26

It was Friday evening and Mark was off for the weekend. After his latest unpleasant encounter with Isabel, Mark felt like he had to get out of Turtle Key for a night or two. He called Sienna.

"Hey, it's Mark. I've been thinking about that hotel in Key West where I think Ricky's parents live.
It's the Casa Bella, with a really nice private beach. I know it's short notice, but what would you think about going on a spontaneous trip to Key West tomorrow with all of the kids, staying overnight and doing some research at the same time? I think I still have a bunch of points and can use them for the room."

It was really a bit short notice, but Sienna liked the idea and why not do something spontaneous? It was unlike her, but there wasn't really that much to plan and they didn't have anything to do on the weekend. "I think that's a great idea," she replied. "Let me ask the kids if it's okay with them. Leo has a girlfriend now so he might not be up for it but I'll let you know."

Since Leo was out with Alana, who already had her driver's license, Sienna texted him. "Leo, sorry to bother you, are you busy this weekend? Mark and I are thinking of going to Key West with all of you and his daughter Sidney."

Leo didn't reply right away, but approximately ten minutes later Sienna's phone bleeped with an incoming text message. "I can go. Alana is going out of town with her family." Sienna was excited. Now she asked Lindsey and Lilly if they wanted to go. Lindsey was excited to go and stay in a nice hotel, something they hadn't done often with their parents, and Lilly nodded profusely, so they were good to go.

Sienna called Mark back. "We can go, actually, we can't wait. What a great idea. What time do you think we should leave?"

"How about we pick you guys up around nine and we stop and have breakfast somewhere? And by the way, I have an old seven passenger van that I barely drive, that should be perfect for all of us."

"Oh, yeah, I didn't even think about transporting all of us, she replied laughing. "I guess we could take our van too, but yours will be fine."

They both laughed. They were giddy about going on a trip together.

*****

Sienna started pulling the kids' and her bathing suits and a change of clothing together for everyone that same evening and couldn't sleep all night because she was so excited. It wouldn't be the same as being alone with Mark but a good test to see how they'd do as a patchwork family and how she could handle it since she was usually rather antisocial. She was glad that the kids had seen her come and go with Mark and their relationship wasn't a surprise for them. They also knew him from the Sea Turtle Sanctuary, just like all employees were old friends for the Flores children.

*****

The next morning, everyone was ready and walking up to the parking lot at the stroke of 9 am with a couple of duffle-bags, a beach bag and a cooler. Mark and Sidney drove up in an old white Chevy Venture that looked like it was barely going to make it across the Seven Mile Bridge.

Sienna looked at the van and asked: "Shouldn't we rather take our van?"

"No, she needs some exercise," replied Mark grinning. "It'll be fine."

So they piled into the old Chevy Venture and off they were. Everyone was in a good mood and Sienna held her breath, excited to see if Lilly would speak with Sidney who was the same age and in the same school but in a different class. She just smiled and nodded though without saying a peep. Just a few minutes later, they stopped at IHOP for breakfast. Sienna was speechless about how many pancakes six people could devour but also what good manners the kids had. The atmosphere was relaxed and happy, Lindsey now had two little girls to boss around and was in heaven and Sidney was good-natured and didn't care. Ethel, the middle-aged waitress with skin that had seen too much sun throughout her life in the Keys and a southern drawl, got them in and out as fast as possible since they were anxious to get on the road.

They climbed back into the van that sputtered a bit as they took off again. Sienna looked at Mark worriedly, but the van merged just fine onto US1 and soon they passed Knights Key with beautiful Coconut Key Beach Resort. Sienna shuddered, imagining Craig might still be there, but soon the chitchatting of her fellow travelers distracted her. The van drove up the Seven Mile Bridge, endless calm waters on both sides beneath them and the old parts of the bridge on the Gulf side that were currently closed due to construction.

Everyone in the van had quieted down and was taking in the beautiful views, well everyone except Leo who was texting Alana and staring at his phone. There were some pelicans on the remaining parts of the old bridge, watching out for a morning snack in the ocean. As they came toward the center of the bridge, Mark explained: "The bridge has a 65 foot clearance here so that bigger boats can pass through. Some parts of the old bridge were removed for that same reason."

He pointed at some land surrounding the old bridge with some dilapidated houses on it. "That's Pigeon Key right over there." Everyone looked curiously out of the window to the right.

After one or two more miles, Mark pointed at a lonely tree on the old Seven Mile Bridge.

"And look, there's Fred, the Tree. Something you haven't seen yet, Sienna. He's quite the celebrity around here and very dear to locals. They even decorate him with lights for Christmas. There's a song about him, by a local musician."

Sienna picked up her phone, googled Fred the Tree on Youtube and played the song by Roger Silvi. They all listened smiling. It was really fun.

"When you come down my way
On the Overseas Highway
Skipping through the islands
In the Florida Keys

Keep an eye out
As you travel about
Along the ridge
On old Seven Mile Bridge

'Cause you're bound to see

Fred the Tree
He's lean and green
As a tree can be
The coolest looking pine tree
You'll ever see

His life can be rough
But Fred hangs tough
Growing all alone
On a bridge he calls home
He's a local Keys celebrity
When the big hurricane swept on through
We bid Fred adieu
'Cause Irma roared into town
To blow everything down

There wasn't much doubt
That she'd take Fred out
But her best huff and a puff
Just wasn't enough
To topple

Fred the Tree
Above the sea
Growing all alone
On a bridge he calls home
He's a local Keys celebrity

Some people driving by tip their hat
Just to say hello
Others light him up for Christmas
Imagine that

A tropical light
Shining bright in the night
With Fred all aglow

An island holiday show

Fred the Tree
Above the sea
Growing all alone
On a bridge he calls home
He's a local Keys celebrity

Growing all alone
On a bridge he calls home
He's a local Keys celebrity

Growing all alone
On a bridge he calls home
He's a local Keys celebrity..."

*****

After a few more miles they exited the bridge and arrived on Little Duck Key. They saw more fishermen and some seagulls soaring through the cloudless sky.

A sign announced: *Entering Key Deer territory. Drive with caution.*

Sienna turned toward the kids and asked: "Have you guys seen any Key deer lately? I remember how cute I thought they were when I was a kid. They are so tiny compared to regular deer. But I haven't seen any yet since I've returned. I hope their numbers haven't even dwindled more since I was a teenager."

The kids shook their heads and started looking out of the window. They hadn't seen any in a while and were anxious to spot one.

Mark commented:

"They used to roam all over the Keys but are so rare now that you can usually only find them on Big Pine and No Name Keys. There is a new free nature center in Big Pine Key in the Key Deer National Wildlife Refuge. "

"I'd love to go there some time," said Sienna and everyone nodded.

Mark continued and everyone listened quietly.

"Key deer had to really adapt to some difficult situations from being hunted to drowning in hurricanes and their fresh water holes becoming useless due to sea water storm surges. Did you guys know that in 1950 there were only about 50 Key deer left in the entire world? A guy named Jack Watson basically saved them from becoming extinct. First he became an officer for the U.S. Fish and Wildlife Service, started educating the government and public about the Key deer and then, when the National Key Deer Refuge was founded, he became its first manager."

A sign pointing toward the Gulf side said "No Name Key". "There are lots of Key deer out there," said Mark. "And a great pub with the best pizza. Maybe we should stop there on the way back." Sienna nodded.

The next Key was Middle Torch Key followed by Ramrod Key, Summerland Key, Cudjoe Key, Sugarloaf Key and a few more and then they arrived in Key West. It was busy in Key West and traffic was heavy. Mark took a left onto A1A South, drove past the airport and soon they arrived at their destination.

Chapter 27

The Casa Bella was an incredibly beautiful resort in an old building with Mediterranean arches on the terrace and high French doors opening to the ocean that Henry Flagler, the founder of the Florida East Coast Railway and builder of the Florida Overseas Railroad from Biscayne Bay to Key West, had built exactly one hundred years ago.

Mark drove the van up to valet parking where it sputtered noisily a few more times. Some smoke came out of the engine and the poor old van died. Mark, Sienna and the kids looked at each other silently with big eyes as a few valets came running up to see what was going on. They were used to more upscale cars at their hotel and wondered what this rather big family in this ancient van was doing here. But Mark didn't care about status symbols or expensive cars. He asked the valets to wait a minute and tried starting the van a few times after letting it cool down for a little bit. It coughed and sputtered but then the engine started up and chugged again.

"She's a bit tired from the trip from Turtle Key," he said grinning at the valet as he rolled down the window and then opened the door to get out. "We're checking in."

Sienna got out of the van as well and opened the sliding back door for the kids who all climbed out, grabbed their duffle-bags and backpacks and ran into the beautiful grand lobby with dark wooden floors and heavy rattan furniture. Big Colonial style ceiling fans created a cool breeze. Old framed black & white photos decorating the walls portrayed Henry Flagler and his third wife Mary Lily Kenan, showing scenes of the Florida Overseas Railroad being built and him boarding the first train to Key West on January 22, 1912.

Sienna followed the kids into the lobby and looked around impressed.

"Wow," she said, "you must have blown all of your points to stay at this nice place."

"I did," Mark replied grinning, "but it was worth it."

They stepped up to the old wooden reception desk and checked in while the kids sat down on the big rattan couches and a nice concierge chatting with them, telling them about all the fun things there were for kids to do at the hotel.

After receiving their room keys, Mark asked the friendly receptionist Ashley:

"Do you know if Mr. and Mrs. Flores are here this weekend?"

"Unfortunately, I can't give you any personal information about Mr. and Mrs. Flores," said Ashley firmly. "They like to stay very private."

That was what Mark had expected. He didn't insist or ask further questions. He and Sienna turned around as Ashley took care of the next guest and Mark said: "We're going to have to find them on our own. I'm not sure how but maybe we can find their cottage and talk to them.

Sienna nodded. "Let's go up to our room first."

They called the kids and stepped out of the lobby. The hotel's gorgeous pool area and beach sprawled out in front of them. There was a path leading along two beautiful pools down to the beach with rows of majestic king palms and water fountains on both sides.

"Let's go up to our rooms first, get rid of the luggage and change into our bathing suits," said Mark to the kids who wanted to run down to the beach immediately that was lined by more palms and hammocks.

Sienna agreed, nodding. "Let's go and check out the rooms, guys. Follow me." She double-checked the room numbers again, followed a sign and took a left to an older wing of the building, walked up a flight of stairs and then she walked down a hallway toward the ocean. It was paradise. The rooms were small but modern and functional and they adjoined in a corner right on the ocean with an L-shaped balcony overlooking both the pool and the Gulf of Mexico. The first room was a suite with a separate living room, so they decided that Leo would sleep on the pullout couch and the three girls on the two queen size beds in the bedroom. Mark and Sienna would share the second room that only had one queen bed. Sienna stowed some perishables in a mini fridge and they all changed into their bathing suits and made their way back downstairs.

*****

The kids were hungry so they decided to have lunch at the pool bar first. Everyone ordered sandwiches and hamburgers and it felt like a real vacation, even though they were only staying for one night. After lunch, they walked down a path heading along the beach that led to a sister hotel. Along the path were more palm trees with inviting hammocks hanging from them. There were also some amazing sand sculptures from a recent sand art competition. They all enjoyed life, took their time, laid down, swung in the hammocks and eventually found a big human size chess game. Mark and Leo, who were getting along fabulously, played a game of chess while the others simply hung out, looking for shells and crabs on the beach. Suddenly, Sienna noticed a nice little standalone stone cottage at the end of the property. *If there's a cottage somewhere on this property, then that must be it,* she thought to herself. She said: "I'll be right back," and walked toward the quaint little cottage.

The cottage was made of coral or some other type of limestone and was surrounded by a chest high wall made of the same material. The yard was beautiful, like an enchanted garden with all sorts of blooming tropical plants with beautiful foliage. There were monsteras, hoyas, birds of paradise, Hawaiian ti-plants, heliconias, various types of ginger, plumerias in all colors and orchids mounted to the trees - it definitely looked like the residents were plant geeks.

Sienna walked up to the closed wrought-iron gate to see if there was a bell or a sign with a name but there was no indication of who might live here. Finally, she saw an older gentleman sleeping on a big rattan lounge chair covered with a blanket on a little covered patio next to the front door. She hated to disturb him so she walked back over to Mark and the kids and told Mark about her discovery.

"I don't know what to do," she said. "We can't really stand at the gate and try to get their attention. I'd hate to intrude on them and be a nuisance."

"Yes, I agree, although we'd be doing them a favor if these three are their grandchildren. Let's just play it by ear."

Sienna nodded.

It was almost time to go back to the room and think about dinner, but everyone was having such a good time that they continued hanging out by the hammocks and the chess set. Nobody was hungry yet after the big late lunch. The sun was low and the girls sat on the beach, building a sand castle while Leo chatted with Alana on his phone and Sienna and Mark just enjoyed each other's company.

*****

Richard Flores, the older gentleman in front of the cottage, had woken up in the meantime. He and his wife had dressed up for dinner and were about to walk down the path toward the main building of the hotel where they usually dined in the restaurant. They watched the happy patchwork family play in the sand and melancholic memories came back as they thought about the time when their son was younger. Suddenly, the older boy looked up. He was a mirror image of their son Ricky at that age. They both saw his unique profile and froze – how could that be possible? Sienna turned around and saw the elegant older couple standing on the path watching Leo. She gathered her courage and walked up to them.

"Mr. and Mrs. Flores?"

They nodded and looked at her quizzically.

"I'm Sienna Brantley. Do you remember me? I used to be Ricky's girlfriend when you lived in Turtle Key."

Mrs. Flores did recognize her and smiled. "Oh, hi Sienna," she said. "It's so good to see you. You haven't changed at all. Are these your children?"

Sienna hesitated. "No, I'm their aunt. They're actually my sister Camilla's." She paused. "And Ricky's."

Mrs. Flores held both hands up to her mouth. "Our grandchildren," she said as she took her hands back down again. They both walked down to the beach curiously. Mrs. Flores walked up to Lilly and Lindsey, said: "My granddaughters, I can't believe it. I think I'm your grandmother, girls" and took them both in her arms. Mr. Flores walked up to Leo, staring at him, then he said: "You look so much like your father, young man," and gave the perplexed teenager a hug.

Sienna had tears in her eyes as she looked onto the scene. Mark put his arm around her shoulder and they just watched as grandchildren and grandparents became acquainted.

Suddenly, Lilly looked up at Sienna and yelled: "Hey, Aunt Sienna! I have a grandma and a grandpa!"

LILLY HAD FINALLY SPOKEN!

Chapter 28

Sienna looked briefly at Mark who was staring at Lilly with his mouth hanging open. She walked down to Lilly who was still standing next to Rose Flores, fell down on her knees in front of her and took her in her arms. She was so happy that Lilly was talking again and that Bianca and Ms. Fisch were right when they said Lilly just needed a special event that would trigger talking again.

"We were about to go and have dinner," said Rose Flores. "We'd love you all to join us, in the hotel's dining-room?" Mark hesitated because the hotel restaurant was very upscale and one of the most expensive places in town. Rose added: "Of course we'd like to buy you dinner."

Mark and Sienna looked at each other and nodded. Sienna said, looking down at herself,: "Unfortunately, we're still in beach clothes, could you give us twenty minutes or so?"

"Of course, we can get a drink and appetizers and wait for you. How many are we?" He counted everyone. "Eight." Richard Flores answered his own question. "We'll get a big table at the window."

They all walked together toward the main building and while Richard and Rose Flores walked into the restaurant, Mark, Sienna and the kids ran up to their rooms, took quick showers and dressed for dinner. They had only brought casual clothes but nobody cared. Everyone ordered from the menu and the group had a happy feast. Mark and Sienna lifted their wine glasses, clinked glasses and tasted the hotel's fabulous wine.

Suddenly, Rose Flores, who was sitting next to Sienna, asked her quietly: "So, where are Ricky and Camilla?" Sienna looked at her and swallowed. She hadn't realized that Mr. and Mrs. Flores didn't know what happened to their son. Of course, the news had protected Ricky and Camilla's real identity. Sienna looked at the kids who hadn't heard the question. She asked Mr. and Mrs. Flores to come with her and stepped out onto the big patio overlooking one of the pools.

"I'm so sorry to have to tell you this, I thought you knew. Ricky and Camilla died in a car accident about two weeks ago..."

Mrs. Flores held her hands up to her mouth and Mr. Flores' face became as white as a sheet.

"So, that bad accident with the tractor trailer a few weeks ago on Overseas Highway was Ricky and Camilla? Oh my God. We haven't even followed local news or been in touch with anyone from here since we just came back from a trip to Europe, but we briefly heard about that accident," said Rose Flores shocked.

Sienna nodded. "Yes, unfortunately it was Ricky and Camilla. I know this is upsetting for you, but I'd appreciate if you could try to hide your feelings from the kids. Just for now. They are orphans and this is the first time they've been a bit carefree since the tragic loss of their parents. I had to take a vacation and come down from Boston to take care of them. Tonight is the first time Lilly has spoken since their death and it is because she was so excited to see you."

They understood and nodded and were happy that they had helped the kids feel better. Even though their hearts were breaking over the unexpected news of their son's death, they pulled themselves together and were going to put on a happy face tonight for the sake of their newfound grandchildren.

*****

Back at the table, Sienna watched the kids chat happily with their grandparents, especially Lilly, and realized she might not be needed here anymore and could return to her job in Boston, now that the kids had some other close relatives besides her. But Mr. and Mrs. Flores weren't the youngest anymore, so who knew if they'd feel up to taking care of three school-age children. Then Sienna looked at Mark who was currently explaining something to Leo across the table. Leo seemed to have a newfound special interest in sea turtles and the Sea Turtle Sanctuary...

Would Sienna leave Mark, the kids and the Sea Turtle Sanctuary and return to the firm in Boston where she'd have to work with Craig again if the grandparents stepped up and took care of the kids?

One of the waiters walked up with a special dessert and everyone looked speechlessly at the chocolate ice cream bomb with sparklers Richard Flores had secretly ordered, pretending to use the restroom.

"This is a cause for celebration," he said, holding up a glass of champagne. "I'd like to propose a toast to our grandchildren Leo, Lindsey and Lilly – and to Sienna and Mark for finding us – and of course to Sidney," he added and winked at Sidney, sitting between Lilly and Mark.

*****

Soon it was time to go to bed and everyone thanked Mr. and Mrs. Flores for the wonderful evening. They all left the restaurant together and stood on the back patio, looking out at the beach, the calm ocean and the beautiful dark sky full of stars. The patio and the pool area were lit up with hundreds and hundreds of twinkling fairy lights. It was a beautiful sight.

"We rented a seaplane to take us to the Dry Tortugas and Fort Jefferson tomorrow. We'd love y'all to join us, there are enough seats for everyone," proposed Richard Flores.

"Snorkeling is really awesome out there," added Rose.

"We have a reservation for breakfast at The Blue Rooster," replied Mark. "What time were you planning on leaving?"

"The plane departs at noon so that would probably work out well if your breakfast isn't too late," replied Richard. "We'd be back around six."

Mark and Sienna looked at each other, nodding. Flying in a small seaplane sounded like a once in a lifetime experience for everyone and they all loved snorkeling. Returning at six would still give them enough time to drive home before it became too late for school the next day.

"We're just going to need everyone's weight," added Richard, "for the seating arrangements. The weight on both sides has to be approximately the same, that's how sensitive the planes react to imbalance."

Sienna laughed. "I really have no idea how much everyone weighs. Do you think there's a scale somewhere in the hotel?"

"Yes, that's no problem. There's one for luggage at the front desk, because people tend to shop too much and then are afraid of having to pay for excess baggage when they fly home," replied Rose, laughing. "Just call or stop by the front desk. Oh, and by the way," she added. "I'll call the front desk and ask if you can stay in your two rooms until tomorrow evening. So you don't have to check out in the morning."

That was huge and made things much easier even though they didn't have much luggage, but they wouldn't have to pack in the morning and their belongings wouldn't have to sit in the van all day.

Mark and Sienna thanked Richard and Rose profusely.

Then everyone said goodnight. They stopped at the front desk and weighed everyone, after that they were off to their rooms where everyone slept like rocks after the eventful day - except Sienna, who tossed and turned all night. What was she doing to do if the grandparents volunteered to take care of the children...?

Chapter 29

It was another beautiful sunny day in Key West. Two chickens scurried across the road and almost brought traffic to a halt as Sienna, Mark and the kids stepped out of the hotel and climbed into a taxi-van that Mark had called to take them to The Blue Rooster, the legendary local restaurant in historic Bahama Village, not far from Duval Street.

"I didn't want to risk taking the van because there's probably no parking in town," Mark said, not mentioning that he was afraid it would break down again and he had already rented a replacement mini-van to get the group home tonight. He was going to have to come down again and take care of the old van, but he could do that when Sidney was at her mom's and maybe Sienna would accompany him. He certainly didn't want to risk breaking down on a Sunday evening with the kids all having to go to school the next day. He continued telling Sienna and the kids about The Blue Rooster:

"This place used to be the sight of boxing matches refereed by Ernest Hemingway. It's famous for its blueberry pancakes and chickens that hang out in the trees and walk all over the place. Also, we can play ping-pong while we wait for our table. You guys are going to love it."

The taxi drove toward Southernmost Point and Mark had the cab driver stop briefly for pictures. The red, black and yellow anchored concrete buoy said "90 miles to Cuba" and "Southernmost Point Continental USA" – they took a few goofy pictures and laughed a lot, then they climbed back into the taxi and Mark explained: "Key West is the closest place for Cuban migrants where they would land after escaping from Cuba, sometimes in homemade boats, to find a better life in the United States. Can you imagine what a dangerous journey that would be in some small nutshell? Lots of people died that way but they were desperate..." He realized that nobody was listening, because now the cab was driving up Duval Street and there was so much to see. Tons of tourists were walking about, some shopping, visiting art galleries and touristy t-shirt shops, eating ice cream, enjoying the beautiful weather. On the left was a sign pointing to the "Hemingway House" on Whitehead Street.

"Ohhh, I wanted to see the Hemingway cats," said Lindsey sadly.

"We'll have to come back to Key West to do that, now that our afternoon is busy with the Dry Tortugas. It's much more important and so awesome that we found your grandparents," said Mark with a serious tone in his voice. There was too much to do in one day and they all realized they'd have to come back soon.

Finally they arrived at The Blue Rooster. They walked into the courtyard of a small unimpressive blue wooden building, checked in at the hostess stand and suddenly stood in the middle of the most beautiful courtyard with trees along the perimeter and a big bar in the middle and a stage where a Reggae band was playing some fun Bob Marley tunes.

The wait wasn't long but Mark and Leo managed to get in a round of ping-pong as the girls danced to the Reggae music in front of the stage.

The restaurant was a wonderful experience with clucking chickens walking between the tables, picking fallen crumbs. The kids had the most delicious pancakes they had ever eaten and the grown-ups had eggs Benedict, a giant fruit salad and the best Cuban coffee.

Soon it was time to leave to be on time for their flight to Fort Jefferson. They walked a bit through rustling and bustling downtown Key West but then they stopped a van-taxi and a few minutes later they were back at the Casa Bella. Everyone had their bathing suits on underneath their shorts and t-shirts. They grabbed a few towels and sunscreen and met Richard and Rose downstairs in the lobby. They didn't have to pack any snacks because Rose had told Sienna and Mark that she'd bring a picnic.

Outside the lobby, a 15-passenger van belonging to the airline was waiting for the guests and drove them to the airport which was less than a five minute drive, where the plane, a de Havilland Canada DHC-3 Otter 10 passenger seaplane, was already sitting on the beach, ready for departure.

The biggest surprise was yet to come when Richard climbed into the small cockpit and put a pair of headphones on his head! He turned around and grinned proudly at Mark, Sienna and the kids as they climbed into their designated seats that had been chosen for them according to their weight.

"Yup, this is my hobby and retirement job. I love flying this old gal," he said, patting the dashboard with countless instruments.

"No worries, she's not that old," commented Rose laughing, as she saw the worried look on Sienna's face.

"Richard is a pretty experienced pilot. He served in the Air Force for years before he became a lawyer."

"Oh, I remember flying with you and Ricky from Turtle Key a few times!" Sienna smiled and said full of excitement.

Richard and Rose nodded. They remembered as well.

Everyone donned their headsets and buckled up as instructed while Richard received his departure instructions from the tower. The seaplane turned and glided through the smooth ocean on its two long floats until it lifted up into the air and slowly reached its cruising altitude of 500 feet.

"There we are, guys." Everyone listened to him through the headphones since the plane itself was too loud. "How did you like this surprise? This is my second career. I really wanted to become a helicopter pilot in Hawaii and spend my days doing stunts along tall waterfalls, but Rose talked me out of it. She likes the Keys and had to take care of her elderly parents in Miami until about two years ago. So we stayed here. This is my copilot Cindy, by the way," he said, patting his copilot's shoulder, "she will take over on the way back to give me a break because I'll be drinking a glass of wine or two during our picnic," Richard said into the intercom system. Everyone laughed.

"Our destination, the Dry Tortugas and Fort Jefferson, is 70 miles west of Key West. It's going to take us about 45 minutes to get there, so relax and enjoy the ride. Our low altitude will allow you a bird's eye view of the ocean and the reefs. Look, right there, at 1 o'clock," he pointed ahead, a bit to the right, "can you see the pod of dolphins?"

Everyone stretched their necks trying to catch a glimpse of the dolphins jumping majestically in and out of the water and oohed and aahed.

"We are now passing over the coral atoll known as the Marquesas and the Key West Flats. You might spot all kinds of marine life ranging from sharks to sea turtles," explained Richard, "so be on the look out guys."

Everyone relaxed and enjoyed the ride with the beautiful views from the air and pointed out some special things they could see because the water was so crystal clear and they were flying at such a low altitude… a fever of stingrays, some big sea turtles amongst other marine life. After a while Richard continued: "We are now passing the treasure sites of the sunken galleons Atocha and Margarita, where half a billion dollars worth of gold and silver were found. It's still an active treasure site where finds of huge emeralds and Spanish gold are not uncommon.

"Wow," said Sienna to Mark, who was sitting across from her, "we could use some of that to rescue the Sea Turtle Sanctuary…"

He grinned and nodded.

Chapter 30

"And here is Fort Jefferson," announced Richard through the intercom system, as they flew toward the massive but never completed coastal fortress, shaped like a hexagon. "It is 150 years old and the largest brick masonry structure in the Americas, built with over 16 million bricks. The building covers 16 acres. During the Civil War, Fort Jefferson was used as a military prison for captured deserters. Among the prisoners held were the four men convicted of complicity in President Lincoln's assassination in 1865, the most famous being Dr. Samuel Mudd."

The plane made a low pass over Fort Jefferson. Richard circled the fort and perfectly executed a water landing on the side that the ferries also arrived on. The seaplane was beached and the passengers climbed out onto the sand. Sienna was happy to be back on the ground. She was the only one who hadn't been a fan of some little flying maneuvers Richard had performed - the kids and Mark had had a blast.

They were still ahead of the first ferry of the day, so they had the entire fort to themselves.

Richard's copilot Cindy handed out snorkeling gear.

"You should go snorkeling first. The first ferry arrives in about half an hour and then it becomes crowded and murky in the water, so you won't be able to see as much. We'll have lunch afterwards," said Richard.

"Where are the best snorkeling spots?" asked Mark.

"You simply follow the outside of the moat wall, then enter the water from the white sand beach on the left side of the fort." He pointed to an area on the left side of the seaplane. "Rose and I are just going to hang out. We don't snorkel that much anymore."

"And I can prepare the picnic for when you return," Rose added with a smile. She loved the idea of hosting her new family and having the opportunity of spoiling them.

Mark, Sienna and the kids waded into the beautiful turquoise water with the fort on their right and some coral growing on the wall and the gorgeous reef with plentiful marine life on their left.

"Don't forget to listen and be on the look out for crunching parrotfish," said Sienna grinning as she and Mark helped Lilly, Lindsey and Sidney with their mask, fins and snorkel and applied some anti-fog lotion to the inside of their masks.

"And don't touch the coral," Mark reminded them. "It's very fragile and protected. Same for any sea turtles you see. All Florida sea turtles are either on the endangered or threatened list so it's illegal to touch them or get within 20 feet of them."

The children and Sienna nodded. They had heard these rules many times and were aware of them. Despite Lilly and Sidney's young age, the kids were all very experienced swimmers and snorkelers since they had grown up here on the ocean. They swam along the fort's wall and kept pointing out special things they saw to each other: a sea horse floating around in between some long seaweed leaves, a bunch of sea urchins they pointed at on the bottom of the ocean but knew to stay in a safe distance, an octopus hiding underneath a piece of coral. They saw a beautiful angelfish and, of course, some parrotfish and cracked up as they heard them crunch on the coral, and they also enjoyed the other beautiful tropical fish and living coral in all colors of the rainbow.

*****

After a while, the first ferry arrived and it quickly became more crowded in the water and lots of the fish went into hiding. The kids started getting restless and hungry, so they all swam back to the seaplane and met Richard and Rose who were hanging out in folding chairs, drinking a glass of wine.

"Well, you guys know how to have a good time," said Mark with a smile as they handed him a glass. "I can only have one, I have to drive back to Turtle Key tonight," he reminded them – and himself.

Rose had prepared a wonderful picnic on a blanket and now Richard helped her retrieve the perishable items out of a big cooler. They had bread, turkey and cheese for sandwiches, potato salad, macaroni salad and fruit salad with tiny marshmallows for dessert and cookies. They had even brought a thermos with coffee and some coffee cups. Everyone was in heaven and not only the kids were beside themselves with happiness to have this new set of grandparents, Sienna was too. She hadn't felt this motherly love in a long time, besides from Bianca of course, and really enjoyed it.

"Well, I have a fun story for you guys," said Richard suddenly as everyone was sitting there, enjoying lunch and looked into the round. "Has anyone ever heard of Cleatus the Crocodile who used to live here?" The kids stared at him in disbelief as he continued: "Yup. There used to be a crocodile here. An American crocodile - not an alligator. Supposedly he swam here from the Everglades in 2003. Crocodiles have been known to swim quite far, but 70 miles seems unusual. Some attempts to capture Cleatus were unsuccessful, but finally in 2008 he was caught and DNA samples were taken. They determined that his mother was from the Everglades and his father possibly from Jamaica. He just lived here peacefully and did no harm, but finally people started feeding him and he became used to humans too much. Park Officials were scared that he'd attack one of the guests so he was relocated to the Everglades. Marine biologists weren't too happy about him being moved. You guys should read up on him and look at the photos. Very interesting. I kind of miss seeing him here."

"Great story," replied Mark. "I've heard of him too but have never seen him."

Unfortunately, it was soon time to go. They explored the fort a little more, imaging where Cleatus had hung out, but then it was time to board the plane and return to Key West. Leo, Sidney and Lilly were so tired that they fell asleep on the flight back. Richard as well who had had more than two glasses of wine and snored so loudly that everyone could hear him despite headphones and the extreme noise of the plane. Rose smiled at their bewildered looks.

"We haven't shared a bedroom in years even though we love each other dearly. Could you sleep with this?"

Everyone laughed, shaking their head. Cindy flew them back safe and sound and soon they landed at Key West International Airport.

*****

Back at Casa Bella, they had to pack and everyone was sad because they didn't want to leave. This trip had been so wonderful and they all wished they could stay longer but Mark and Sienna had to work tomorrow and the kids had to return to school. Richard and Rose went back to their cottage to give Mark, Sienna and the kids time to pack but Rose said insistently: "Make sure you don't leave without saying goodbye, we have something to make you feel better, for now."

They took their luggage to a newer van that Mark had rented instead of using the old one and walked back through the lobby and up the beautiful palm tree lined path to the cottage.

Richard and Rose were waiting outside in their beautiful enchanted garden with a cat and three little kittens. One of them, the sweetest black and white spotted kitten that reminded Sienna of the cat she and Camilla had as little girls, was in a cat carrier. The girls and even Leo went crazy as they saw the cats and picked them up and petted them profusely.

"Well, we should have asked Sienna and Mark first, but we wanted it to be a surprise... this little black and white kitten is polydactyl like the famous Hemingway cats, that means he has six toes instead of five. We thought since you couldn't go to the Hemingway house this time, we'd let you take him home. His name is Ernest." Sienna looked at bit bewildered at first, but what was she going to say? Ernest was adorable and he'd fit right into the cottage in Turtle Key.

The girls had tears in their eyes and hugged Richard and Rose. "Is that okay, Aunt Sienna? Can we keep him?"

"Do I have a choice?" asked Sienna laughing.

"Can't you come with us?" asked Lindsey her new grandparents. "We have enough space in our cottage."

"No, not this time, but we'll figure something out, okay?" said Rose and gave her another hug.

Richard and Rose walked Sienna, Mark and the kids to the rental van, handed them a little cooler with sandwiches and drinks for the road and stood there smiling and waving, as they departed. Everyone in the van waved and blew kisses.

The kids were quiet on the way home, thinking about their adventures and their newfound grandparents.

Ernest sat on Lindsey's lap purring, obviously content with his new family.

Chapter 31

Sienna stepped back in shock and almost fell over Leo and the girls as she walked into the kitchen and discovered another white orchid on the kitchen table along with some messed up paperwork. Again, it could be the orchid from Bianca's shop, but Bianca would have probably told her if she had brought it over. Sienna didn't feel safe in the cottage, wondered if someone else was there and every shadow or tree scratching against the windows made her jump. She wondered if she should call Craig but would rather not speak with him and what if it wasn't him? But who else would be doing this? The homeless guy? But he wouldn't be buying orchids. Should she call the police? Should she ask Mark for advice? Even though it was late, she decided to call Bianca after she and the kids had brought the luggage inside and the kids had gone upstairs to get ready for bed. Lindsey had taken Ernest upstairs in his cat carrier and Sienna was going to have to find some type of box and fill it with sand that Ernest could use as his litter box tonight.

Bianca was still up and answered her phone right away.
"Hi Bianca, I'm sorry to call you this late."
"Oh, hey honey! I'm glad you called. I was wondering when you guys would get back. How was Key West?"

"It was actually great. Believe it or not, we found Ricky's parents."

"Oh my gosh, that's fantastic. So, are they in good shape? Maybe they could take the kids if you want to go back to Boston?"

That was the question Sienna had been having a headache about.

"They are young for grandparents and also seem to be wealthy. So that does make a lot of things easier."

"That's awesome! And how did things with Mark go?"

"Oh, Bianca. He's wonderful. And so is Sidney. All of us got along really well."

"I'm so happy for you and for the kids. Wow, those grandparents must be beside themselves with happiness too."

"Of course they were shocked, they didn't even know Ricky and Camilla died. But they were definitely happy about the kids. Richard Senior is a pilot and took us to Fort Jefferson. And Rose just spoiled us. You should have seen the picnic spread she brought to Fort Jefferson. It was such an amazing day."

Sienna paused briefly.

"But the reason I'm really calling you is there was another white orchid here in the house when we got home. Did you happen to bring the one from your store over?"

"No, sorry, I wouldn't just go into your house when you're gone, I'd give it to you personally," Bianca replied. "Boy, but that's starting to get creepy. Is anything missing or something else changed? I wonder if you should call the police."

"Yeah, maybe, but then I have to talk to Mark's ex-wife if she answers the phone."

"That's true too," replied Bianca. "Do you know what? I have Ben's cell phone number, he's another officer at the Turtle Key police. Just let me know if you want to call him.

We could ask him to treat it discreetly and not talk to her about it."

"Good idea, thanks," said Sienna. "Okay, let me think about it. I'll let you go, it's late."

"Okay, sweet dreams and call me anytime if you need to,"

"Thanks, Bianca. Good night."

After speaking with Bianca, Sienna felt less spooked and brave enough to walk out to the parking lot in the front and check if the same car from a few days ago was parked in the parking lot again. She walked out front but the parking lot was empty besides the familiar cars. Everything was calm. Everything was fine on the back patio and in the backyard as well. It was a beautiful starry night.

Sienna suddenly realized that Craig hadn't texted her in a while. She checked when she had received his last message. Friday evening, the evening at the Coconut Key Beach Resort. Did he know about her schedule or was that a coincidence? She didn't want to text him this late. If he was indeed in London it was about 4 am, but she decided to call him in the morning to see how he'd react.

*****

Meanwhile, Mark and Sidney had arrived at home after dropping off Sienna and the kids. They were tired after the long day and glad to be home. Sidney had barely made it home without falling asleep and she walked up the stairs of Mark's two-story condo leading to her bedroom to get ready for bed, while Mark went back outside to get the rest of the luggage out of the van.

Suddenly, Isabel drove up in her police car. She got out looking extremely unhappy.

"May I ask where you're taking my daughter this late on a school night?" she asked in an antagonistic tone.

This could only mean trouble, but Mark tried to remain calm and friendly.

"We were actually in Key West for the weekend and just came back. Are we not allowed to go on trips when she's with me for the weekend? And it's not that late, by the way. It's 9 pm."

"I hope you didn't go with that *puta* from Boston?"

"Oh, come on Isabel, do you really have to talk like that? That just reflects badly on you. I don't think it's any of your business who I go to Key West with, is it?"

"What about the baby? You're going out with other women?"

"I'd like a paternity test when the child is born because I very well think that this child could have been fathered by your Coast Guard lover."

"What makes you think that?"

"You've been dating him longer than three months now, haven't you?"

"If you don't get back together with me when I have the baby, I'm going to make sure you lose custody of Sidney too," she said a bit too loud, got back in her car and drove away.

Mark sighed, locked the van and walked back to his apartment. He hated this drama and wondered what to do about the situation with Isabel.

Chapter 32

The next morning, Sienna had an idea. She called the Coconut Key Beach Resort and asked to be connected with Craig Wilson. The operator informed Sienna that he wasn't a registered guest there anymore. Of course that didn't mean anything, he could be staying somewhere else in the Keys, since it was seriously unaffordable to stay there for more than a few nights. Then she called the firm in Boston, pretended to have misplaced his cell phone number and asked for Craig's contact information in London.

"Oh, hey Sienna," said Margaret the receptionist. "He didn't give us any contact info for London. He said to just use his cell phone. But, as far as I know, he left London already."

That didn't give Sienna much more information either so she called Bianca and asked her for Ben's phone number, the local police officer who worked with Isabel.

"Do you think I can trust him to keep this confidential?" she asked Bianca.

"Yes," she replied, "you can trust him. He doesn't like her very much, trust me, nobody does…"

She called to ask when she could file a complaint against an unknown person and how the police would help her in a case like this. Usually there was nothing the police could do until someone or something was actually harmed.

"Hi Ben, this is Sienna Brantley, can I speak to you in private? I'd like you to keep this confidential, if possible. Bianca said I could trust you."

"Oh, hello. Sure. Let me step out for a second."

That meant Isabel was probably in the back, listening.

"So, what can I do for you?" he asked after a few minutes. He had stepped out of the office and was officially walking to a Starbucks across the street to get some coffee. "And why don't you want Isabel to know about this?"

"I'm dating Mark and she doesn't seem happy about it. I just feel that she'd be biased and it would be awkward discussing something like this with her. The strangest thing has been going on. My ex-boyfriend was in town, not accepting that I broke up with him but supposedly he left already. Since the evening I saw him, someone has been breaking into my cottage and leaving orchids in different locations. On the lanai, the kitchen counter, the kitchen table. He or she has also been moving stuff around and rifling through the drawers. It's super creepy. Obviously someone knows how to get in and knows I like orchids. He or she isn't doing any harm but is obviously trying to scare me."

"Hmmm... that does sound creepy and of course we can help you. First of all, is there a key somewhere accessible that this person might know about?"

"Ummm, yes. You know, it's so safe here, there has always been a key under a rock in a planter by the front door. Ever since I was a kid."

"Well, you should get rid of that immediately. Maybe give the key to the receptionist at the Sea Turtle Sanctuary if it needs to be somewhere where the kids can get it. Second, can you install a camera and exchange the locks in the house?"

"I'll look into it, good idea, thanks."

"Third, we can have someone watch the house day and night, but the problem is if I'm using our office's manpower, I'll have to inform Isabel."

"Okay, why don't we wait with that and I'll talk to Mark and ask him what he thinks about it."

"You could always hire a security company or private investigator but that would be expensive," said Ben. "But, other than that, of course there's not much we can do if we don't know who's doing this."

"Thank you very much, Ben, you were a great help. I'll get back to you about what Mark says about letting Isabel know about it."

"Okay, keep me posted. Talk to you later. And please call me if you feel threatened in any way or if it gets worse."

*****

Sienna wanted to call Mark next, but she didn't want to bother him at work because she knew how busy everyone in the Sea Turtle Sanctuary was. She sat down at her laptop and looked out onto the patio where she already had an impressive orchid collection that the mysterious person had left in the cottage. Strange. He or she knew that this was her favorite orchid and they also knew exactly when nobody was in the house. Craig knew that she liked this type of orchid after seeing them in her apartment in Boston. Sienna also wondered where this person was getting the orchids. Bianca's flower shop was the only place around that had a bigger selection. Sienna typed orchid shops and nurseries in the area into the search engine of her laptop. There were a ton in Homestead but the closest one was in Islamorada. She checked if it was open and called the phone number. There was no reply so she wondered if the employees were busy working in the nursery and decided to go for a drive. She looked at the time on the upper right of her screen. It was 10:30. She had until three to pick Lilly up at the bus, so plenty of time.

As Sienna was leaving the cottage, she took the house key out from underneath the rock and brought it to the front desk at the Sea Turtle Sanctuary. It was a bit risky because the receptionists were usually interns and college students and they switched quite a bit according to how busy it was and whether they had to help in the back with the turtles. Sienna called Bridget and asked her to inform everyone that the kids would be stopping by to pick up the key and to put it in an easy accessible place. Then she texted Lindsey, Leo and Bianca, letting them know that the key wasn't under the rock anymore. Lilly didn't have a phone yet but whoever picked her up from the bus stop would know where the key was.

As she walked up to her rental car, she was surprised that she couldn't find the key fob in its usual spot, a little side pocket. She dug through her purse and finally found it at the bottom in between some other things. She was surprised at herself – what had happened to her usual almost obsessive organization?

Sienna also found the velvet bag she had stuck in her purse containing the conch pearls from Camilla's office. Deep in her thoughts, she played with the bag in her hand feeling the round pearls inside and put it on the passenger seat next to her purse so she wouldn't forget about it. She looked up Jewelry Appraisers and also found one in Islamorada.

The GPS led Sienna to a smaller yet really nice upscale nursery specializing in orchids in Islamorada, "The Orchid House". There was a showroom and two greenhouses and everything appeared really tidy and well kept. There wasn't a dead leaf or dirt anywhere on the ground. The showroom was empty and Sienna had to walk through the first greenhouse and into the second to find a younger gentleman, the nursery owner, who was giving a customer a tour. "Hi. Welcome to the Orchid House. Let me call my wife," the owner said. "She can come out and assist you."

"Thanks," replied Sienna. "I'll look around in the meantime. I just have a few questions."

Sienna walked up and down the rows and rows of various orchid species and finally found an area with white Phaleonopsis in beautiful planters. This place was a score because she immediately recognized the unusual clay pots with a lot of holes in them that looked handmade and that were exactly like the pots the Phals were in that had been left at her house.

A woman in her late twenties or early thirties with short curly hair, denim overalls and crocs came out and greeted Sienna with a cheerful face.

"Hi, welcome to the Orchid House. I'm Bella. Can I help you?"

Sienna felt a little strange with her request and hoped she wouldn't come across as crazy but she told the young lady the creepy story and that she was trying to find out who was doing this to her.

"That's why I need to ask you, can you remember anyone buying a lot of these white Phals? You might remember the guy's British accent if it was my ex-boyfriend? He's from England. The first one was a really nice arrangement of several plants in one of these pots, but the others are just one plant. The pots are always this type. I already have an impressive collection at my house."

"Wow, that is a bit creepy," Bella replied. "At least that creep is leaving something nice in your house," she added, "but I'm really sorry, we sell so many orchids, especially these white Phals, that I could never remember who bought them, even if it was just recently. We sell large amounts to the hotels in the area, so I'm guessing that person could have also bought them in one of the hotel gift shops."

"Is Coconut Key Beach Resort one of your clients?" asked Sienna.

"Yup. Huge. They always have a big orchid display in the lobby and in the restaurants. One of us goes over there to rearrange them once a week. They also sell orchids in the gift shop out front."

"That's probably where he got them from," replied Sienna. "Thanks very much." She thought she'd thank Bella by buying something and asked: "I have a friend who's really into big spotted and unusual Cattleyas. Can you recommend something nice? I owe her a gift."

"Sure," said Bella and led Sienna into the showroom where she let her choose one of the gorgeous orchids in bloom.

Sienna carefully hung the beautiful mounted Cattleya she had purchased for Bianca onto the handle in the passenger side door and typed the address of the jewelry appraiser into her GPS. Sienna's car was immediately filled with the wonderful scent of the orchid and she looked up, surprised. Wow, I might have to get another one of these, she thought to herself.

*****

In less than five minutes, Sienna arrived at the jewelry appraiser's shop. Islamorada was small. A customer was just leaving the store and the appraiser, John Campbell, was about to go out for his lunch break, so Sienna was lucky to find him in his shop.

"I have ten minutes for you but would appreciate if you called ahead and made an appointment next time, Ma'am," said the Bahamian man in his late fifties.

"I'm sorry, I happened to be in town and realized I had the conch pearls with me, so it would be great to kill two birds with one stone," replied Sienna. "I've been wanting to have these appraised for a while now."

She got the velvet bag out of her purse and spilled the twelve pearls in all different sizes and colors onto a tray with velvet lining that Mr. Campbell had placed on the glass counter. Sienna could tell that he was rather impressed as he held his breath for a few seconds and reached for a magnifying glass without taking his eyes off of the pearls.

"These are very impressive, Ma'am," he said. "May I ask where you got them? They are one of the rarest and most expensive types of pearls in the world."

"They have been in my family for a while," Sienna replied. "I think my grandmother began collecting them when my grandfather brought her beautiful conch mollusk shells home from his fishing trips to the Bahamas. My mother, who lived here in the Keys all her life, found a few and even my sister and I found one or two when we were small. I recall finding a gigantic one with my sister almost thirty years ago but that one has been missing."

"You need to find it urgently," replied Mr. Campbell. "The historic Queen Mary Conch Pearl Brooch," he showed her a photo, "features two natural pink conch pearls weighing 24.9 and 28.1 carats. Excellent pearls today can cost as much as $15,000 per carat and more, but those are the exceptionally rare ones. Top-grade conch pearls are more typically around $4,000 - $7,000 per carat. So, if you do the math, if it were 24 carat and the most exceptional type, it would be worth $360,000. A lower grade but still top notch would be worth almost $100,000."

Sienna felt like she had to sit down. She was getting a bit dizzy listening to these astronomical numbers.

John Campbell could tell that she needed a chair and said: "There's a chair right over there, why don't you pull it up and sit down," he said with his soft Bahamian accent.

He started looking at the individual pearls through his magnifying glass. He made an "ooh" sound as he picked up a very dark pink pearl that was a perfectly symmetrical oval.

"This shape is the most desirable," he said and showed it to her, "oval because you can make the best jewelry out of them." He pointed at the photo of the brooch again. Both pearls were oval. He put the pearl on a small jewelry scale. "Okay," he continued, "this one is three carat and the perfect color and shape, look at this wave-like "flame" structure on its surface, the creamy porcelain-like appearance and unique shimmer," he paused, "it might be worth $40,000 - $45,000. And trust me, Ma'am, there is a big market for these."

Sienna was speechless. She had assumed that the pearls might be worth a few hundred or even thousand dollars but not nearly as much as Mr. Campbell was now telling her.

"You should put these into individual bags," Mr. Campbell said, as he turned around and grabbed a pile of black velvet drawstring bags out of a drawer, "otherwise they will scratch each other. If you will allow me, I'll put them into individual bags and attach a price tag to each bag." He stuck the biggest pearl into a bag, pulled the drawstring and labeled a price tag with the price he had mentioned and pushed it over to Sienna's side. Then he picked up the next pearl. All of the others were smaller and not as exceptional as the first one, but Mr. Campbell appraised them all between $2,000 and $10,000. He was now extremely helpful to Sienna, hoping she'd let him sell one or two pearls for a commission.

Sienna's head was spinning as she got up. She shook Mr. Campbell's hand as she thanked him and left the store. The twelve conch pearls she had in her purse and that had been scattered about in Camilla's office for years had a value of approximately $100,000 and that was without the missing big one that she and Camilla had found; she knew it still had to be somewhere but feared it might never show up.

Mr. Campbell gave Sienna the name and phone number of a very reputable gem dealer in Key West who would sell them for her but also offered his assistance.

"Also, one of the most renowned pearl appraisers in the world works for them, an old friend of mine," he added as Sienna walked out the door.

Chapter 33

Sienna arrived back at the Sea Turtle Sanctuary and was so excited that she grabbed her purse and the orchid for Bianca and went inside to tell Bridget about her discovery. The Sea Turtle Sanctuary was safe for at least another three months if she managed to sell the pearls.

"Can you come to my office when you're done?" asked Sienna as she found Bridget in the back, filming a video of another one of the turtles that was almost ready to be released.

"I'm actually done with this part of the video," replied Bridget and followed Sienna. "Cool orchid," she said, pointing at the orchid Sienna was holding up. "What's going on?"

Sienna made motions for Bridget to follow her and closed the door tightly behind them. Without saying a word, Sienna got the big velvet bag out of her purse containing the other individual velvet bags, placed the bigger bag neatly on her desk and started carefully emptying all the other pearls onto the velvet, making certain to keep them with their individual bags with the prices on them.

Bridget just watched, her eyes growing wider and wider with anticipation.

"Do you have any idea how much these conch pearls are worth?" asked Sienna.

"Nope," said Bridget blatantly.

"They've been lying around here for years. I found some in the glass cabinet over there and some in these drawers. I know that my grandmother used to own some of these and my mother collected them too," she said, pointing at the drawers of the desk in front of her. "I just had them appraised in Islamorada. They're worth approximately $100,000."

Bridget's lower jaw dropped. She was speechless.

"And there's a really big one that Camilla and I found when we were kids. I gave it to my mom back then, but can't find it anywhere. Of course someone might have sold it already but it could also be floating around here somewhere. That one is worth even more, I'm talking like a quarter million or so."

"Oh my gosh! I can't believe things of such value have been just sitting around here like that," said Bridget in complete shock.

"Yeah, I'm flabbergasted too. I had no idea they're worth that much. They are incredibly rare and it's actually unusual that they made their way all the way here. They're usually found in the Caribbean. I'm going to try to sell them. The appraiser gave me a contact in Key West who deals with them. That will keep us afloat for around three months. I mean, I guess a bit less after paying all the debt."

Bridget's face lit up. She walked around the desk and gave Sienna a huge hug.

"Boy, Sienna, you are such a blessing!" she said. "I'm so glad you're here!"

In that instance, Bridget's phone bleeped. There was an important call for her on her landline and she had to go and take it.

"Gotta go, but you're awesome!" she said.

*****

Sienna was so excited that she texted Mark, asking if he had a few minutes to come to her office. He was actually on his way out to check on the turtle that was being released in a few days, but he had a few minutes and knocked at Sienna's door. Sienna stood up and gave him a kiss. He looked at her, surprised. She seemed happier and more relaxed than usual. She took him by the hand and led him to her desk where the beautiful pink conch pearls were lying on the bigger black velvet bag. The desk lamp's light was shining on them and their unique shimmer was highlighted. He just stood there, staring at them. Just like Sienna, he had heard about pink conch pearls but he had no idea how valuable they were.

"Mark, I just had these appraised in Islamorada. Just this little handful is worth about $100,000!"

Just like Bridget's, Mark's jaw dropped. "Wow, is that guy sure? That's crazy!"

"He seemed to know what he was talking about and gave me the contact info of a dealer in Key West." Sienna picked up the biggest pearl that was worth almost as much as all the others combined. "This one is really big and desirable and worth about $40,000."

"Wow, do you have a safe somewhere? You need to put those away in a really safe place," Mark said. "But that's amazing. Where did you find them?"

"They've been floating around in this office for years, I guess. Some were in that glass cabinet with the shells over there, some were just lying around in these drawers. I might actually find more if I empty the entire thing. I'm actually going to start searching the cottage and this office obsessively because there's one missing that Camilla and I found as kids. That one was almost the size of a quail's egg."

Mark looked at Sienna, flabbergasted.

"Okay, I'm exaggerating, but it was more than four times as big as this one," she said grinning, pointing at the big one.

"Well, congratulations," said Mark, "that's really awesome." He stepped closer and kissed her. He had missed being together with her 24/7. For a second, it was only them again and the kiss made them want more, but they jumped apart as someone knocked at the door and Bridget walked in, looking for Mark.

Bridget grinned and said: "I'm heading out to see Oscar. Can you join me, Mark?"

"Sure, I'll see you later, Sienna?"

"Yes, I need to talk to you, can you call me after work?"

"Sure," said Sienna and started putting the pearls back into their bags without mixing up the price tags.

*****

Sienna picked up her phone and called the contact in Key West that Mr. Campbell had given her, Pearls and Gems International. A receptionist answered the phone.

"Pearls and Gems International, how may I help you?"

"Hi, this is Sienna Brantley. I received your number from Mr. Campbell in Islamorada, may I please speak with Natalia Romero Contreras?"

"She is in a meeting right now. May I ask what it's in regards to? She'll call you back as soon as possible."

"It's regarding some valuable conch pearls that Mr. Campbell just appraised for me. He said you might be able to confirm the appraisal and sell them for me."

"Can you please give me your contact information? I'll have Ms. Romero Contreras call you back as soon as possible."

Sienna gave her number to the receptionist and ended the call. She had some time before she had to pick Lilly up from the bus so she started emptying the drawers in the desk, curious if she would find some more forgotten pearls. She found all sorts of junk and clutter but no more pearls.

Ten minutes later, Natalia Romero Contreras with Pearls and Gems International called her back. Sienna answered the call.

"Hi, this is Natalia Romero Contreras with Pearls and Gems International. You had called?"

Sienna had thought the gem dealer's name sounded Hispanic but she had a strong Russian accent.

"Hi, yes, this is Sienna Brantley. I just had some conch pearls appraised by Mr. Campbell in Islamorada that have been in the family for generations and he told me you might be able to help me sell them."

Ms. Romero Contreras replied, her deep voice trying to sound professional but she couldn't hide her excitement. Pink conch pearls were very rare since they didn't often make their way to Florida and jewelry dealers in the United States were constantly on the lookout for them.

"Yes, Ms. Brantley, the market for pink conch pearls is really hot. We can guarantee that we'll achieve top dollars for you. May I ask where you're located? Could you stop by and show them to me and my internal appraiser?"

"I'm in Turtle Key. About an hour away from you."

"Hmmm. Let me check my schedule," said Ms. Romero Contreras, "could you stop by tomorrow at eleven?"

"Yes, that would work out perfectly," replied Sienna. "Can you give me your address?"

They exchanged information and Sienna was all set to drive into Key West the next day to show Ms. Romero Contreras the conch pearls. She wondered if Mark had already arranged for his old van to be fixed and whether he'd be able to join her...

*****

At 3 pm sharp, Sienna went and picked Lilly up from the bus stop. Lilly was now a different person and chattered non-stop. She couldn't wait to see Ernest the kitten and had barely made it through the school day because she had been thinking of him. She took Sienna's hand and Sienna had this warm fuzzy feeling in her heart as she looked down at Lilly and saw how much happier she was now that they had found her grandparents.

They unlocked the front door and walked upstairs to Lindsey's room where Ernest had spent the day. He had had an accident and Sienna quickly walked over to the bathroom to get some cleaning supplies and clean the mess. She had no idea how to train a kitten to use a litter box but she knew they had to find a pet shop and go and buy a real litter box, cat litter and some other items for Ernest. She felt bad for leaving him by himself all day. She had been so busy that she forgot.

Suddenly, Lilly, who had been playing with Ernest, started crying, ran over to her room and threw herself on her bed. Sienna followed her, sat down next to her, took her in her arms and asked: "what's the matter, Lilly?"

"I shouldn't be this happy when my mom and dad are dead," she said sobbing. Sienna took her in her arms. "You'll never get over your mom and dad dying, Lilly, it's okay to be sad sometimes and mourn. But they'd want you to be happy. You will always have these sad moments but I hope they'll get better. Also, now you have Ernest who needs you to take care of him."

"That's true," Lilly said very maturely for a five year old. "Let's go take him outside so he doesn't have another accident."

"That's a good idea," replied Sienna. "Maybe we should keep him outside on the lanai for now.

Lilly went and picked Ernest up and they both walked out to the lanai. Sienna watched Lilly take the kitten outside and her eyes filled up with tears as well, but she quickly wiped them away so Lilly wouldn't see them.

*****

As they walked through the family room onto the lanai, Sienna discovered a new orchid on the coffee table. She rolled her eyes but looked around anxiously. This was getting old...

She called a local locksmith to take the first step and exchange the locks.

Chapter 34

Sienna had to talk to Mark about whether she should involve Isabel or not in the case of the "orchid intruder". She texted him and asked if he could stop by the cottage after work.

"Sure! I'd love to see you anytime. Sidney has soccer practice until 5:30 pm, is it okay if I bring her? Shall I bring some pizzas?"

"Sure!" replied Sienna. "Lilly will like that."

She always welcomed a break to not make dinner and thought about Mark's question to bring *some* pizzas. One was never enough anymore. The amount of food the kids ate was amazing.

As soon as Lindsey was home, Sienna made a run with her and Lilly to the pet shop down the road. There were some cats in crates for adoption from the humane society, hamsters, guinea pigs and Russian tortoises and Lilly and Lindsey ran back and forth, wanting to look at them all.

"We should get a second kitten so Ernest has some company, Aunt Sienna, don't you think?" asked Lilly sneakily as she looked at a beautiful Siamese kitten from the Humane Society.

Sienna grinned. "No, I don't. We just got Ernest. Let's see how he adjusts first."

It was hard for Sienna to remain firm but she did. She didn't want to mention the fact that there was still a small chance they'd all move to Boston.

Instead they splurged on a really nice litter box, a cat bed, some toys and treats. Ernest was going to be one spoiled kitten.

*****

Mark and Sidney arrived just as everyone was doting on Ernest again. Even Leo had stayed home since he had heard that Mark was bringing pizza. Sienna took note of how much Leo admired Mark and how much he seemed to crave a father figure like him. She wondered if Ricky had spent much time with Leo.

It was always time for pizza, so they had an early dinner and the two large pies that Mark had brought were barely enough for all of them. Finally, the kids went to their rooms to do their homework, Sidney went to hang out with Lilly and Sienna and Mark sat down on the lanai with a drink.

Just as they were sitting down on the big weathered rattan couch, they heard rustling in the bushes next to the lanai and then saw someone run away down the path toward the beach. All they could see in the dark was that the person looked like he or she was wearing a dark hoodie with the hood up. Instinctively, Mark set his drink down, ran down the stairs, through the backyard and down the path toward the dock, trying to follow the intruder. He or she was gone but Wayne was there again. He had just found a conch shell in the area where the tide had receded around the dock. He pulled out the raw meat with his finger, stuck it in his mouth, swallowed it with pleasure and licked the salt off of his lips.

"Hey, man, did you just see someone in a dark hoodie run down the path?" asked Mark not mentioning the fact to Wayne that conch shells were protected.

"No, sorry, man," replied Wayne, "I was over there, looking at the ocean. But trust me, I'm keeping an eye open for the lady. Her sister and sister's husband were good souls. Helped me out a lot. Said maybe one day I could get a job here because I know a lot about turtles..."

Mark didn't know what to say. He had previously heard about Wayne and knew that Camilla and Ricky had fed him sometimes.

"Okay, thanks, man. Someone's messing with her house and coming in so you might want to stay low key because you know you'll be the first one the police accuse..."

Wayne looked at him bitterly.

"Sure right about that..."

Mark got a $10 bill out of his wallet and handed it to Wayne. Wayne was so thankful that he almost started crying.

"God bless you, man. Thanks. I'll keep an eye out for the person in the dark hoodie."

Mark returned to the cottage and wasn't sure if he should mention Wayne to Sienna. She had followed him to the backyard and stood there, waiting for him as she saw him walk back up the path.

"Mark, this is getting creepier and creepier," she said. "This is exactly what I wanted to talk to you about."

"What do you mean?" he asked quizzically. "Let's go and sit back down, I can really use that drink now."

"So what's going on?" Mark asked after they had situated themselves back in their seats and picked up their drinks again. He put his arm around Sienna's shoulders.

"I don't know if I told you, but someone has been breaking into the house and leaving all these orchids and moving other things around, almost as if to make me paranoid and frankly, they're succeeding. Actually he or she is not breaking in, they either have access to a key, have a key or knows how to get in without a key."

She pointed at the orchid collection that had already grown voluminous on a table in the corner.

"This person knows that these are my favorite flowers and knows exactly when nobody's home. I think it might be Craig, who isn't getting over the fact that I broke up with him. He seems to have anger issues..." She didn't want to go too much into detail and tell Mark about the last evening in Boston when Craig had grabbed her wrists in a violent manner and the evening at the hotel.

"Wow, that's scary. I wonder if I should move in for a couple of days. I'm sure the kids wouldn't care. By the way, Wayne the homeless guy was in the back again. He obviously chased the intruder away but he also said Camilla and Ricky fed him sometimes and they had said something about getting him a job at the Turtle Sanctuary..."

"Hmmm. I wonder what he'd do and if he's reliable..." She looked out into the backyard. She still didn't feel comfortable with him back there. "You staying here might not be a bad idea. The only thing is that the intruder is a coward, he or she only comes when nobody's home."

"I wonder if you should inform the police," said Mark.

"That's why I wanted to talk to you. How do you think is your wife going to react if I go and file a complaint? I don't think she's going to be very sympathetic toward me."

"Although her job does require her to be impartial. But I know what you mean."

"To be honest with you, Bianca told me to talk to Ben and I already did. He had a few different ideas, like switching out the locks, setting up a monitoring system and watching the house 24/7. He said the police would do that, but since Isabel's the one who makes the officers' schedules, she'd have to know."

"Yeah, I can see that." He set his glass down with an unexpected bang, hit his knees with his hands and looked as frustrated as he felt.

"If only she wasn't such a bitch." He looked at Sienna who was looking at him a bit shocked about the unexpected outburst. "Excuse my language."

He sat there and thought for a minute.

"I really wish we could take care of this without Isabel." Why don't we try installing a camera first. I'll help you with that. And you said you already called a locksmith to switch out the locks?" He thought about it for another while. "But, do you know what? Once we know who it is, we're going to have to report them anyhow, right? So we might as well speak with Isabel, whether we like it or not."

Sienna thought about it and agreed. It was unfortunate that Mark's ex-wife was the local police detective but she assumed she'd still have to be somewhat professional.

"Okay, I'll call tomorrow. It's late now."

Suddenly, Sienna remembered her trip to Key West to the jewelry dealer tomorrow.

"Oh, Mark, I was wondering if you already organized to have your van fixed? I have to go to Key West tomorrow to show the conch pearls to a jewelry dealer."

He laughed. "Well, as a matter of fact, I took the day off and am going there tomorrow since Sidney has soccer practice again right after school and it's not my turn to car pool. I guess we'll be going together! When's your appointment?"

"At eleven."

"Are you telling the kids? I don't think they'd be too happy if you told them you're going to Key West."

"I haven't thought about it yet. Well, it's work-related, that's different. And if I return later than three, I'd have to have Bianca pick Lilly up anyhow and they'd wonder where I am...."

"Yeah, I guess you're right. So, that works out really well. Can we leave around 9:30 and you drop me off at the parking lot of the Casa Bella where I can meet my buddy?"

"Yes, maybe we can have a quick lunch with Richard and Rose afterwards. I'll call them and let them know we're coming."

Chapter 35

The next morning, Sienna called the Monroe County Sheriff's Department to talk to someone about the intruder and of course, with her luck, Isabel answered the phone.

"Good morning, Detective Baldwin, this is Sienna Brantley. I've had a problem with an intruder coming into my cottage. Could I speak to you about it?"

The line was silent for a minute. Obviously, Isabel was pulling herself together and trying to be professional and not say anything nasty.

"Sure. What's going on?"

"Someone is breaking into the cottage every time nobody's home and, strangely enough, not only leaving orchids but also moving stuff around and opening drawers as if searching for something."

Isabel laughed briefly. "So, he's leaving things and not stealing anything? Well, that's hardly a criminal offense."

Sienna already regretted calling and felt that Isabel wasn't taking her seriously. "I feel like someone's stalking me."

"Is there a reason for you to think that?"

Sienna just hated talking to Mark's ex about it.

"Yes, I recently had a bad break up with a boyfriend."

She heard Isabel click her tongue in a derogatory manner.

"Aren't you from Boston? What would the ex-boyfriend be doing down here? Are you sure you're not imagining things?"

Sienna realized that this whole conversation didn't help at all and that the more she told Isabel, the worse it was going to get. She really didn't want to be discussing these intimate details with her, of all people.

"I'm sorry to bother you with this. Why don't I wait a little and see if it stops. Thank you very much."

"Okay. Have a nice day."

Sienna ended the call and sat there for a minute, her heart pounding in her chest, really mad at herself for calling Isabel. She'd talk to Mark and see if they could handle it on their own.

*****

Sienna and Mark made their way to Key West after Lindsey had left for school. The sun was shining, they opened the top of the convertible and they were giddy about going on a little drive together without kids. She briefly told Mark about her conversation with Isabel and he became upset for a second, but then they decided not to let her ruin their day.

"We'll figure something out," he said. "You can count on me."

As they came up to the Seven Mile Bridge, Sienna remembered her and her friends riding up to the old part of the bridge on their bikes. She had been so proud of her first "real" bike with the banana seat and pink streamers hanging from the handlebars and had stolen away with her friends Tina and Julia so many times when her parents found it much too dangerous to drive along the main road, US1. Of course, Camilla had never done that and never got into as much trouble as Sienna… or at least she never got caught.

"We used to go fishing here under the old part of the bridge, but of course that's missing now after it was blown up for "True Lies". I remember that loud explosion as if it were yesterday. It totally changed where we hung out. After that we went to Knights Key where lots of migrant workers lived. And that's a giant luxury resort now..."

Mark smiled at her. "Yeah, that movie must have brought a lot of excitement to the lazy Keys. A lot has changed in the past years."

"Yeah, if the kids rode their bikes along US1 now, I'd have a heart attack, despite sidewalks. Of course it was less busy back then, but it was still dangerous. I can't believe we did that. Now it's even hard to turn onto the other side of the road unless you're at a traffic light. But it is spring break right now…"

Mark nodded. "Yeah, this is one of the busiest times of the year."

They enjoyed the scenery silently for a while until Sienna asked:

"When did you move here?"

"Exactly ten years ago. I was only going to stay at the Turtle Sanctuary for my internship but then I met Isabel and she got pregnant, so I accepted their job offer. I'd probably be living and working in Orlando now if I hadn't met her. One of my uncles owns a big veterinary clinic there and wanted me to join him, but that's not my thing, a big office where the animals are just numbers."

"So we basically have to thank her for making you stay here," laughed Sienna, "otherwise we would have never met…"

"And of course I'm glad I have Sidney," he added thoughtfully. Again, they were talking about Isabel. He wanted to change the subject and pointed at a pod of dolphins, jumping in and out of the water. "Look."

Sienna glanced over to the right without taking her eyes off of the traffic for too long. The endless turquoise-colored water stretched out on both sides of the bridge, so clear and shallow that they could see the darker reef in some areas.

"It must be strange for you to be back after such a long time," said Mark.

"Hmmm." Sienna didn't want to talk about why she had left and never returned. She put her hand on his leg and squeezed it a little. "I'm so glad to be back and that I met you," she said. Mark put his hand on hers and she swerved a little, as she got too excited.

"Wow, wow, wow," laughed Mark as he pulled his hand away and held onto the top of the dashboard.

"Okay, let's pay attention to the road again," she laughed and put both hands on the steering wheel, looking strictly straight ahead, her jaw set sternly.

They both laughed. They left the Seven Mile Bridge behind and countless further Keys and in less than an hour, they arrived in Key West, took a left onto Highway A1A, South Roosevelt Avenue, passing the airport on their right. A few minutes later they passed Smathers Beach and arrived at the Casa Bella.

"So, do you think you can join me, Richard and Rose for lunch?" Sienna asked Mark as he climbed out of the car in the parking lot to join his friend Gary who was already working on the old van.

"I think Gary should be done by then," Mark replied and called out: "Hey Gar, do you want to come and meet Sienna?"

Mark's friend Gary, a hippy in his late fifties with an old checkered bandanna around his longer grey hair and weathered tanned skin from living in Key West all his life, stood and looked up, came over to say hi to Sienna and Mark.

"Howdy. Sorry, I can't shake your hand," he said, pointing at his greasy hands, "but very nice to meet you."

Sienna smiled and nodded. "Nice to meet you too, Gary. Good luck with the old gal here."

All three of them laughed.

Looking at Mark, she said: "I'll text you when I'm done."

The men waved as they walked back toward the van, Gary obviously saying something flattering about Sienna as he jabbed his elbow into his friend's ribs in a friendly manner. He was glad to see his friend happy again.

*****

Sienna took a left into a little residential neighborhood, drove along the ocean and past several "southernmost" landmarks toward the Southernmost Point and then took a right onto Duval Street. She wished she could stay longer and just walk around, but then again, she had a feeling this wasn't the last time she'd be here.

She checked her GPS. Her destination was just one hundred feet away and so she took the first available parking space that she could find even though it was still an entire block to get to Pearls and Gems International. Surprised, Sienna stepped up to the upscale looking jewelry store with items in the window that were far beyond her budget and tried to walk in, but she actually couldn't - she had to ring a doorbell and wait until a security guard in a dark blue suit and tie came and unlocked the door. She hadn't expected such an upscale shop on rinky-dink Duval Street, but that's what Duval

Street was all about: Bargain t-shirt shops next to exquisite and costly art galleries, jewelry stores and luxury real estate agents.

"Hi. Sienna Brantley," she introduced herself to the security guard. "I'm here to see Natalia Romero Contreras at eleven."

He nodded. "Please follow me." He walked up to an elevator, pressed the button. He and Sienna got in and rode up to the second floor without exchanging a word. The elevator opened up to a beautiful sunny foyer with giant monsteras and other tropical plants framing both sides of a big sliding glass door and a very contemporary looking waterfall in the middle that created an incredibly zen atmosphere. The glass door opened silently, the employee had disappeared and Sienna stood in front of a tall very simple but expensive looking reception desk with another discreet employee behind it, this time a beautiful young girl, also wearing a dark blue suit. Sienna who was wearing a nice but plain green linen shift dress that was a bit wrinkly from the drive started feeling a little underdressed...

Sienna didn't have to say anything. "Ms. Romero Contreras will be with you shortly, Ms. Brantley," said the receptionist. "You can take a seat if you'd like."

Sienna looked at some beautiful large contemporary paintings hanging in the foyer and, before she had a chance to sit down, Natalia Romero Contreras stepped in. Natalia Romero Contreras was so full of energy that Sienna FELT her presence in the room before she saw her. She was a petite Russian woman in her mid to late thirties with a platinum blonde bob, a beautifully shaped face with a pointy nose, green cat eyes and, how could this surprise Sienna, a dark blue business suit with six-inch expensive dark blue stilettos Sienna recognized as the stunning work of designer Gianvito Rossi. Natalia's voice and commandingly strong Russian accent were so loud and she talked so fast that Sienna had a hard time following her.

She walked toward Sienna and took her hands into both of hers. "It's such a pleasure to meet you, Ms. Brantley. Did you find us okay?

"Yes, no problem," answered Sienna. "It's nice to meet you too. What a beautiful office," she said as they entered Ms. Romero Contreras' office and sat down on a beautiful contemporary white leather sectional with a big glass coffee table in front of it.

"We just moved in. What a pain that was. But I'm so glad we're here now. We used to be near Mallory Square and the offices were tiny and dark with low ceilings. I finally have space to breathe," she said in a theatrical manner, pointing her arm up to the airy high ceiling and waving over to the floor to ceiling windows with a view into a beautiful tropical backyard oasis. "Can I offer you something to drink? I think we should have champagne to celebrate our possible cooperation. You don't come across pink conch pearls every day."

"Oh, I really shouldn't, I have to drive," replied Sienna.

"One glass will be fine," said Ms. Romero Contreras commanding the conversation as she pressed an intercom button on a big modern phone that resembled a spaceship and said something in Russian to her assistant. Two minutes later, the assistant, also in a blue business suit, stepped in, carrying a tray with a bottle of very expensive bubbly in a silver bucket and two expensive Ukrainian crystal champagne flutes.

"Ah, the old widow," said Ms. Romero Contreras smiling happily. At first, Sienna didn't know what she meant but then she realized that the champagne was Veuve Cliquot, widow Cliquot in French.

Irina carefully poured champagne in the two glasses and left the office, Ms. Romero Contreras said "Spacibo,

Irina" and lifted her glass to propose a toast to Sienna. "To our cooperation. Why don't you call me Natalia?"

Sienna nodded. "Sure, please call me Sienna. Cheers."

"Poyekhali!" said Natalia and took a big sip. "Now, please show me what you've got."

Sienna was a bit more careful because she knew the champagne would go right to her head since she wasn't used to drinking champagne and she also wanted to savor every sip. She set the champagne flute down, fished the big velvet bag containing the twelve smaller bags out of her purse, set it down on the big glass coffee table and opened the drawstring. Natalia got up and retrieved a large elegant velvet tray out of a sideboard. Sienna poured the beautiful pink conch pearls onto the tray one by one. Natalia was delighted and beside herself with joy as she saw the size and colors of the pearls. "They are perfect," she almost shouted with joy. Then Sienna poured out the biggest oval shaped pearl and Natalia was finally speechless. "May I?" she asked breathlessly and picked it up very carefully with a pair of padded gem thongs and held it up to the light, examining it carefully with one eye and the other one closed. "This reminds me of the dark pink pearl that Elizabeth Taylor wore in a necklace and is now missing. Its color is just beautiful and I can even see its "cat's eye effect" without looking through my jewelers' loupe! I'll have my appraiser explain that to you. I'm going to call him now, okay? Where did you get these, Sienna?"

Before Sienna could answer, Natalia got up and pressed the intercom button. She said something in Russian again, obviously asking Irina to send in the appraiser, because a few minutes later, an older gentlemen stepped into the office, the only one besides Sienna in the entire building not wearing a dark blue suit. He was dressed in a colorful Hawaii shirt, comfortable looking slacks and flip flops. He looked like he was a native from the Caribbean Islands, maybe Jamaica, and that's where he had obviously learned his specialty, appraising the value of these beautiful rare pearls. He was obviously the only one who didn't have to adhere to dress code. He shook Sienna's hand as Natalia introduced him to her.

"This is Winston Lewis from Jamaica. He is one of the most renowned pearl appraisers in the world. He learned under John Wright in Bermuda but worked in Kingston for over twenty years. He is an eminent authority in his field."

Mr. Lewis sat down next to Natalia. His eyes seemed to widen as he first caught sight of the conch pearls, but he remained calm and quiet and tried not to show any reaction. He was strictly professional. He put a headband magnifying glass jeweler's loupe with a lamp on his head, was wearing white gloves, set down a pair of calipers and a jewelry scale and then he quickly transferred the pearls from the black velvet tray onto one with white stretched silk. The white background helped determine the quality of the pearls' luster.

He had a grading sheet with entries for size, luster, shape, color, surface and weight and went through all these categories pearl by pearl, which he carefully held up to the light, measured, examined and weighed. Sienna and Natalia sat there quietly, watching him during the entire process that took almost an hour. Natalia had several glasses of champagne but they didn't seem to have any effect on her, while Sienna barely drank half of hers and already felt tipsy. Finally, the appraiser picked up the biggest one he had saved for last.

"This one is truly magnificent," he finally said, looking through his jeweler's loupe. "Not only because of its tremendous size, but also color, luster and shape are highly desirable. This will fetch a very good price."

Natalia asked: "Can you please explain the "flame structure effect" for Ms. Brantley?"

Winston Lewis explained: "Some very rare pearls have the spectacular chatoyancy effect known as the "flame structure" which appears as a silky sheen on the surface of the pearl. Chatoyancy effect comes from the French and means "shining like the cat's eye." He showed Sienna and Natalia. "See, right here...Can you see that it looks like a flame here?"

Sienna nodded. "Amazing."

Winston Lewis took off his headband, picked up his tools, nodded at Sienna and said: "it was a pleasure meeting you." He handed his assessment sheet to Natalia before he left the office.

The prices he had entered into the sheet were even a bit higher than those of Mr. Campbell in Islamorada.

"I'm sorry, I interrupted you earlier. Where did you say you got these pearls, Sienna?" asked Natalia.

"They have been in my family for a long time. My grandfather was a fisherman and he and my dad would go to the Bahamas a lot and bring big queen conch shells back for my grandmother and mother. And also pearls. But some are also from the Keys, as far as I remember. I guess some rare ones make their way over here. When I was about five years old, my sister and I once found a gigantic one on one of the beaches in Turtle Key. That one's still missing."

Natalia's eyes widened...

Chapter 36

After Sienna and Natalia had discussed their cooperation and had a chat about Sienna's work as a lawyer, Natalia walked Sienna to the door.

"Think about it, professionals like you are needed in the Keys," said Natalia. "Boston has enough lawyers, but the ones down here are all shady." They shook hands. "We'll be in touch. I'll send you an offer. And look for that other pearl," added Natalia.

"Bye, it was nice to meet you and Mr. Lewis," said Sienna and walked back to her car, caught up in her thoughts. There were really more options for her to stay here and work in the Keys than she had thought, especially remotely.

She was already a little late for lunch with Richard and Rose, so she hurried to her car and drove straight back to the Casa Bella. Mark was already there, sitting with them at the pool bar. He grinned as he got up and gave her a kiss to greet her. "Well, lucky you, you'll have the honor of me driving back home with you to Turtle Key. Gary couldn't fix the van and it had to be towed to a garage. So, I'll have to come back and get it this weekend. If I can avoid junking it one more time," he said and grinned.

She laughed. "Well, that's too bad. I was offered really nice champagne and only drank half a glass because I thought I had to drive..."

They all laughed. "Well, why don't you have another glass now," proposed Richard. "I think we have a lot to celebrate."

He lifted his hand, calling a waiter. "George, please bring us a bottle of your best champagne and four glasses."

A few minutes later, they clinked glasses. Richard made an announcement.

"Well, even though Rose and I are heartbroken about Ricky and Camilla's accident, we are ecstatic about the three grandchildren we had no idea existed for all these years. And about you too, Sienna."

Mark and Sienna looked at each other quizzically, wondering what Richard and Rose were up to.

"After we broke it off with Ricky seventeen or eighteen years ago, we rented out our house in Turtle Key and moved to Coral Gables to be closer to the firm but after that I retired to Key West. We never sold the house in Turtle Key. So, we'd like to propose that we move back to that house and take care of the kids as long as you need us to, Sienna. You can go back to Boston and just come and visit on the weekends or whatever you decide to do. But we want to let you know that we're ready to step up and do our part. I can even help and give the Sea Turtle Sanctuary legal advice if you need me to since I've kept my license active despite being retired. But I guess you can take care of that yourself, Sienna."

Mark looked at Sienna, surprised. He knew that she was only on vacation right now and had her job in Boston, but he had never taken into consideration that Sienna would really go back. He thought she was happy here with him and the kids and was ready to start a patchwork family, despite his ex-wife.

Sienna looked from Richard to Rose, then at Mark and then back at Richard. She was speechless and didn't really know what to say. She did what she had to do and thanked

Richard and Rose. It was true, her two weeks in the Keys were almost up and she had to go back to Boston, no matter what, but she had been pushing the final decision ahead of her like a ton of bricks.

"Thank you, guys. I'm sure the kids will love that. And it certainly gives me some piece of mind when I have to return to Boston."

Mark frowned and looked down at his plate. His mouth was twitching. He didn't want to broach the subject now with Richard and Rose present, but he was upset and Sienna could tell.

They finished lunch and Richard and Rose looked at each other, wondering why their generous proposal hadn't found more excitement. But they presumed Sienna had so much going on that she probably just needed some time to digest the news.

*****

Mark drove the convertible since Sienna had had two glasses of champagne after Richard had informed them of his and Rose's plans. They drove quietly out of Key West and onto US1, not talking much, both deep in their own thoughts. Suddenly, after passing a sign for "Little Torch Key", Mark took a right off of US1 and drove down a small road leading to a square wooden building with a thatched roof. The building was surrounded by smaller palm trees and had a circular driveway in front and a small dock in back of it. Mark walked around the currently deserted building, sat down with his legs hanging from the dock and made signs for Sienna, who had followed him, to sit down next to him. An old turquoise colored boat named "Island Girl" was anchored next to the dock.

They just sat there for a while in the shade, looking out at several tiny beautiful islands, little green speckles in the ocean, some boats cruising in the distance. A great white heron jumped up at the end of the dock. Mark and Sienna had interrupted his afternoon break. He spread out his majestic wings and squawked while taking flight.

"This is the Welcome Station for Orchid Island. I worked here one summer long as a waiter because I needed some real money after interning in the Sea Turtle Sanctuary for two summers. Great experience. I really learned how to deal with people who know what they want. These people spend a lot of money but they also demand a lot in return and they have the right to."

Sienna wondered what he was trying to tell her.

"I'm sorry," said Mark, "I'm just jabbering. When I'm here, I always remember that great summer. I actually wish I could take you out there one day, but it's quite pricey. What I really wanted to say is that we really have to talk. What are your plans, Sienna? Where is this relationship going? I really thought we're hitting it off and you just seem to want to go back to Boston. What future does that give us?"

"Well, I have to face that I have my home there and my job. Even if I quit my job, I'd have to give them notice and would have to work until my contract is over. The fact that Richard and Rose want to come to Turtle Key and assist with the kids is really helpful. That means the kids can stay here no matter what and don't have to come to Boston with me."

"So, what do you think are you going to do, Sienna? Are you really returning to Boston?"

"Well, I love you and I really love the kids and being down here, but..."

In this instance, an employee stepped out of the Welcome Station. Mark and Sienna's conversation was interrupted.

"Hi, folks. Can I help you? Are you waiting for the next ferry?"

They both jumped up like teenagers caught doing something forbidden. Then Mark recognized his former coworker Peter. "Oh, hey Pete, remember me? Mark."

Peter looked at him, hesitated for a while but finally remembered.

"Of course, Mark! That was a fun summer when you worked with us and we were all allowed to stay on the island. That's not possible anymore, it's too busy, and every inch is needed for the paying guests."

Mark nodded. "Hey, this is my friend Sienna. Sienna, this is my old coworker Peter. We had a blast that summer I worked here."

Sienna nodded, a bit taken aback that Mark was just calling her a "friend". "Nice to meet you, Peter."

"Well, we're trying to make it back by three, Sienna has an elementary school kid that she has to pick up from the bus," Mark explained. "I usually do too but my daughter has soccer practice today. Did you hear Isabel and I got divorced?"

"Yeah, I heard. Sorry to hear that," replied Peter.

They all looked at the time on their smart phones and realized it was already past three.

"Well, I guess I'm not going to make that," said Sienna. She felt bad. She had even forgotten to ask Bianca to pick Lilly up for her. "Excuse me guys, I'm going to call Bianca and ask if she can go and check on Lilly."

She stepped aside and called Bianca while the men chatted a few more minutes.

"Hey, Sienna," said Bianca as she answered the call. "I had to pick up Sammy and since you weren't there, we took Lilly home with us. She and Sammy had a snack and are doing their homework together now, so take your time."

Sienna apologized. "We totally lost track of time. I'll be home in about forty minutes."

"No worries."

*****

The atmosphere between Mark and Sienna was a bit tense and they didn't restart the discussion about their relationship as they drove the last forty minutes home to Turtle Key. Mark took a left into the parking lot of the Sea Turtle Sanctuary, said goodbye to Sienna immediately and drove away in his pick-up truck, mumbling something about going to watch Sidney's soccer practice. She could tell that he was upset. I guess he won't be moving into the cottage for the next few days, she thought...

*****

Slowly, Sienna walked to the back of the Sea Turtle Sanctuary and up to the cottage. She urgently needed some time to herself. Usually, rather antisocial and content with being alone, she felt like she had had to constantly step out of her shell during the past twelve days. She had certainly enjoyed watching the kids change and warm up to her, but she also just needed a breather. She looked at her watch. It was 3:40. Lilly was safe and sound at Bianca's house and Lindsey wasn't going to be home until six after cheerleading. She walked into the house, filled a metal bottle with water, quickly changed into her bathing suit and grabbed a towel.

She walked down the path toward the dock, spread out her towel and sat down at the end of the dock. She sat there for a few minutes, enjoying the beautiful view and drank her water. Suddenly the whole situation and decision-making overwhelmed her and she burst out in tears. It was basically easy. She wanted to stay here, but could she give up her safe and lucrative career in Boston? *Why did you die, Camilla,* she thought to herself, *how I wish I could have talked to you one more time...*

Suddenly, Sienna jerked up. Someone had come up quietly in back of her and sat down next to her. It was Lilly.

"What's the matter, Auntie Sienna?" she asked. "Why are you sad? Don't you like it here?"

"Oh, yes I do," replied Sienna, pulling up her nose and trying to stop crying, but she couldn't. "You know, grown-ups are sad sometimes too. This whole situation hasn't been easy for me."

"Would this make you feel better?"

Lilly put her hand in her pocket and fished something out. She put it into Sienna's hand. Sienna looked at it. It was the giant pink conch pearl that she and Camilla had found as little girls. "Bianca said you were in Key West trying to sell these pearls. Do you want to sell this one too? Maybe then you don't have to work and we can all stay here together?"

Sienna couldn't fight the flood of tears any longer, facing this sweet innocent child, and she let them flow. She took her in her arms and said:

"Oh, Lilly, that's so sweet of you! Where did you have this?"

"I had it in my room the whole time but forgot about it. Mom gave it to me when I wasn't feeling good one day and Ernest was playing with it when I came home. By the way, he didn't have an accident and used his litter-box."

Sienna examined the pearl with its exceptional chatoyancy.

"If it's important you can have it," said Lilly. "I don't need it."

"Do you know that your mom and I found this together when we were kids at Coco Plum Beach? It was in a conch shell and fell into the water when we picked it up. And then it almost got washed away."

"So it's a nice memory."

"Yes," replied Sienna sadly. "But we don't have to sell it for me. I can work. We have to sell it to save the Turtle Sanctuary."

Lilly nodded. "That's important. The turtles are the most important."

Sienna smiled a bittersweet smile. Even Lilly already thought that the turtles were more important than her. She took her in her arms again.

"No they're not, Lilly. They're very important but you, Lindsey and Leo are more important. And I love you all very much."

Chapter 37

Natalia, who was always on duty and loved her job, said she would jump into her car immediately and drive up to Turtle Key when Sienna called her to inform her that the big conch pearl had been found.

"That thing belongs in a safe if it's as big as you say," Natalia said, her Russian accent commanding the conversation as she walked up to her car. There was no backtalk. "It's only an hour drive both ways, and a pretty drive at the same time. It's five thirty now and I'll be home by eight – and I have a fun car to drive," she said, caressing the light brown leather wrapped steering wheel of her white antique 507 BMW Convertible.

"Okay," replied Sienna who realized that she wouldn't be able to dissuade Natalia from coming so late, "just punch Turtle Key Sea Turtle Sanctuary into your GPS and it'll lead you right here. We live in back of the Sea Turtle Sanctuary. There's a path on the right leading down to the cottage. You can't miss it. It's a light green cottage on stilts right on the Gulf."

"Okay, see you around 6:30," replied Natalia. She wrapped a colorful silk scarf around her head and put on a pair of gigantic sunglasses, looking like a film star from out of a fabulous fifties movie and was on her way.

*****

Sienna walked through the cottage like every day now, checking to see if the intruder had been there. There was no sign of a new orchid or any items in the cottage being in disarray. Maybe changing the locks had worked. She sighed a big sigh of relief.

Since Mark had promised to stay in the cottage, she called him, hoping he wasn't cross with her anymore. There was no answer. Maybe he was upset or maybe he was just busy and hadn't heard the phone.

In that instance, her phone bleeped. It was Bianca asking whether Sienna and the kids wanted to come over for dinner.

Sienna returned Bianca's call right away.

"Hey, Bianca. Yes, we'd love to come over for dinner. I just have to be home by 6:30. I'm expecting someone. Is that okay?"

"Yes, dinner's ready, come on over. I didn't realize how much I was making and then my two granddaughters Jenny and Lynn cancelled."

"Thanks, I appreciate it, I haven't been home all day so it would probably be pizza night here again."

"I know, that's why I called," replied Bianca, grinning about how Sienna's healthy eating habits had changed in these past two weeks.

"Oh, and my orchid friend Louisa is here, I hope you don't mind. You'll love her."

"Okay, see you in a second," replied Sienna, called Leo and Lindsey and texted Natalia to let her know when she was about five minutes away.

"Guys, Bianca invited us over for dinner. We don't have to stay long but she is already done. Can you join me right now?"

"Alana's picking me up to go over to her house," replied Leo. "Is that okay? Oh, and Aunt Sienna, did you forget about my court hearing tomorrow?"

She froze and looked at him. She had forgotten but didn't want to admit it.

"No, I didn't," she replied slowly. "10 am, right? Don't come back too late, okay, so that you're not too tired tomorrow?"

He grinned. "That'll be sleeping in for me, bruh. I usually get up at 6:30."

Sienna grinned. She thought it was hilarious being called "bruh" but she took it as a form of endearment. It was going to be a long night for her. She still had to look at Leo's file as soon as Natalia left.

*****

The girls followed Sienna down the path and walked the few hundred yards to Bianca's house. She and her friend Louisa, a beautiful woman in her early sixties, her long black silver-streaked hair pulled up to a tight bun, were under the pergolas in the back, talking orchid shop. Louisa, who had come to Florida as a young girl with her parents from Cuba over fifty years ago, ran a coffee shop right next to Bianca's flower store and was also the President of the local Orchid Society. Louisa was Bianca's best customer and teacher. She knew everything about orchids and helped Bianca where she could. She could barely walk due to an autoimmune disease and used a cane but had more energy than most other people Bianca knew, including herself. Besides orchids, Louisa also knew everything else that happened around town. She was fully aware of the situation with Sienna, the kids and Mark and his ex-wife Isabel. She shook Sienna's hand and hugged her like an old friend as Sienna walked up to her and Bianca.

"It's so nice to finally meet you, chica! You are doing such a great job with the kids! You should definitely stay here and join our orchid society. We need more true conches around here. I was at the service for Ricky and Camilla but you probably don't remember."

Sienna was a bit overwhelmed but nodded and smiled. She hadn't heard that expression forever and loved being called a "conch", the slang for natives in the Keys, and said: "Thank you, it's nice to meet you too."

Louisa reminded Sienna of Maria in the café in Key Largo, a cordial Hispanic mama or abuela who would give her right arm for others but didn't take crap from anyone and spanked her kids with her chanx, her flip-flops.

They all walked inside Bianca's house. Bianca had made fresh empanadas and chili con carne and it was very noisy in the kitchen with everyone talking at the same time, laughing and enjoying their meal. Bianca had made her signature margaritas again and Louisa lifted her glass and proposed a toast to Sienna. "Salud - to new friends!"

Sienna held up her glass and clinked it with Bianca and Louisa and took a sip. It was sour but made her feel warm and relaxed.

Louisa continued chatting with Sienna as she ate a couple of empanadas.

"I heard about the conch pearls. We had some of those in Cuba but they were lost when we came here."

Sienna wasn't happy that everyone suddenly knew about the pearls. Who knew, maybe the intruder in the cottage was looking for them and not just trying to scare her...

*****

At 6:25, Sienna's phone bleeped with an incoming text message. It was Natalia letting her know that she was just getting off of the Seven Mile Bridge and was almost at the Sea Turtle Sanctuary. Sienna, already a bit tipsy on her second margarita, looked around, checking where the girls were. Bianca noticed her look and said: "They're upstairs with two of my girls. I think they're watching TV. They're fine if you have to go. Hey, come back and bring your friend when you're done with your business. The more the merrier!" She and Louisa were having a great time and walked Sienna out front to look at some more orchids Bianca had there and where Sienna was going to wait for her guest.

"Thanks for dinner, Bianca, and for the drinks," said Sienna as she walked into the parking lot to greet Natalia.

*****

Just as Natalia in her antique BMW was pulling into the parking lot, a person wearing a dark hoodie with the hood up came running up to the other end of the parking lot. He or she had tried to leave through the back and along the beach as usual but Wayne had blocked the path and followed him or her. The mysterious person had to turn around and was now panicking and out of breathe as Wayne ran toward him/her.

It was the same person that Sienna and Mark had seen the other night in the back yard and it looked like a woman, not a man. Sienna couldn't tell for sure but he or she was much shorter than Craig. The person jumped into an older dark sedan at the other end of the parking lot and drove away with squealing tires. Wayne stood there, shouting: "Follow her!"

In a panic, Sienna ran up to Natalia's car, jumped inside and yelled: "Follow that car!"

Natalia immediately stepped on the gas pedal and followed the dark sedan down the road, heading toward the Seven Mile Bridge. Sienna called the police station. Ben answered and said he'd be on his way, then he immediately informed his colleagues in Key West to see if anyone was driving around the lower Keys and could come to the other side of the bridge.

"Vehicle traveling south on Seven Mile Bridge, dark older model sedan. Driver has been breaking into local house. Assistance needed on south end of bridge ASAP," he said into his radio.

"Copy," replied a colleague, currently cruising through Little Duck Key. "I'm on the south side of the bridge. Will have bridge shut down and be waiting for that vehicle. Requesting assistance of further cars to block road."

Natalia, right on the dark sedan's tail, but in the meantime with Ben in his police car following her with flashing lights, looked at Sienna from the side as they drove over the beautiful bridge with the sparkling early evening ocean on both sides. The south end of the bridge had been shut down in the meantime, so no cars were coming toward them. Natalia slowed down a little to let Ben pass her.

"What's going on here?" she asked as she slowed down to a more comfortable speed, not having to keep up with the dark sedan anymore. "I didn't expect to get involved in a car chase tonight. I thought only Russians do that," she added and grinned.

"It's a long story," replied Sienna. "This person has been breaking into my house. I'll tell you the whole story later. Sorry, it was bad timing – or good, because I wouldn't have been able to get my car keys and follow the car so fast."

She patted the front pocket of the white linen shorts she was wearing. "By the way, I have the pearl with me. I was much too nervous to leave it anywhere, so I just carried it on me."

Natalia's eyes widened. "Show me," she said.

Sienna got the pearl out of her pocket. It was wrapped in a soft little cloth napkin. She carefully unwrapped it and held it up so that Natalia could see it. The evening sunlight broke on the dark pink pearl almost as big as a quail's egg and accentuated its beautiful shiny luster.

Natalia was speechless for a second, but then she had to watch the road again and said nervously: "Put it away, fast! I can't stop staring at it because it's so beautiful! And what if it you drop it!"

Sienna wrapped the pearl back into the napkin and put it in the pocket of her pants.

They had now arrived at the end of the Seven Mile Bridge that was closed by several police cars with flashing lights, blocking all of the lanes in a right angle. The volatile driver in the dark sedan that had been driving in a breakneck speed had no other choice but to stop. He or she just sat there, defeated, waiting to be arrested.

Ben and another police officer walked up to the dark sedan, got the driver out and handcuffed him or her. In the meantime, the hood had slipped off and Sienna recognized who the person was: It was not *CRAIG*. It was *ISABEL,* local Turtle Key Detective and Mark's ex-wife. Not only Sienna was in shock about this discovery but also Ben and the other police officers were speechless. Isabel was led away and assisted into the backseat of Ben's police car. Ben looked around and discovered Sienna in Natalia's car. "I'm going to have to ask you to come back with me and file a report. Is that okay?"

"Yes, can you hold on a second?"

She took the pearl out of her pocket and handed it to Natalia. "Can you write me some type of receipt? Ben, can you please witness that I'm giving this pearl to Ms. Romero Contreras?"

Sienna held the pearl up again and Ben nodded, staring at the precious object in her hand.

Natalia leaned over, opened the glove compartment of her BMW and found a pad of post-it notes in there. She wrote a quick note:

"I confirm receipt of one pink conch pearl from Sienna Brantley. Approx. 45 carats. Natalia Romero Contreras. 3/20," and handed it to Sienna.

"Great doing business with you," said Natalia and waved briefly as she accelerated her car and drove off of the Seven Mile Bridge that was just being opened again by the police officers.

Sienna waved and got into the front seat of Ben's car. She sent a text message to Mark: "Can you please pick me up at the police station in half an hour?" He didn't reply again, so, after filing a report, Sienna texted Bianca to come and pick her up.

"I still have some margaritas left, why don't you come over and have another one," said Bianca.

Sienna needed another drink to celebrate that the intruder had been caught, but she was still shocked that it was Isabel and not, as she had suspected, Craig.

Bianca parked her car in the parking lot and they both walked up to Bianca's cottage. Suddenly, Bianca had a thought. “Shouldn’t we go over to your house and check what Isabel did this time?”

“Yeah, good point, maybe better than me going over by myself and finding something really creepy.”

“I have to let Louisa know that we’re going to your house, she’s still waiting at mine. Oh, and by the way, I feel really bad. Isabel is a good friend of Louisa’s and comes to Louisa’s shop every morning to get a coffee and Louisa tells her every day what’s going on in Turtle Key. I think she might have been unintentionally telling Isabel what you have been up to every day. After I told her. And after being questioned in a smart way that Isabel has learned as a police detective and Louisa just telling her, thinking nothing bad of it.” She paused for a second. “To think that good-natured gossip can lead to something like this,“ Bianca continued. “I’m so sorry, I’ll never talk about you or what you’re doing with other people again.”

Sienna swallowed. That made sense. That’s how Isabel had known exactly when nobody was in the house. But Sienna wasn’t someone to hold a grudge and Bianca seemed truly sorry.

“No worries, Bianca. It’s not like Louisa was talking bad about me. It’s fine. And I’m sure Isabel knows exactly how to get the information she wants out of someone. Do you know what? Let’s just go to your house and have another drink with Louisa. Now that I know it was Isabel and she’s in police custody, I’m not nervous about going back to the house by myself later. And the kids are probably already home too.”

Chapter 38

Leo's court hearing was scheduled for the next morning. Since one margarita had turned into two and it had become a very late night, Sienna got up early and looked at Leo's file and what was to be expected. Sienna had a splitting headache but had to pull through another busy day. Lilly and Lindsey were sent off to school, Leo put on a collared shirt and khakis to make a good impression. Leo and Sienna drove over to the Monroe County Courthouse, which was just about five minutes away from their cottage. Sienna's phone started bleeping with incoming text messages from Mark who was now realizing that he had missed her messages and had heard about Isabel's arrest. But Sienna had to concentrate on Leo's case and just texted back: "At court with Leo. Call you later."

The courthouse and room were very plain and no-frills, not like a big fancy courthouse in the movies, thought Leo to himself. The courthouse was a plain peach-colored building with a white roof at the end of a strip mall and the interior of the room was just a few tables set up in U-shape. The judge, an older motherly looking lady in a suit, a representative of the county, Leo's lawyer as well as Leo and Sienna were the only people in the room. Of course, Isabel wasn't present after the incident last night.

The judge read the file while everyone waited with baited breath. She looked up and said:

"Well, I guess this case is pretty cut and dry. A young man lost his parents, is in need of attention and therefore gets in trouble. Does anyone have any further explanations or questions?

Sienna and Timothy looked at each other. Sienna whispered something into Timothy's ear and he got up.

"Your honor, I'd like to add that in the meantime we have found Leo's grandparents who will be moving up here to spend more time with their grandchildren after being estranged from their parents for many years. So he will have much more supervision than before and is certainly not at risk of repeating his mistake."

The judge nodded. She looked sternly at Leo.

"Leo, considering that your parents just both died and you have a new pair of grandparents taking care of you, I will simply give you a warning. Shoplifting is something that shouldn't be taken lightly. It hurts the storeowner and the community. How would you like something being stolen from you? It's the same thing. I don't want to see you here ever again, is that understood?"

Leo nodded. "Yes, your honor."

The judge hit her wooden gavel on the sound block and closed the file folder. "Winn-Dixie has pressed no charges against Leo Flores. Case of Leo Flores vs. Winn-Dixie Liquor Stores is closed."

Leo, Sienna and Timothy stood up. Sienna took Leo into her arms with a big sigh of relief.

"As soon as I'm back home," she said as they left the court building, "I'm going to make an appointment for your driver's license test. And please ask Alana if she's available tonight. I'd like to take you all to the Thai place to celebrate."

Leo's face was beaming.

*****

Sienna drove Leo to school. As soon as she had dropped him off, she sent Mark a text message. *Can you talk?*
He replied almost immediately: *Busy day today. How about lunch?*

Ben at the police station still had some questions for Sienna, so she stopped by on her way home.

She sat down across from him in the back office. Since Isabel wasn't there, he was in charge now and, as Sienna could see, he seemed pleased and happy about it.

"So," he said, "this will be considered *stalking."* He read out load from some notes he had made. "Defined as: willfully, maliciously, and repeatedly follows or harasses another and makes credible threat with intent to place another in reasonable fear for own safety of his/her immediate family." He took a break and continued: "Punishment/Classification: 1 year in county jail and/or $1,000; if probation granted or sentenced suspended, counseling required."

He looked up at Sienna. "Now it's entirely up to you if you want to press charges. She is at home and suspended from her job now but will be taken into custody again, depending on your decision."

"I don't want to press charges," said Sienna. "I just hope this will be a lesson for her and she will stay away from me from now on."

Sienna signed the form confirming that she wasn't pressing any charges against Isabel and left the police station.

Even though she was shocked that Isabel was the perpetrator, she was happy to know it wasn't Craig. She was going to have to face him when she went back to Boston...

*****

And there it was again... the nagging thought that she not only had to return to Boston in two days but that she also had to make up her mind as to what she was going to do. These past two weeks had been a whirlwind of activity and events: upsetting events, threatening events, happy events and life-changing events. Camilla and Ricky dying, meeting Mark, Craig showing up, becoming extremely attached to her nieces and nephew and finding their grandparents. Not to mention being back around these fascinating sea creatures, the sea turtles and the entire Sea Turtle Sanctuary that needed her help and had to be saved. If anyone could do it, it was without a doubt Sienna with her background as an attorney along with the children's grandfather, Richard.

Deep in her heart, Sienna knew what her decision was, even though the children's grandparents wanted to move up to Turtle Key and take care of the kids. That was fine, even if Sienna stayed. After all, it takes a village.

*****

As Sienna walked to her car in the parking lot in front of the police station, she bumped into Isabel who was arriving and had just climbed out of her car. There was an awkward silence as they walked toward each other but they both had to keep walking to not appear immature. As they were about to pass each other, Isabel stopped and apologized for what she had done.

"I'm really sorry. What I did was really childish and mean of me. I promise I'll leave you alone and find my peace with you and Mark being together. We are not good for each other. And I'm not pregnant either, by the way. You can tell him."

Sienna was speechless yet thankful that Isabel had found the strength and courage to apologize. She said: "Thank you" and they both continued walking. They would never be best friends but they might be able to tolerate each other.

*****

Sienna drove to the Sea Turtle Sanctuary and saw Wayne sitting on a bench in the parking lot. She walked over to him and said: "Thanks for everything, Wayne. We wouldn't have caught the intruder without you. I need to discuss it with the manager first, but would you be interested in helping in the Turtle Sanctuary? We could use another set of hands around here."

Wayne was speechless and beside himself with happiness to be given another chance. He stared at Sienna for a second but then he replied:

"Would love to, Ma'am."

"Please stick around," Sienna said and continued walking into the Sea Turtle Sanctuary.

She walked past the reception desk, nodding at Cynthia, the intern, bumped into Bridget and gave her a quick hug and said: “Hey, can I talk to you about something in a bit?” but she continued walking toward the treatment rooms. Bridget could tell she was on a mission and nodded, smiling silently. Treatment Room 1 was empty and so was treatment Room 2. Sienna walked out back the big outdoor basins and there was Mark, standing at one of them, checking Olivia’s vitals. He looked up surprised and saw Sienna walking toward him looking very determined.

“I do have to fly to Boston the day after tomorrow.” she blurted out. “But that’ll be to quit my job and sell my condo. I’ve decided to come back and stay…”

His face lit up and he took her in his arms as if he never wanted to let go of her again. Then their lips met each other and they locked for a long tender kiss.

Everyone in the Sea Turtle Sanctuary, who had seen Sienna storm through, was watching through the windows in the back and started clapping and cheering.

It looked a little bit like Olivia in the basin was winking.

TO BE CONTINUED…

Made in the USA
Columbia, SC
07 September 2021